A STRONG COLLECTED SPIRIT

Pvt. Edward Gersh assumes his fighting stance in the training ring at Fort Bragg, North Carolina, in 1944.

A STRONG COLLECTED SPIRIT

A FIGHTER'S MEMOIR

EDWARD I. GERSH

with

STUART A.P. MURRAY

A LILY BOOK

*To my wife, Holli Gersh, my best friend and
the love of my life, and the best sparring partner
any man ever had – with all my love.*

EDWARD GERSH

LILY PRODUCTIONS
3850 Hudson Manor Terrace
Riverdale, New York 10463

PROJECT EDITOR: Aaron R. Murray
PRODUCTION ASSISTANT: Rachel D. Murray

ISBN: 0-9645433-3-8

Contents

"Whoever has courage and a strong, collected spirit in his breast, let him come forward, lace on the gloves, and put up his hands."

—ATTRIBUTED TO THE ROMAN POET VIRGIL

Preface

IOFFER MY HEARTFELT THANKS TO THOSE WHO SHARED their memories with me for this memoir of my careers in boxing, teaching, and day-camping: they include Wilfred Avellez, Andy Moskowitz, the late Larry Kent, Roger Dorian, and most of all my wife, Holli Gersh, who shared so many of the years and experiences related in these pages.

I am also grateful for the support of my friend and partner of fifty years, the late Norman Schnittman, and to my wonderful family, for whom this book has been written.

My thanks go to Stuart Murray for all his hard work during our four-year collaboration to complete this memoir. We both sincerely hope the results of our efforts will be entertaining and informative – a window into a time that I am profoundly grateful to have experienced and enjoyed.

Edward Gersh
Woodstock, New York

Prologue

ROAD RAGE IN BOCA

E DWARD GERSH WAS ENJOYING A FINE SPRING DAY in March of 2000 as he eased his new Lexus through the busy traffic of Florida's State Road 441. The car radio played softly, old standards, and the tinted windows and air conditioning kept South Florida's heat at bay. A robust 80 years of age, and as fit as a man twenty years younger, Gersh was heading to his home in the gated community of St. Andrews Country Club in Boca Raton.

The Lexus stopped for a traffic light, where a construction barrier just ahead made the highway's three lanes merge into two. When the light turned green, the cars advanced slowly, taking alternate turns moving into the narrower roadway. Then came Gersh's turn, but another car suddenly pushed in from the right and cut him off, forcing him to jam on the brakes.

Annoyed, Gersh rolled down the passenger window and called out, "What's the matter with you? It's my turn to go."

The other driver, a middle-aged, heavyset fellow, yelled back, "Aw, go to hell!"

Gersh seethed with anger. Shortly, both cars turned right onto another road, and Gersh decided to annoy this guy a bit. The Lexus passed and then cut sharply in front of the other car, without using directionals. Soon, Gersh was back in the left lane with the other car alongside at the right, the driver yelling and cursing at him.

Gersh rolled down the window again and hurled an expletive of his own.

The other driver shouted, "Get out of your car and say that to me!"

"Okay!" Gersh answered, and pulled over onto the shoulder.

The other car followed, and the fellow jumped out and rushed Gersh, who was getting out of the Lexus. The man grabbed Gersh by the shoulders and viciously tried to knee him in the groin, just missing. Gersh threw up both arms, breaking the other man's grip, and followed with a sudden left hook.

"The guy's eyes went wide," Gersh later recalled. "I held off with my right, which was cocked, because I realized the ground was macadam, and a knockout blow might result in serious injury."

The left hook was enough, however, and the fellow crumpled into the fetal position.

Gersh bent over him, demanding, "What's the matter with you, you dumb sonofabitch?"

From the fetal position came a whimper: "Why didn't you turn on your directional signals?"

"Next time," Gersh said, straightening up, "don't pick on a former prize fighter."

Still angry, Gersh returned to his car and pulled away. In a little while, the air conditioning had cooled him, and a soothing tune played in the background. Gersh reflected on his left hook, and how he hadn't thrown one like that in years. Always was his best punch. He'd won tough bouts with the left hook and had taught some very good young boxers to throw it. He was pleased that he still had it when he needed it. Gersh's hand absently touched the miniature pair of golden boxing gloves that hung from a watch chain at his belt. When he pulled in at St. Andrews, he was still smiling.

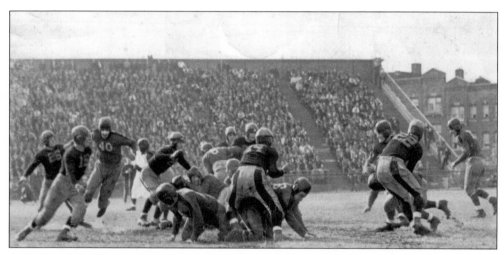

On his way to block for the DeWitt Clinton ball carrier against George Washington High, lineman Gersh, 40, was also on his way to becoming an All-Metropolitan first-team selection.

Chapter 1

'AS TOUGH AS I COULD BE'

CHESTNUT HILL ROAD IN WOODSTOCK, NEW YORK, is beautiful in summertime, following a rushing brook and winding its way beneath overhanging trees. At the start of the road, there's a golf course on the right, and after half a mile or so, another expanse of grass opens on the left. A driveway turns in here, a long track running along the edge of the trees and leading to a large fieldstone house that looks down on a perfectly maintained estate.

This part of town is far from the beatnik, hippie legacy of artsy Woodstock village, which for generations has been an artist's and musician's haven that attracts thousands of tourists. The Chestnut Hill Road house, built of cut stone and trimmed with white in Federal style, is part of another Woodstock legacy – one from the 19th and early 20th centuries, when such grand estates were established, inspired by impeccable taste and paid for by old New York money. Inside, the rooms are spacious, handsomely furnished, hung with art, and decorated with collectibles varying from rows of delicate antique tea cups and saucers to imposing Remington cowboy bronzes on pedestals. In a small front room that looks out over the grounds, the walls are covered with black and white photographs, mostly of boxers, some of them autographed to Edward Gersh, owner of the house. Also hanging here are framed newspaper clippings with pictures of young boxers in fighting stance or wearing robes, towels around their necks, and grinning for the news photographer. Most of the boxing-news pictures are of Gersh, himself. One, from a 1943 *New York Post*, shows him barely slipping under an overhand right thrown by a tall, black fighter. "It Pays to Duck," says the caption title. Another, headed "Champ," is of Gersh a couple of years later, posing in gloves and trunks, his wavy dark hair combed back neatly in the style of the day. He is in a sparring ring at Fort Bragg, North Carolina, and it is World War II.

One of the most prominent pictures shows world heavyweight champion Joe Louis, in trunks and robe, sitting on a locker room bench and signing a boxing program for Gersh, also in trunks and robe, sitting beside him. This is the locker room at Fort Bragg, where Louis has just given an exhibition for thousands of cheering troops. Gersh, too, was on the night's card, fighting in a preliminary bout.

Boxing was the sport and passion of their generation. Sixty years later in Woodstock, now in his early eighties, Gersh has the rugged look of a former fighter. His barrel chest and easy gait show that he keeps fit. He works out in the gym in a converted garage on the estate, sweating at the heavy bag and honing his timing on the speed bag. His room with the old pictures is an ex-boxer's den, with an ex-boxer's best memories on the walls for visitors to see and for him to remember. The memories are of a day far removed from Chestnut Hill Road, but those memories are still alive to Gersh.

Between the era of the pictures and the Woodstock estate came a long teaching career at one of the toughest schools in East Harlem, and a parallel career as a businessman who made his fortune in real estate and day camps. There was also third career,

2

more recently, as the hard-working manager of professional boxers, many of them very good fighters.

The varied careers that brought Edward Irwin Gersh to Woodstock began in 1941, just before the United States entered World War II, a time when New York University had a topnotch football team. A preseason training picture from the *New York Times* that year shows NYU coach Mal Stevens in tie and waistcoat, kneeling, hand on a football, in front of 60 players in practice uniforms. Eddie Gersh, a 21-year-old sophomore, is on the far right, wearing a lineman's number "50." Gersh remembers it well, as he tells a guest. . . .

❧

MOST PLAYERS AT NYU'S TRAINING CAMP that summer of 1941 had full athletic scholarships, but I didn't, and I needed a scholarship more than any of them.

I'd already borrowed from friends and family for the previous spring's tuition, but I couldn't afford to pay for the coming fall. The only way I could stay in school was to win a football scholarship, so I had to impress the coaches during those few weeks in camp. I was determined, but the odds were against me. I had to at least make the second team because they didn't give scholarships to third-stringers. Another fellow already assumed he'd be the second-team guard, thought he'd already sewn up that spot right at the start of camp. I was desperate. Really desperate. Without a scholarship there'd be no college at all. My whole future depended on how I played in camp, so I was as tough as I could be.

When we scrimmaged intra-squad, I fought like a sonofabitch.

Two years earlier, I'd been an all-Metropolitan lineman as a senior at DeWitt Clinton High School in the Bronx. NYU had offered me a full athletic scholarship then. As one of the top players in New York City's five boroughs, I was a prime college recruit – 195 pounds, about six foot tall, and I knew how to battle because I'd spent much of my life on tough city streets. Off the football field, I was easy-going, quiet by nature, and I wore wire-rimmed glasses, but I knew how to take care of myself.

When I'd graduated from high school, NYU wasn't the only college to offer me a football scholarship. So had George Washington University in Washington, D.C., which had a stronger football program. I had hopes of turning professional one day, so I chose George Washington instead of NYU. As it turned out, George Washington was an unhappy place for a New York kid with no money, living only on the two meals a day provided at the football team's training table.

After attending classes during the day, I had freshman football practice for three hard hours, followed by dinner at five p.m. Afterwards, I had to study late into the evening, and I had no money for extra food. At George Washington I used to go to bed hungry every night. Teammates who were better off had food sent to them from home, or they bought their own – and they hoarded it. I was too proud to ask my parents to send me money, because I'd always thought they were broke – or so I heard at home.

For the past seven years, I'd worked every summer at hotels in the Catskills, but I'd always given my parents every penny I made, so I'd nothing saved for myself. I thought it was normal to give your parents everything you earned. That's how my father brought me up. His name was Henry Gersh, and was actually my stepfather, although I called him my father. He never showed me any affection or took any interest in me. He always degraded everything I did. He ridiculed my high school football-playing, saying I was too rough, that I liked body-contact sports too much. I never could do anything right for him. He never worked. He had a pension from military service in World War I. He said he'd been gassed. The pension wasn't much, and we had to move around a lot, usually just ahead of the rent collectors. When I was 18, I finally saved up and bought a car for $35, but I left it with my father when I went to college. He later sold it for $20 and kept the money.

When I went to George Washington, my father gave me only $25, even though I'd earned $175 that summer, which I'd given to my parents. After I left home for George Washington, I never went back again.

That freshman football season was long and lonely, far from home and from my girlfriend, Gertrude Margolies. Gertrude wrote me, pleading for me to come back to New York, and whenever we talked on the phone, she cried. Once, she came down there to try to convince me, but I stayed on through the football season, even though I was unhappy and hungry. At the end of the season I had an argument with a teammate, who sucker-punched me, and I got a broken jaw. The next day, I took a bus back to New York. My face was painful and swollen, and for days I was only able to drink and eat through a straw. I was utterly miserable. By now, my parents had moved back upstate, to the Catskills.

❧

THERE I WAS, IN NEW YORK WITH A BROKEN JAW, not a penny to my name and nowhere to live. I moved in with Gertrude's family, sleeping on a cot they set up at night in the kitchen of their East Bronx apartment, which was very small. Gertrude's parents had the bedroom, and she slept in the living room with a maiden aunt. Gertrude worked as a bookkeeper and secretary, contributing $10 a week to the household. I had no money to give because I was attending NYU, studying Physical Education, but I was becoming one of the family. I was able to attend the spring and summer semesters at NYU by borrowing from everyone I knew.

Sixteen credits cost $169 in 1941. The country was just coming out of the Depression, so my friends and relatives couldn't afford to loan me much, if anything. Well, somehow, I got that tuition money together, and in March I went to spring training, but I twisted my ankle so badly that I couldn't play. The head coach, Mal Stevens, said that since I hadn't made the team, NYU couldn't give me a scholarship. I had to try out again in summer camp at Lake Sebago, north of New York City.

In those days, we went both ways, offense and defense, and I fought like hell on every play. It was the same determination I had later when I was fighting in the boxing ring. I told myself, "Nobody's going to stop me!" I played like I'd never played before. I devastated my opponents. When I was playing defense, I broke through the line several times and upset the ball carrier before he could get started. After the very first scrimmage, they moved me up to second team guard, and Coach Stevens promised me a scholarship, which was full tuition with meals after practice during the season.

I was on my way.

I did so well in camp that I was eager for those first scrimmages against other schools so I could measure myself against competition on the field. NYU had a solid football program, and a few years previous had been nationally ranked. There was still a chance I could eventually play professionally, but one way or the other, I would finally get that degree I was after. In 1941, a college education was hard to get, and having one meant a far better future for a young man like me, who'd never had much in the way of worldly possessions. My Physical Education studies would make me a school teacher – whether or not I also played professional football. In those days, most football pros had other jobs anyway, because the National Football League didn't offer its players much wealth and fame.

Our team went up the Hudson for a pre-season scrimmage against the cadets at West Point, a beautiful campus. The backdrop to the field full of players wearing NYU's violet uniforms and West Point's black and gold was a panoramic view of the river. This was what college football was all about.

During that scrimmage, we kicked to West Point, and I ran downfield after the kick returner, who cut to the left sideline. I turned to go that way, but somebody blocked me from the side and behind.

On my left knee. I went down, and I couldn't get up, couldn't even move that leg. I was in tremendous pain and had to be helped off the field. I was badly hurt. I couldn't go back into the game.

For the next two days, I had to lie in bed. The knee was swollen, and I was in agony. I had serious cartilage damage, but in those days surgery wasn't advanced enough to repair those kinds of injuries. The knee had to heal by itself, without medical help, so I spent the rest of that training camp on the sideline, leaning on a pair of crutches, in constant pain.

After a couple of weeks, the knee seemed to be getting better, although the leg was stiff, and I couldn't straighten it. When I finally got rid of the crutches, I was able to walk only on the toes of my left foot, and I had a limp until I finally could straighten the knee. In spite of it all, I was anxious to get back to the football team that season. I tried to play again, but whenever I dug hard, the knee buckled, and I'd fall down. I'd be in agony for days and could hardly walk. I wanted to play, but I couldn't. I realized that my football career was over. I was horribly disappointed.

My college days might've been over, too. I'd known guys at George Washington University who'd lost their football scholarships after they were injured. I expected that my scholarship to NYU would be taken away if I couldn't play anymore. Then I got a letter from the dean saying that NYU would let me keep the scholarship, even though I couldn't play football. As long as I got the grades to stay in school, they said, I'd have the scholarship. Not too many schools would have done that for a football player who got hurt like I did. I was always grateful for that.

❧

I GREW CLOSE TO GERTRUDE'S PARENTS, Ruby and Tillie Margolies, who treated me like a son. I wanted to contribute something financially to the household, but I had to study, and there was very little time to work. Sometimes I put in a few hours with

Ruby's furniture-moving business, and at lunchtime I worked in the NYU cafeteria, earning 35 cents an hour and my lunch.

Gert and I had first met when she was a summer guest at the Hotel Hoffman in Naponach, New York, in the "Borscht Belt," where I worked as a waiter. I was going into my senior year of high school then. She was at the hotel for two weeks with her uncle and aunt, who were supposed to chaperone her, although they didn't do such a good job of it. She was pretty, five-foot-two and a brunette. We became close, and after she went home to New York I'd drive a few hours to the city to see her. I'd then turn around that same night and drive back to Naponach in time to work the hotel breakfast shift at eight-thirty in the morning.

In 1941, it was a family arrangement in the Margolies household, but Gert and I slept in different rooms, of course. Her father, Ruby, thought the world of me, and he was more like a father to me than my father was. Then one day in November, Gert announced that we'd be getting married in a few weeks. I was surprised, but I agreed. I had no choice. After all, her family fed me. I slept there. They were supporting me. So, Gert and I got married at Bronx City Hall on December 6, 1941. At the time, I didn't have the money for a wedding ring, but I later bought one for $10 from my friend Herbert "Iggy" Chaitin, who worked part-time in the jewelry business. The wedding was a civil ceremony, and we just went home afterwards. There was no party to celebrate the wedding, no honeymoon – that was it, except that we went to the movies the next day.

That day was Sunday, December 7, 1941.

When Gert and I came out of the movies, we heard people in the street talking excitedly about a Japanese air attack on Pearl Harbor. Everyone was shocked and angry, and at the same time no one knew what was going to happen next. We waited by our radios to hear what President Franklin D. Roosevelt would say to the country. On Monday, NYU classes were canceled so we could hear him address Congress, which went to war with Japan,

Germany, and Italy. I had my studies to do, so I signed up with the Enlisted Reserves, which allowed me to finish college before being called up – unless there was a special emergency and I had to go in.

I continued with my Physical Education studies at NYU, and by mid-winter my knee seemed to have healed. I was eager to play a sport, so I went out for wrestling, but when I drove hard off the leg the knee buckled again, and I was in agony. The pain lasted for days, and the knee would swell up. It was almost unbearable, but what was worse was the thought of never being able to play sports again. That really troubled me.

I'd been an excellent speed skater and had taught ice skating as a part-time job in New York City. When I was on the hotel staff in the Catskills, I taught horseback riding. But now it seemed I was finished with sports for good. As time passed, the injured leg progressed, the pain finally left it, and I walked without a limp. Still, it seemed I'd never again be involved in competitive sports.

AROUND THIS TIME, THE MARGOLIES FAMILY moved to a larger house at 1229 Evergreen Avenue in the South Bronx. It was a street of single-family homes with driveways in between, typical of the kind of good South Bronx neighborhood New York City families aspired to. Gert and I had the porch, and later we moved into an apartment that was built above the garage.

One winter's day early in 1942, I was walking on University Avenue, near NYU's uptown campus, when I met high school friend Bernie Gladstone, the fellow who'd convinced me to come out for DeWitt Clinton's football team. Bernie was wearing a brand new watch he said he'd earned by doing some amateur boxing at Jamaica Arena in Queens, on 169th Street, off Jamaica Avenue. I admired that watch. Bernie told me fighters got a $15 watch if they won their fight, and a $10 watch if they lost. I figured

I could use a watch, and I thought: I'm a pretty tough guy, and I've been in plenty of fights. I wanted a watch, and I wanted to give boxing a try. So I went over to Jamaica Arena to see if I could get a fight. There were fights every Friday night in those days.

When I got to the arena, I went up to the ticket booth and told the ticket-taker I wanted to fight. He asked whether I'd ever fought before. Since I hadn't, he said I had to train first, and he suggested Bobby Gleason's gym in the South Bronx. He said there was a fellow there named Larry Kent, who trained amateurs. After I trained a while, he said, I could come back and get a fight and earn a watch. I went over to Gleason's Gym, which was on 149th Street and Third Avenue, above a sandwich shop. It was quiet as I went up the stairs, because the fighters and trainers hadn't arrived yet. Most usually came in the late afternoon, after their regular jobs.

The place was almost empty. Then I saw a tall, thin fellow there, and I asked him about Larry Kent. He answered gruffly, "Who wants to know?" I told him who I was, and he said, "I'm Larry Kent."

After I explained that I wanted to learn to box, Lolly, as he was nicknamed, asked whether I'd ever fought before. I told him that as a kid I'd had lots of fights. He became more friendly and we talked a while.

Gleason's Gym looked down on the street from the second floor. Big windows were across the entire front of the gym, so the fighters could look down on the street and the people could look up and see them in the windows. There were no high-rises in the neighborhood then. The gym had one very large room, and two heavy bags were by the windows. On the right as you came up the stairs was a small boxing ring and three rows of spectator seats, about thirty folding chairs. There was a speed bag near the ring. Bells were constantly going off. They rang at three minutes and at one minute, then at three minutes again, nonstop. When boxers trained, they worked out for three minutes and then took a one-minute rest. The bells told when to stop and start. The clock with the bells was over near the ring so the boxers always could see the time.

Lolly managed and trained several fighters, but didn't have a heavyweight, which I could be. He'd never fought, himself – he had a bad hip that gave him a limp – but he was a student of boxing and was an experienced trainer. To make a living, he worked part time as a taxi driver. Lolly was in his early thirties, and was making a name for himself as a trainer. He'd worked with Sugar Ray Robinson, Henry Armstrong, Jake LaMotta, and Patsy Spataro – the best. He was also recognized as a handler of promising young amateurs. What did he see in me? He said he didn't want a heavyweight who was fat, who couldn't move. I was well-built, and could take a punch. I was a complete beginner, but I liked to box, liked to fight, and I liked Lolly.

As Lolly and I spoke, I felt he knew what he was talking about. After a while, he told me, "If you want to start fighting, then come here on Monday, bring shorts, sneakers, and seven dollars for gym dues for the month." Well, by the time I left that day, I was enthusiastic about getting a fight at Jamaica Arena and earning that wristwatch.

When I told Gertrude I planned to train and then have a few fights, she encouraged me to do it. Neither of us imagined my boxing would take on a life of its own. Larry Kent would train me, but he wouldn't allow me to box at the Arena until I was ready, and that would be after almost 10 months of hard work.

The photos bear the following handwritten inscriptions:

From a Heavy to a good one, Keep punching Eddie, your Pal, Joe Baksi

JOE BAKSI

1/29/44 Best wishes To Eddie Irwin a very good fighter. Sincerely "Beau Jack"

BEAU JACK
World's Lightweight Champion

Best wishes To my Pal Eddie, Sincerely Allie Stolz

ALLIE STOLZ
Outstanding Lightweight Contender

To Eddie Best of luck to you. Your Pal Phil Terranova

PHIL TERRANOVA
World's Featherweight Champion

Edward Gersh knew many of the top prize fighters of the 1940s and 1950s, including, clockwise from upper left, Joe Baksi, Beau Jack, Phil Terranova, and Allie Stolz. Pictured together at Grossinger's resort in the Catskills in 1951 are, l-r, Rocky Graziano, British middleweight Randy Turpin – then training to fight Sugar Ray Robinson – and Jake LaMotta. Turpin had recently won the title from Robinson in Britain, but would lose it in a return bout in New York.

Chapter 2

TRAINING AT GLEASON'S

THE SOUND OF A SPEED BAG rattles through the fieldstone garage near the house on Chestnut Hill Road. Here, Edward Gersh has his gym, which is simple, with no fancy equipment. There's a heavy bag, sets of sparring gloves, weights – a place to stay in trim and to sweat. Gersh wears a T-shirt, practice gloves, shorts, and sneakers. He is smooth as he taps in synch with the speed bag, a natural rhythm acquired after years of practice. It's quiet here other than the clatter of the bag.

When a guest asks Gersh about boxing technique – how to punch hard – Gersh demonstrates on the heavy bag, showing how one leg pushes off when the punch is thrown, adding weight, adding hitting power. Gersh doesn't hit too hard, though. He warns that unless your hands are properly taped, punching the heavy bag too hard, even with practice gloves on, can damage the hands.

In the distance across the expanse of lawn, several deer browse leisurely in the grass. Beside the house, gardeners are grooming the flower garden inside a white picket fence. Summer is kind to

Woodstock's hills and woods. Sunlight gleams off the quartz in the stone walls of the house. At a kitchen window, the house-keeper, who is also the cook, can be seen moving back and forth while he prepares lunch. In the garage gym, Gersh thuds a fist into the heavy bag. He holds back when he hits, but there's power in the punch, a studied strength.

During a break, Gersh recalls the fall of 1941, when World War II was raging in Europe, and the United States was drifting ever closer to the conflict. Roosevelt supported Britain, providing warships and military supplies. There were reports that Europe's Jews were being rounded up by the Nazis and imprisoned. . . .

≀≀

I WAS AWARE OF PERSECUTION OF THE JEWS over there. I wasn't religious, but I was culturally a Jew, as were both my parents and my natural father. Neither of my parents was religious, and I was never bar´ mitz´vah'd as a boy, but we would always celebrate Passover and the other Jewish holidays – in a party way. I had no religious training and never attended temple, but I considered myself a Jew.

I was born in New York, in the Lower East Side, on March 6, 1920. A few years after I was born, my mother divorced my natural father, whose name was Samuel Ellman. I don't remember much about him, except that he was a lawyer. I met him only a few times later in my life. When my mother left him, she went upstate to Monticello, New York, where she moved into a "kochallein," a Yiddish term for a boarding house where there was a community kitchen, and you would cook for yourself – "cook alone," kochallein means. I remember my mother using Yiddish sayings. There was one in particular she would say to calm me when I was extremely upset with somebody or something: *"Mit gutches, mein Kind,"* meaning, "Handle it with goodness, my child."

14

That expression stayed with me all my life.

My mother's maiden name was Koven. She was progressive for her time. She was very conscious of what we ate and always made sure we had only fresh food, never anything from cans. Whole wheat bread and brown sugar. I never knew what white bread was until I was a teenager. We had fresh carrot juice every day, and when she cooked vegetables, like spinach, she had me drink the broth. Maybe that helped get me in shape for football.

It was at the kochallein that she met Henry Gersh, and they started an affair. Eventually, they moved into an apartment together, and we lived in Monticello. I had a half brother, Gabriel, who was seven years younger.

We moved back to New York City when I got older, and my mother sent me to DeWitt Clinton because it was an all-boys school. A schoolteacher had told her I was too fond of the girls and would do better academically at an all-boys school. Otherwise, I could've gone to George Washington High School in upper Manhattan with Iggy Chaitin and Bernie Jovans, two of my "blood brothers," who both played football. It was sports that kept me in high school when I thought about dropping out, like my other two blood brothers did: Frankie Ganger and Walter Carroll. We were blood brothers because we cut our wrists and mixed the blood as a show of loyalty. Frankie was my closest friend.

Well, I failed my sophomore year in high school and had to stay back. That's when I started thinking about working full-time instead of finishing high school. By working I'd finally have some money of my own and could begin to make my way in the world. In the late 1930s, money was hard to come by, and since I always gave all my earnings to my family, I had nothing for myself. When I first wanted to play football, I couldn't even afford the five cents it cost for carfare to go the few miles to DeWitt Clinton's practice site. I couldn't pay the carfare, so I didn't go out for the team.

After I failed, I seriously considered leaving school and going to work, until Bernie Gladstone talked me into coming out for the

DeWitt Clinton football team. Gladstone was an important influenced on me several times in my life. Now, I went out and became a lineman. In my senior year we won every game but one, and that one we lost to George Washington High because Iggy caught the winning pass for a touchdown to beat us. He was an all-scholastic end – an all-star for the five boroughs of New York City. By then, I'd become pretty good myself and was an all-scholastic lineman.

Sports meant everything to me. That's the reason I eventually gave boxing a try.

᳒

WHEN I GOT TO GLEASON'S THAT FIRST DAY TO TRAIN, after classes at NYU, I was anxious, wondering what it would be like. A small sign was posted at the front door, telling which well-known fighters were sparring upstairs that day. Spectators paid 50 cents to come in and see the action in the ring. I went up and entered that world of the boxing gym, with the ringing bells, the sound of speed bags, the thudding of leather gloves on heavy bags and on bodies and on the head gear boxers wore when sparring. Right away I could see it was a businesslike mood at Gleason's. That mood was set by the fighters, who were ambitious and aggressive, and so were their trainers and managers. A passion for boxing, dreams of title fights, of fame and of big money, brought the fighters and trainers to Gleason's. Promoters and gamblers and hangers-on were there, too.

In early 1942, Gleason's had a reputation for quality boxing, and world-class fighters trained there. These included featherweights Mike Belloise and Phil Terranova, and an up-and-coming middleweight, Jake "The Bronx Bull" LaMotta. Gleason's Gym had been established in 1937 by New Yorker Robert Galiardi, who changed his Italian name to Gleason because his gym was in an Irish neighborhood, or so they say. There was constant rivalry, often open hostility, between the various ethnic groups in New York. Like Lolly Kent, Bobby Gleason also worked as a cab driver to make ends meet.

Every serious fighter was under the eye of a trainer who was watching, evaluating, criticizing, encouraging, scheming. Gleason's had some of the best trainers, such as Chickie Ferrara, Freddy Brown, and Ray Aarcel. Morris "Whitey" Bimstein was highly regarded, and he often was at Gleason's, too, but Whitey was more of a regular at New York's other leading place for boxers, Marshall Stillman's Gym, on Eighth Avenue in Manhattan. Stillman's had two rings for sparring, was larger than Gleason's, and had more boxers training there.

Gleason's was kept spotless. If anyone ever spit on the floor, they'd be thrown out. There was no smoking, and the place was always swept clean. Bobby Gleason was fastidious about that. There was an elderly Italian man named Phil, who kept the place clean. The neighborhood bookie was usually there every day, taking bets on the horses. Local men would come up to the gym to see the bookie and place bets.

In the back of the gym were several small rooms with training tables for the star fighters – the pros who could afford the rooms. There, fighters were massaged after a workout, and they had their own private lockers. Jake LaMotta, who they later called the "Raging Bull," had his own room. Mike Capriano was LaMotta's trainer and manager then.

Lolly didn't have a room of his own. We used a section of metal lockers that were in the back of the gym. There was a shower back there, too.

Otherwise, every fighter started out equal in the gym, no matter who he was down on the street. Everyone paid the same basic monthly fee to use the equipment, whether they were world champions or boxing neophytes. What counted at Gleason's was boxing – training and managing, conditioning and commitment and dedication. Some would be shadow-boxing – moving around the gym, punching at imaginary opponents – improving technique, loosening up for a session in the sparring ring or a workout with the heavy bag. Many of these fighters met each other in the professional ring as opponents in hard-fought matches that could make or break careers. Young amateurs skipped rope next to seasoned pros pounding the heavy bag. Meanwhile, sparring in the ring might be a former contender whose best days were gone, but for that three-minute round he gave everything he had in hopes of getting another shot at the title.

Fighting, boxing, is the most difficult sport and profession in the world. There's nothing more difficult. And to be good, you have to be completely dedicated. Nobody can be very good without dedication, although some people are more natural than others.

I didn't have the degree of coordination that say Sugar Ray Robinson, or Joe Louis, or Sugar Ray Leonard had, but what I lacked in coordination, I tried to make up for in determination. Determination, dedication, hard work, and the ability to absorb physical pain without complaint and to dish it out without malice – this attitude was fostered at Gleason's. Inspiring quotes and sayings were hung or painted on the walls. One that Bobby Gleason favored was attributed to the Roman poet Virgil:

"Whoever has courage and a strong, collected spirit in his breast, let him come forward, lace on the gloves, and put up his hands."

To succeed, a boxer not only had to work hard, but he also had to mentally wrestle with defeat and triumph, which could alternate from one day to another. Victory and loss meant elation followed by frustration. These emotional extremes confused and disillusioned young fighters, often ruining them before their potential in the ring was realized. To make a career out of boxing, a fighter needed the right attitude – and also the right trainer.

At the outset of my training, Lolly taught me the proper stance. I was left-handed, and he changed me from leading with my right to leading with my left. For one thing, a left-handed – "southpaw" – boxer would have problems getting fights because other boxers considered a left-hander too difficult to get used to in the ring. Being left-handed, I had the potential to have a powerful left hook, a punch many top boxers had perfected.

Most natural southpaws changed their stance, and some of the best fighters were left-handed – Joe Louis, Jake LaMotta, Sugar Ray Robinson, Al "Bummy" Davis, all were southpaws, and when they changed their stance, they developed great left hooks, usually their best punch. As soon as Lolly saw I was a southpaw, he said, "No, no, you've gotta switch."

So I started training, and he began to teach me that left hook, but it was very difficult to learn. I practiced at it all the time. Even when I was walking down the street, I'd be throwing that left hook, trying to get it. My neighbors on Evergreen Avenue knew I was training to be a fighter, and they understood it when they saw me walking along the sidewalk, firing off left hooks into the air. Try as I would, that left hook wouldn't come to me the way I wanted to feel it, and this was frustrating. The knee I'd injured held up, though, and didn't trouble me when I boxed.

When I wasn't in class or studying, I committed myself to boxing, just as I'd pushed myself to be a good football player. As a teenager, I'd built up my strength for football by pushing my car while my brother, Gabriel, steered. Now, I went to the gym almost every afternoon, working on the heavy bag and the speed bag, skipping rope, exercising, practicing punches, and learning defensive techniques. The conditioning and bag work I did mainly on my own, and technique was usually under Kent's supervision.

Kent taught me the fundamentals – the jab, blocking punches, the right cross, uppercuts, and that elusive left hook. He also insisted I learn to box rather than charge out eagerly and start swinging away at opponents. Kent wanted his fighters to be patient, to score points by boxing and only swing away at decisive moments in the fight.

One of the first things I learned was that you have to take care of yourself, especially your hands, and bandage them before you

*Gersh enjoyed horseback riding while working
on the staff of Catskill Mountain resorts.*

hit the bag. Every fighter is concerned about bandaging his hands
before he works out. I taped my hands to protect them when I
punched. I learned that from Lolly, who told me how to do it.
When you hit the heavy bag – if you hit it properly – you can hit
it so hard that your hands can't take the power of the blows, and
you'll damage them. If I tried hitting the bag when my hands
weren't bandaged, I felt the painful results. I quickly learned that
I had to bandage them because the bones aren't constructed to
withstand the power of a real good punch.

I was learning the boxer's ways, and at the same time I was
becoming impatient for my first fight. Lolly was firm, though,
and insisted I'd have to wait until he knew I was ready.

I met lots of first-rate fighters in those days – welterweights Bummy Davis, Beau Jack, and Tony Genero, middleweight Steve Belloise, and heavyweights Arturo Godoy, Steve Dudas, Joe Baksi, and Gunnar Borland. American boxing fans – and almost every young guy wanted to box in those days – knew these names well. After a while I was allowed to spar with some of them, going three rounds, three-minutes each. You learn a great deal by sparring, by actually boxing, and if you do something wrong, you suffer for it immediately.

Great 20th-century Jewish prize fighters included, clockwise, from top left:
Henry Armstrong (at left); Abe Simon, shown on a Joe Louis fight poster;
Bummy Davis; Maxie Rosenblum (at right); Barney Ross (at right);
Max Baer; Benny Leonard; and Bob Pastor, center.

Chapter 3

JEWISH BOXERS

AT FIRST, LOLLY got a professional to spar with me, someone who'd take it easy on me. Of course, if you're training with somebody like that you're not going to try to hit him very hard, because if you did then in another 10 seconds he'd be mopping the floor with you. The pros themselves have an understanding when they're sparring, not to hit too hard. I once saw Bummy Davis and Tony Genero sparring, and Genero sat Davis down, as the saying goes. Well, Davis got up, there was a war. It finally had to be stopped by fellows jumping in between them.

In 1942, Bummy Davis was a top welterweight, fighting at around 147 lbs. He was Jewish, from a Jewish neighborhood in the tough Brownsville section of Brooklyn – the birthplace of the gangster organization known as "Murder Inc." Davis, whose real name was Abraham Davidoff, was nicknamed "Boomy," which his manager, Johnny Attell, changed to "Bummy," in keeping with the tradition of boxers assuming names that made them sound tougher – like "Kid This" or "Battling That."

But Davis needed no nickname to embellish his reputation as

a rough character. He grew up as a hot-tempered street tough, a fearless brawler. He'd been discharged from the army as a troublemaker. His enlistment lasted just a couple of months. By 1942, Bummy had been suspended from fighting in New York State because he'd become enraged in the ring when an opponent was fouling him and the ref didn't stop it. As a pro, he had a 35–3–2 record, but his temper had put his career on the ropes, though he was only 21.

When I met him, Davis was training for a comeback, and New York City's Jewish fight fans were eager to see him again. There were a tremendous number of Jewish fight fans in the metropolitan area, so Jewish boxers were always good draws. Historically, some Jewish fighters had been among the world's best boxers. Jackie "Kid" Berg was the British lightweight champion in 1934–36. "Battling" Levinsky was the world light-heavyweight champion in 1916–20. Another light-heavyweight world champ, from 1930–34, was "Slapsie" Maxie Rosenbloom. Abe Simon was a great heavyweight – in March 1942 Simon lost for the second time to Joe Louis for the heavyweight championship, which ended his career. Natie Brown was another top heavyweight contender who also lost twice to Louis.

And of course, there was the great Benny Leonard.

Leonard is considered the best lightweight champion in boxing history and one of the finest boxers of all time. In his heyday, from 1915–32, he was probably the most famous Jew in America. Leonard was a New Yorker, too.

More than any other ethnic group during the first two decades of the 20th century, Jewish fighters dominated boxing in the United States. There were top-flight Jewish prize fighters right through the 1940s, including professionals and Olympic champions. There was Barney Aaron, Maxie Berger, Sam Berger, Teddy Gordon, Leo Center, Joe Choynski, Leach Cross, Sam Mosberg, Georgie Abrams. Maxie Rosenbloom, who was from Connecticut, was one of the most outstanding fighters ever. Rosenbloom had an astonishing record of 223 wins in 299 career fights. Before retiring in 1939, he fought more title defenses than anyone in boxing history. He got the nickname "Slapsie" because he used a certain punch that was something like a slap.

Other than Abe Simon, the two most famous Jewish heavy-weights of the 1930s–40s were the brothers Max and Buddy Baer, who came from out West. Max wore the Magen David on his box-ing trunks and called himself Jewish, although the Baers had only one Jewish grandparent and were not practicing Jews. Nevertheless, Jewish fight fans packed the arenas whenever the Baers fought. Max was world heavyweight champion in 1934–35 and retired in 1941 with a career record of 72 wins – 52 by knockout – and 12 loss-es. Buddy had 46 wins and 7 losses, with two of those losses to Joe Louis. That second loss to Louis was a first-round knockout in January 1942, about the time I was taking up boxing.

NYU has compiled a list of more than 350 notable Jewish pro-fessional and amateur boxers – including Edward Irwin Gersh, I'm pleased to say. I did have something in common with at least one Jewish professional heavyweight in the Forties: Bob Pastor, a New York City native. Pastor, whose father was Jewish, had attended NYU, and earned a degree in Commerce from the School of Business in 1935. Always a dangerous opponent, diffi-cult to hit, Pastor fought Joe Louis for the heavyweight crown in 1939, and Billy Conn for the light heavyweight title in 1940. In both fights he was knocked out in the late rounds. By early 1942, Pastor was looking for another shot at the heavyweight title. By then, his record was about 50 wins in 60 or so decisions.

That April of 1942, Pastor defeated Jimmy Bivins in a 10-round decision. At the time, Bivins was ranked as the number-one contender in both the light-heavyweight and heavyweight divi-sions. Pastor would never get another title shot, however, because he retired later in the year at the age of 28.

Well, I passed month after month training at Gleason's under Lolly Kent and also worked out on my own. I got up at 5:30 a.m., took the subway to Pelham Parkway, and ran two or three miles at the track there. I did this two out of three days, with one day to rest. After running, I'd go back to have breakfast with Gert at the Margolies house and then leave for class. I worked lunch at the cafeteria for two hours, then went back to class.

Late in the afternoon, I was working out at Gleason's. In the evenings, weary and often banged up, I studied for hours. Gert would rub baby oil onto my bruised ears to prevent them from swelling up into the boxer's typical cauliflower ear.

ॐ

I KEPT AFTER LOLLY, ASKING WHEN I was going to get a fight, when was I going to get my chance, but he didn't pay any attention to me. Other guys had different ideas, however, and wanted to take on this eager young college kid. They were out for some malicious fun.

There were these two Jewish brothers named Jackson, who sometimes trained at Gleason's, and they were pretty good amateur boxers. One of them had been a Subnovice heavyweight and had won the New York Golden Gloves. Being a Subnovice meant you had fought twice before entering the Golden Gloves competition, which was only for amateurs. A Novice had never had a fight before entering the Gloves. The Open category was for boxers who could have had any number of amateur fights.

So, those Jackson brothers sometimes were at Gleason's, and the Subnovice Gloves champion kept asking me to spar, but Lolly always refused to let me go in the ring with him. This happened a few times. Then one day Lolly wasn't there, and the Jacksons came in, and the one who had been Subnovice champ asked me to spar with him. I didn't want to seem afraid of him, and so I said, "Oh what the hell!" We got into the ring, and Jackson's trainer put my head gear on, and my gloves on, and gave me my mouthpiece, and we started boxing.

Well, when Jackson got me in the ring, he just beat the living daylights out of me. He pummeled me from corner to corner. We boxed two or three rounds, and he beat me up mercilessly. At the end, my face was all bloody.

I learned a lesson: I should do what my trainer says.

When Lolly heard about this, he was furious that his fledgling heavyweight had been taken advantage of and viciously beaten up. These things happened, of course, but they went against the boxers' code of honor. More experienced fighters were expected to be mentors to hard-working young boxers, not bully them.

I was angry, too, and I often thought of one day taking revenge on Jackson. Before then, however, came my first real fight.

ૐ

MY FIRST BOXING MATCH was in mid-June 1942, at Jamaica Arena, the venue that'd been my original objective from the start. By now, however, Jamaica Arena was no longer giving wristwatches to the fighters. They awarded medallions, one to the winner and one to the loser.

After a fight, the boxers or managers would go to the arena office and sell back their medallions – the winner's was worth $15, and the loser's $10. This way, the fighters technically remained amateurs, although they did earn something for fighting. Amateur boxers in most weight classes fought three rounds of three minutes each, but heavyweights were different. Heavyweights fought five two-minute rounds. They were the main event, the last fight of the evening, called a "special event."

My first fight was an extra bout, added by the management to the normal card. My opponent was Tony Cole of Rockville Center, also a relatively inexperienced boxer. Cole had had several fights before, and he was well known in the arena. I was fighting under the name, "Eddie Irwin," using my middle name as my last name. That was Lolly's idea.

It was a Friday night, and the place was filled, jammed. There were fights every Friday at Jamaica Arena, which used to have great amateur bouts, often outdrawing the professional bouts held in other venues. On this particular night the arena was packed with about a thousand spectators.

When I came out of the dressing room to wait in the doorway to the arena, the house lights were low, and the crowd was in the dark. I stood there a few moments, waiting to go down to the ring. I was very nervous, just as every fighter's nervous before a fight. Then I started to walk down the aisle toward the ring, and as soon as the spotlight hit me, following me all the way down, all my nervousness left me, and I felt calm.

A hardboiled New York sports reporter described my first battle with humor, recognizing the lack of experience and ability that combined with the raw eagerness of us young fighters:

Both boys did the best they could but it became apparent as the thing progressed that, while each lad's spirit was willing, the flesh was weak. Both boys endeavored to slug but the exhibition was pitiful. Cole ran into a left jab that was intended for Sutphin Boulevard, and got a bloody nose. This was in all truth a crime, since here was one contest where blood should never have been shed.

Well, it was a close fight, and I never was so tired in my life, but I thought I was winning by points. I kept punching, kept swinging away, and at the end, I sat there worn out on my stool, thinking I'd won the decision.

The reporter didn't mince words:

At the final bell the two dog-tired gladiators literally collapsed in their respective corners while the judges proclaimed Cole the winner. Irwin appeared too tired to register any disappointment at the decision and Cole could not have walked over to get his gold watch [sic. medallion] if his very life depended upon it.

I was disappointed and completely exhausted – so exhausted that when I left the ring, I almost fell down the steps.

But Lolly was saying to me, "You did a good job, you showed a lot of guts. You did a good job." And as I went back up the aisle, people kept saying, "Good fight, kid. Good going." A lot of different people said this, and that felt good. It was good to hear what they were saying, and I felt proud of my performance.

Suddenly, I didn't feel exhausted anymore.

ès

I KNEW I HAD TO WORK HARDER on my conditioning, so I jumped rope and did extra roadwork, building up my wind and stamina. I trained at Gleason's almost every day, working out as I would have at a job, and all the while I wondered whether I was really improving. I fought again, a week after my first bout, this time against Lloyd Scott of Harlem. The reporter called me the "Bronx Dreadnaught," referring to the massive battleships of the First World War.

"Irwin, who dropped a decision to Tony Cole at the local club last week, looked a little better last night. . . ." The writer called it "a slugfest."

Both lads were hard hitters, and when either connected, the "oofs" could be heard out on Jamaica Avenue. Many wicked body blows found their mark on Scott as the massacre progressed, and . . . it was slug-slug all the way, with both boys never pausing for a breath. At the end of the fifth and final round, the judges smiled on Irwin and the crowd smiled, too.

So I not only won for the first time, but I pleased the reporter, and the crowd also agreed with the judges' decision. My ability to deliver body punches from close in made the difference in this bout.

≥●

I sparred with some of boxing's finest of that day: light heavyweight champion Tami Mauriello, of New York City; Joe Baksi, also a New Yorker, one of the top heavyweight contenders of the 1940s; heavyweight Lee Q. Murray, from Norwalk, Connecticut, who would win 60 fights in his career, 43 by knockout; and Lee Oma, from Chicago, a heavyweight with immense talent, but who drank and womanized too much. Heavyweight Gunnar Borland of Syracuse was also at Gleason's at this time, having just lost to Mauriello, kayoed in the third round.

These fighters were about the same age as me, but they had three or four years' more experience, a tremendous difference in the ability of a boxer. One New York sports columnist later wrote about me and mentioned my notable sparring partners, saying, "Against them all he proved . . . that he knows his way around the 'squared circle,' once he gets into it."

Early in my career, I still had plenty to learn. One thing I knew by now was the importance of short punches to the body, delivered relentlessly from close in. I learned both how to deliver them and what it meant to receive them. One of my most memorable experiences was sparring with Joe Baksi, whose final professional record would be 59-9-4.

Joe was getting ready for a 10-round main event at Madison Square Garden, and I was at the training camp with him, as one of his sparring partners. He was a devastating body puncher. We were sparring, and all of a sudden he hit me right in the solar plexus.

I was paralyzed.

I didn't fall down, but I couldn't move. Now, if he wanted to, Joe could've hit me on the jaw, or hit me anywhere – because I couldn't move my arms, I couldn't move my body. And it took me maybe 10 seconds to catch my wind, to be able to continue boxing. But Joe didn't take advantage of me after he hit me, because he saw that I was paralyzed.

So, that's what often happens to you when you're a fighter – you can be paralyzed by one body punch.

ॐ

I CONTINUED TO STUDY HOW so many great fighters, from Joe Louis to Bummy Davis and Jake LaMotta, used a destructive left hook to get knockouts. I wished I could master that punch myself. At times, when I was LaMotta's sparring partner, I found myself the target of the Bronx Bull's own unique and crushing left hook.

LaMotta was very tough, and in great condition.

I often sparred with him and learned a lot from him. He'd come in at you with a leaping left hook, a devastating punch, and it came at you so quickly, you weren't prepared for it. I tried it myself, but never could master it.

LaMotta always made it clear that he was boss in the ring when we were sparring. If you hit him hard, landed a solid punch, he'd try, usually successfully, to land two or three solid punches in return. When the bell rang at the end of a three-minute round, LaMotta kept punching. He fought on. He didn't give you any rest – and he'd do this for three rounds straight, for nine or ten minutes straight. You just had to punch back. It was really good for your conditioning. John Thomas, his regular sparring partner, sometimes took severe beatings from him. Thomas sparred with LaMotta almost every day, and as a result had a head condition. Thomas was a good fighter himself and would usually fight on the undercard – the second fight – when LaMotta fought in a main event. LaMotta was a top middleweight contender by 1942, but a lot of boxers in his weight class wanted to avoid fighting him because he was so tough.

I worked hard on my own left hook, trying to make it come out naturally, to make it feel right. Over and over again, I threw it, practicing the footwork, the proper balance, the twist of the hips that gave power, the timing and the quickness. . . . It was difficult to master this punch. Then, one day, while I was walking home down Evergreen Avenue, hooking at imaginary opponents, I felt something good.

There! That was it!

I had the left hook.

"Gee, this is great," I told myself, throwing lefts all the way to the Margolies house.

It was like an awakening.

Next, I had a fight in the Jamaica Arena. I was up against a fellow named Phil Brady, who was six foot three and 215 pounds. I was about six foot and 185 pounds. He was from Long Island City, and a champion in the Navy, and his manager, Al Weill, had big plans to have him turn pro as soon as he got out of the service. Weill managed several world champions over his own career.

Brady was strong as a bull. I took a lot of punches. In the middle of the first round I got hit on the nose with a right hand. I felt my nose move over, and it started bleeding. At the end of the round I went to my corner and sat down. Blood was all over me. Lolly just grabbed my nose and moved it back, then he put cotton up my nostrils, patted me on the head, and said, "Go back out there! You're winning." The bell rang, and he said, "Keep it up! You're winning!"

In those days, if you didn't quit, the referee would never stop the fight. Today, if they ever saw anything like that, they would stop the fight immediately.

Well, a boxer breathes through his nose, and I couldn't breathe with the cotton plugging it. I kept fighting, the cotton fell out, and blood was all over me, all over the ring, all over Lolly, and all over the other fighter.

Then, suddenly, I hit Brady with that left hook, and he went down. I was so surprised – the hook had come out all by itself. I was standing there, staring at Brady on the canvas, but I was supposed to get back to a neutral corner, and the referee wouldn't start counting Brady out until I did.

I heard Lolly Kent shouting at me, "Go to your corner! Get to your corner!"

So, I won my first fight by a knockout. Most of my kayos would be by that sudden left hook that came out all by itself. As for the broken nose, I was used to having my nose banged up when playing football, because in my day players wore no face masks. I always had a scar on my nose during football season. Actually, after the Brady fight and Kent's quick work, it seemed to me that my nose was straighter than ever.

In 1942, there were a dozen or so more fights, and I won most of them, many by knockout. By the end of the year, few amateur fighters were willing to get in the ring with me. When they did, I won. By now, the reporters termed me a "hard hitter," who "packed a dangerous punch." Before long, they would be saying I carried "dynamite in both fists."

One reporter thought highly enough of me to write, "Every manager of a heavyweight believes he has a 'white hope,' and Eddie Irwin's backers were sure they had a future champ. While it's still too early to tell, there've been events which provide reason for such confidence."

I began to think seriously about entering the Golden Gloves Open Division in the spring of the following year, 1943. At the same time, I was studying for my NYU degree while working in the university bookstore. I was a newlywed husband, but as I watched the progress of the war, I knew I'd be in the service before long. During this time, there were many Nazi and Japanese triumphs over the Allies. I'd have to stop my studies if the situation became worse and college men in the Enlisted Reserves were called up. My blood brothers didn't go to college. Iggy Chaitin joined the Marines and became a pilot, and Bernie Jovans joined the Army. Walter Carroll became a fighter pilot in

The five "blood brothers" in 1936, back row l-r: Gersh,
Iggy Chaitin, and Frankie Ganger; front, Bernie Jovans
and Walter Carroll.

the Army Air Force, and Frankie Ganger worked in the war industry, at an aircraft factory in Pennsylvania, so he didn't have to enlist.

Then came deep sorrow, with the news that two of my blood brothers, Carroll and Iggy, had been killed in the service.

Carroll had been in the 15th Air Force, flying P-38 "Lightning" fighters in the Mediterranean theater. He'd been an ace, with eight kills to his credit. He'd returned to the U.S. for additional training and wanted to get into action against Japan. Instead, he'd been killed in California during practice for low-bombing missions. Carroll's parents called to notify me about his funeral. I was in disbelief because I'd heard he was back in this country, and I thought he was safe. He'd become an ace fighter pilot and had survived. We all thought he'd settled down in California with his wife, Andrea, who was a lawyer., but Carroll always was wild, crazy, always a troublemaker. He was trying to get sent back overseas, this time to the Pacific.

On that practice low-bombing run he was ordered not to fly lower than 500 feet, but he purposely, daringly, went lower, hit a power line, and blew up.

I went to Carroll's funeral – it was only a small funeral. Frankie Ganger was there, too. There was snow on the ground, and the hearse got stuck in the cemetery. Frankie and I had to push the hearse to get it through the snow.

Iggy Chaitin had been a top pilot in the Marine Air Corps. He was shot down in the Pacific, crashing on some remote island. He was missing in action and declared dead, and his body was never recovered. Iggy's funeral was in a big New York City temple. I was closer to Iggy than to Carroll, who'd drifted away from our group in our last years in school. I've remembered Iggy all my life. He was a very handsome guy, and a great athlete. After he died, I'd wake up in the middle of the night, dreaming I saw him in a subway train. He'd ignore me. I had those dreams almost every night back then. I encountered him a couple more times in my dreams, and we realized we'd never be friends anymore.

I still dream about Iggy from time to time.

Gersh slugs the heavy bag with a hard left while training for the Golden Gloves. (N.Y. Daily News)

Chapter 4

SWEET REVENGE

STROLLING WITH HIS GUEST from the garage gym back to the Woodstock house, Gersh is quiet, as if lost in thought. A towel around his neck, he's cooling down after the workout. Gardeners are busy raking the lawn and tending flowers. In the middle distance, the deer browsing near the fenced tennis court pause and lift their heads. The guest asks Gersh about being a student at NYU in 1942, with service in the war waiting for him.

Whatever the future held, and whatever World War II would bring, Gersh says, he worked hard as a student and a fighter. Eddie Gersh studied at NYU, and Eddie Irwin kept winning bouts from Jamaica Arena to the New York Athletic Club, St. Nicholas Palace, and the Downtown Athletic Club. He recalls changing his major from Physical Education to English Education, and that required lots more reading – not always easy when his body throbbed with the aches and bruises of sparring or from the previous night's match.

ॐ

I OFTEN ATTENDED CLASS WITH MY NOSE bandaged or an eye puffed. People in school must have thought I was crazy, because I'd come in with a black eye, or a cut eye, or bruises over my face. Here I am, an NYU student with other students, and I looked like some street bum. But after a while, they found out why I looked the way I did, and they used to come to the fights and root for me.

Gertrude didn't want to watch me fight, but she accepted my commitment to be a boxer. She didn't have much choice. I was resolved to do it. I also stuck to my studies in order to get that NYU degree, which would qualify me as a schoolteacher. Boxing became a way of life for me, and I began to think about turning pro. I was winning fights, so it was understood I'd turn pro. There weren't any other up-and-coming Jewish heavyweights in those days.

I was a good athlete in good condition, even if I didn't have the great natural coordination of fighters like Joe Louis or Sugar Ray Robinson. There was one white fighter I knew who had it, the heavyweight Lee Oma. I always wished I'd had that great coordination, but I was successful mainly because of my determination.

They were mostly victories, those 20 or so fights I had from late 1942 through the first weeks of 1943. Though I was officially an amateur, the money I made selling back the $15 winner's medallions helped Gertrude and me pay some of the bills. This was a time when an average day's wage was $5-10. Lolly Kent shared in the income. As manager, he took a third of either $15 or $10, and a dollar for expenses, such as car fare and first-aid supplies.

Lolly was very kind to me, although he was always fooling around, always teasing everybody. He was a practical joker and very noisy in the gym, but he was serious and concentrated when he was watching me sparring, and he was always there for me during fights. He was protective of his fighters, but demanding, too, bringing the best out of us. He pushed us to realize our potential – potential that he saw, though we often didn't. Lolly wasn't always gentle. He wanted fighters who could stand on their own feet, who could take care of themselves, even with their trainer driving them hard – especially with their trainer driving them hard. And he was rowdy and loud when he was in his fighter's corner during a bout.

Lolly once said, "Later in my career, television broadcasters had a rule: do not put an open mike within a mile of Larry Kent's corner, because the language I used was beautiful – I called my fighters all the sons of bitches in the world. I insulted them, I abused them, I cursed them – and it worked!

"Sometimes, when Eddie came back to the corner during a fight, he'd say to me, 'Don't swear! Don't curse!'"

❧

I WAS BECOMING WELL KNOWN IN NEW YORK, and some people at the Downtown Athletic Club in Lower Manhattan decided to bring in a ringer from Chicago to fight me. They planned to bet heavily against me, since I'd be no match for the heavyweight they were putting up. Everybody else would bet on the local boy, me, and they'd be cleaned out if I lost.

Lolly would have none of it.

"Those Wall Street guys at the Downtown Athletic Club thought they could pull a fast one," he said. "Eddie was a big favorite in New York, and these guys figured they'd make money off their friends at the club because they knew Eddie would lose – he'd get killed. But I refused. I told them, 'Who is this guy you're bringing in? I don't know him. My fighter doesn't fight anybody I don't know.'

"Somebody offered me $5,000 if Ed would fight their heavyweight. I told him, 'You can't give me $25,000 for this fight!' Well, those guys at Downtown got mad at me."

Lolly knew I'd willingly have fought that Chicago heavyweight. When I heard he was against it, I argued with him, saying I wanted to do it, but he refused to let me.

"Eddie didn't care, he'd fight anybody, he had no fear," Kent once said. "He went through a lot of rough sessions in training – got hit a lot. He used to think that when the bell rang you had to come out swinging, but I told him over and over that he had to box."

Lolly said I was a smart fighter. I tried to anticipate what the opponent was going to do, or to make him think I was going to do something – for example, I'd feint a left jab and then throw a right hand. I tried to out-think my opponent. At the time, I didn't realize that was one of my attributes as a fighter. My strategy also was to avoid getting hit, which didn't always work out of course.

Just how good I was getting became clear one day when I was working out at Gleason's, and in came the Jackson brothers. The Subnovice champ, the one who'd beaten me up a few months earlier, offered to spar. I said, "Sure."

We started boxing. Well, Jackson didn't realize how much I'd matured, how much I'd learned, and how much I'd progressed. This time, when I got him in the ring, I had no mercy – it was a heyday for me. This time, I beat the living daylights out of him. Whatever he'd done to me before, I gave it back to him in spades.

The first time around he had hit me with everything. The second time he couldn't lay a glove on me. Couldn't hit me on the ass with a broomstick. I didn't try to knock him down, but I battered him from pillar to post and back again, until he finally said, "Well, that's enough."

He was shocked.

Afterwards, he said to me, "Gee you got pretty good!"

That was very gratifying.

He said, "You've really improved a lot since last time I saw you."

I thought, revenge is sweet.

❧

IN THIS TIME, I BEGAN STUDENT-TEACHING as part of the NYU School of Education training. I taught at James Monroe High School in the Bronx, and I thoroughly enjoyed it.

As a boxer, I impressed the boys, of course, and since I wasn't much older than the students, some of the girls liked to flirt with me. One of them once stared so hard at me in class, that eventually she got me flustered. Then she looked over at her friends and grinned, as if to say to them that she'd got me – as if she'd just scored points in a contest with her friends.

Some of the girls, like her, were quite beautiful. Since they weren't much younger than me, at times they were hard to resist when they flirted, but I didn't let myself get involved.

More than anything, I was looking forward to entering the New York Golden Gloves Open Competition in 1943. I was ready, and if I was successful there, I'd have a path to the pros.

If I got through the first stage of the Gloves tournament, winning the New York championship, I might get to Madison Square Garden, which was the venue for the finals of the Intercity Golden Gloves Eastern championships. The Garden was where the top boxers fought. Success in the Gloves was a goal Lolly Kent kept in front of me. Afterwards, there would be opportunity to turn pro. A white, Jewish heavyweight contender was an ideal attraction for the fans – many who were for me and many who came to see me beaten. I could generate a lot of money at the gate, part of which would be my purse. Even if a contender lost a big fight, he could do very well. Heavyweight Jimmy Bivens got $40,000 in his loss to champion Joe Louis in 1941.

Of course, everything hinged on the war situation, which was gloomy. At the end of 1942, the enemy still had the military advantage. I well knew I might not be given enough time to graduate from NYU because the Enlisted Reserves, which I was in, could be called up. There was also talk of moving up my class's graduation date so the reserves could be inducted a couple of months sooner. In fact, graduating from NYU meant as much to me as boxing did just then. I'd worked too hard in school. I had a wife, probably a family would be started before long, but with the war on, nobody knew what would happen next. I had to graduate.

After all I'd gone through, borrowing the money for tuition, which had to be repaid, the injured knee, working in the cafeteria for 35 cents an hour and lunch, those grueling late night hours studying. . . . I wanted that degree from NYU.

ॐ

THE 1943 NEW YORK GOLDEN GLOVES tournament had eight weight classes, from 112-pound to heavyweight (above 175 pounds). It was an elimination, with the winners going on to the next fight, and the losers were out. The bouts were all three rounds of three minutes each. The USO, the charity that entertained the troops, received the profits from the Golden Gloves tournament, which was sponsored by the *Daily News* Welfare Association. The *Daily News* had sponsored the Gloves since 1927. The paper's sports department described the Golden Gloves as "the greatest of all amateur boxing events."

The boxers represented athletic clubs, some civilian, others from military bases. I fought for Roman Sports Club, a New York organization that Lolly Kent knew, and which had several fighters in the tournament. The bouts were held in Ridgewood Grove, a popular sports facility in the Ridgewood section of Brooklyn. New York City had a dozen important venues for boxing events, most of them community athletic clubs. These included the Pelican, the Irving, the Broadway Arena, the Pioneer, the Greenwood, the New Polo, Atlantic Gardens, the Bleecker, the Lion, and Jamaica Arena. A ticket to a 10-bout card cost about two dollars. The New York Athletic Club and the wealthy man's Downtown Athletic Club assumed airs of social superiority, but most of the fight venues could described as "dimly lit dens" wreathed in a fog of tobacco smoke.

People in the know could tell how well a boxer was doing by where he fought. Many young pros got their start at Ridgewood Grove, including Ruby Goldstein, Tony Canzoneri, Johnny

Huber, Danny Terris, Kid Rash, and Bummy Davis. The next level was the Broadway Arena in Manhattan and then St. Nicholas Palace at West 66th Street and Broadway. Everybody hoped one day to fight their way up to Madison Square Garden, the city's top boxing venue – the country's top venue – which then stood at Eighth Avenue and 50th Street.

Before you got to the Garden, you had to win in places like Ridgewood Grove, which was the centerpiece of a bustling Brooklyn-Queens neighborhood of mom-and-pop stores, movie houses, and gas stations. The Grove had a few stores, a pool hall, and food stalls. A number of different ethnic groups lived in the Ridgewood district, as could be seen by the restaurants, from Chinese to Italian, but the area around the Grove was predominantly German. Before the war, a Jewish fighter like Bummy Davis – especially Davis, who was pugnacious and proud – could be sure the Ridgewood fight fans would be cheering for his opponent and booing him mercilessly because he was a Jew. Davis would bring a hundred or more of his Brownsville neighborhood fans to cheer for him, and the moment he was announced they raised the roof with their roars.

In the 1930s, many a New York German had openly supported Adolf Hitler and the Nazi Party, but things had changed by 1943. No one dared voice pro-Nazi sentiments in public anymore. Still, I was glad to have friends from NYU and from my DeWitt Clinton days come to cheer for me at Ridgewood Grove.

Coast Guardsman Edmond White was the overall favorite to win the title. White was the previous year's Subnovice champion. Everyone who knew boxing and knew amateur fighters had anticipated that White and I eventually would meet for the championship, because they felt we'd beat everybody else. As it turned out, the draw matched us against each other for our first fight. I well knew how tough it would be.

White was about 205 pounds, and I weighed about 185, so he was quite a bit bigger than I was. When we came out to the center of the ring for our instructions from the referee, White tried to stare me down, because he was the champion. He tried, but he didn't psych me out at all. Well, we started fighting, and all of a sudden I saw bright light – I saw a million stars and I heard a tremendous roar. And then I heard the referee saying quietly, "Two, three . . . "

Then, I heard him much louder: "FOUR!"

Actually, he'd been shouting all the time at the top of his voice, but because I was stunned, I'd heard the first numbers as if he was whispering.

My first thought was, "Where are you, Eddie? You're sitting down."

"FIVE! . . ."

"What are you doing sitting down? You're supposed to be fighting! . . ."

"SIX! . . ."

The crowd was roaring now.

"Oh, you got knocked down! Okay, take a count."

Taking a count means that you stay on one knee until the count of nine, and then you stand up. Getting stunned like I did, I didn't feel anything, but I saw those million stars, and the big roar that I heard was the crowd yelling when I was falling. At the count of nine, I got up and the referee brushed off my gloves. I kept him between me and White to give myself another couple of seconds, and then we started fighting again.

The NYU sports reporter, Irv Kintisch, later described the action, saying White had hit me with a "vicious overhand right to the jaw."

Somehow, Gersh got to his feet and weathered the terrific onslaught of the aggressive seaman. This round went to White. To win, Eddie Gersh had to take the next two rounds – or knock out the burly White.

44

I gradually took control of the fight, winning the second round and outfighting White throughout the third. I was pressing him harder and harder until at last he was groggy, and I had him up against the ropes, with his hands down, and I was hitting him, boom, boom, boom, with left hooks and right crosses – and then the bell rang. But if the fight had continued for another 15 seconds, I would have knocked him out.

Kintisch wrote:

> Putting out all the way, our boy won an uphill battle to win a close decision over the Coastguardsman. This bout was really a thriller.

Eddie White went on to fight professionally, quite successfully. His trainer, Charlie Goldman, wanted to take me on, but I was loyal to Lolly Kent and wouldn't go. Goldman later became the trainer for world heavyweight champion Rocky Marciano.

The Eddie White fight wasn't the only thriller I had in the Golden Gloves tournament. The next bout, also at Ridgewood Grove, was for the New York Open title, and I was up against Jimmy Stift of the merchant marine. The *Daily News* reported on the fight and described how I was able to get inside and use short, hard, body punches alternating with my left hook.

> They fought through three fairly fast rounds, with Irwin doing the heavy smacking. He reddened the merchant seaman's middle with lusty shots and chopped away at his chin with equal facility.

I defeated Stift by a decision. The *Daily News* writer said:

> The [New York] Heavyweight Open title fitted nicely on the head of Edward Irwin of the Roman S.C., a former all-scholastic tackle from DeWitt Clinton High.

That tournament brought me considerable attention. I gained popularity with New York fight fans, and I was noticed by professionals – fighters and trainers.

❧

Irv Kintisch opened his next sports column in the NYU newspaper by writing about "one Eddie Irwin," who'd won the New York Golden Gloves:

Strange, isn't it that I mention boxing and, stranger still, somebody who many of you don't know. Perhaps, though, you know him as Eddie Gersh. Ah! that's right. Now you know him. The bespectacled Ed is an English major here at the School of Education.

Kintisch recalled my football injury:

It was doubtful if he would even walk again, much less play. But Gersh was too much of an athlete to let an injury get him down. . . . A year is all that Eddie has been at the game, but in that short time he has blasted his way right thru the amateur ranks, to the coveted title of "Amateur Heavyweight Champion of New York."

Another NYU student reporter, David Metzger, wrote in the school newspaper, *Washington Square College Bulletin*:

After seeing Eddie Gersh winning the Golden Gloves heavyweight championship at Ridgewood Grove last Wednesday night, I had to essay a bit further on one of New York University's finest athletes.

Metzger flatteringly described me "wading through strong contenders" and talked about my "brilliant victory" over Stift. Metzger also spoke of the upcoming Golden Gloves Eastern "Tournament of Champions" the following week, and about my hopes to win and go on to the national East-West competition in Chicago later in the month:

It seems like a long way to go, but after viewing an incident which occurred on the night of the finals, this correspondent feels sure he's got the stuff to go through undefeated.

Metzger then told about 135-pound Golden Gloves contender, Russell Hawkins, "a cock-sure fighter" who'd been flooded with public praise and compliments in the days before his fight for the division championship. "But it seems his opponent, Max Grothe, had failed to read of Russell's prowess. And before one round had been completed, the colored boy was flat on his back." The disap-pointed Hawkins was "weeping alone in the dingy hall," wrote Metzger, who saw me preparing to leave the dressing room to meet Jimmy Stift. Someone commented that Hawkins "was a good little fighter, but he let those press clippings go to his head."
Metzger wrote:

Turning to his manager Lolly Kent and Carl Moskowitz, a junior who has been Eddie's constant companion, Gersh confided, "If I get through this fight tonight, I won't let that happen to me. No matter what the papers say, I won't read a word."

Metzger continued:

Knowing Eddie, this further substantiates our original idea that he will be the same clean-living, modest, well-mannered

Gertrude and Edward Gersh, left, pose with friends while crowding into a bed frame on an outing in the Catskills.

boy we were acquainted with before all this sudden glory came to him. And, might we add, it couldn't happen to a nicer guy.

I enjoyed all the attention, but I refused to let the praise go to my head. I didn't speak about my boxing very much. Boasting went against my grain. Athletes of those times were taught to be dignified, reserved. That was how a man showed character. You just did your work and did your sports and that was it. It wasn't that I was so modest, but in those days, if you were a good athlete, you didn't brag like they do today. Fighters weren't loud and boastful. They lived up to certain standards of an athlete, quietly, and let their actions do the talking for them.

Dave Metzger gave himself credit for predicting "a great

future for Eddie Irwin. If you recall, we said that Eddie might take the place of Bob Pastor as the university's representative in the prize ring. Well, so far we're on the right track."

Being compared to Bob Pastor in March 1943 was a mighty compliment for any young fighter, but could I live up to that kind of billing? That was yet to be seen at the upcoming East Coast Intercity Golden Gloves competition, which would be at Madison Square Garden, before 19,000 howling boxing fans. Whether or not I continued to win, NYU had brought itself considerable good publicity by keeping me on scholarship back in 1941. New York's fight fans were following the Gloves, and now they knew about Eddie Irwin from NYU.

*Eddie Irwin ducks under an overhand right from Bill Gilliam
of Newark, on the way to the Eastern Regional Golden Gloves
heavyweight victory in 1943. (N.Y. Post)*

Chapter 5

'THIS SUDDEN GLORY'

PPROXIMATELY 30 bouts were held on each of the first two nights of the 1943 East Coast Golden Gloves "Tournament of Champions" in York City. The venue for March 15th and 17th was Ridgewood Grove, with the finals at the Garden on Friday, the 19th.

There were two categories of fights: a military-only tournament involving 30 servicemen, and the Golden Gloves "Tournament of Champions," which had 53 fighters, all on teams representing their home cities. Newspapers sponsored the various Golden Gloves city teams, which were named after the newspaper that was backing them. The *Philadelphia Inquirer* fighters were favored to win the team title, as the *Daily News* reported on Wednesday, March 17, the second night of the tournament:

> Despite the rainy weather, another near-capacity crowd subwayed to the Grove to see surviving boxers from the squads of the *Washington Times-Herald, Trenton Times, Charlotte* (N.C.) *Observer, Newark Evening News,* [*El Mundo* and *El*

Parcial of] Puerto Rico and the [*Daily*] *News* Welfare Association try to overhaul the iron-fisted, steel-nerved *Philadelphia Inquirer* outfit in the race for the team championship and trophy.

In the first stage, I drew a bye.

All eight of the Philadelphia fighters won their matches the first night, Monday. Their heavyweight, Danilee Yorkis, won by a knockout. Yorkis was described by the *Daily News* as a "19-year old power-punching student." On Wednesday night, I met Trenton's Hal Evans, whom I kayoed to reach the championship bout. In years to follow, the Evans bout would pass from memory. It was diminished by comparison with the ferocious fights against Eddie White and Jimmy Stift and then the Golden Gloves championship at Madison Square Garden.

The night I fought Evans, Yorkis was the favorite over Newark's Bill Gilliam. The *News* called Gilliam

> . . . a hard-hitting colored giant who upset Charlotte's Bob Burns, a paratrooper who used to perform for Chicago's Gloves champs. Yorkis and Gilliam were fighting for the right to meet New York's dreadnought, Edward Irwin, a 22-year-old NYU student.

Gilliam won that night, making Yorkis one of only two Philadelphians who didn't reach the tournament finals. Six Philadelphia boxers would fight for championship titles on Friday night at the Garden. Their team already had earned enough points to win the team title, but Philadelphia wouldn't win the most prestigious Golden Gloves title of all – heavyweight champion.

That title would go to either Newark's Bill Gilliam or to me.

On the evening of Friday, March 19, 1943, Madison Square Garden was crammed with 19,000 fans. I'd never boxed in front of so huge a crowd before. Some friends and relatives were in the seats, but Gertrude wasn't there because she couldn't stand to watch me in the ring, punching and getting punched. My mother's brother, Bill Koven, was there that night. Uncle Bill was eager to see his nephew fight for the championship. It was big news around New York.

Also in the crowd was the fast-rising professional welterweight contender, Sugar Ray Robinson. Sugar Ray had come to cheer for Lolly Kent's prime amateur, Eddie Irwin. Lolly had worked as one of Sugar Ray's trainers, and used to tell Ray about me, and me about Ray. At the time, Sugar Ray was 43-1. His only loss had been to Jake LaMotta on February 5th of that year. Robinson met LaMotta again on February 26th and won the rematch.

Lolly worked with Ray Robinson for 14 years and considered him the greatest fighter, pound for pound, who ever lived.

Before the fight, I was in a small dressing room downstairs from the Garden boxing arena, methodically preparing myself. I sat on the trainer's table, bare-chested, in shorts and boxing shoes, while Lolly taped up my hands. The Gloves tournament went on above us. The noise of the crowd rose and fell in waves, then would erupt in cheers as the boxers went at it. And there would be a great shout when a man was knocked down.

The previous two bouts had been short, both ending with knockouts in the first round. The 175-pound fighters were boxing now. The heavyweights, Gilliam and I, were next, the last fight of the tournament, the main event. There was no greater place for a boxer to be than Madison Square Garden, fighting for the championship in front of a packed house. Tonight, I was a long way from Ridgewood Grove in Brooklyn and from the football fields where I'd earned my first reputation as an athlete.

Even with the crowd noise above us, there was an atmosphere of profound mental concentration in the dressing room. Kent made comments now and again as he worked on my hands. He drew the robe over my shoulders, then pushed the gloves onto my taped hands, lacing them tight. Up above, the ringside bell clanged to start the third and final round of the 175-pound class. The noise surged and rose to a crescendo as the fighters battled with all they had. I was excited, nervous, eager. The gloves felt good as I bumped them together a few times. Then came a sudden roar from the arena.

It was only a minute into the third round.

Now the bell was ringing and the crowd was cheering wildly. There'd been another knockout. The 175 fight was over.

I stood down from the trainer's table.

Someone called for me to come up. I left the dressing room and walked down the hall toward the door of the arena, Lolly and a couple of friends from NYU were with me. The long robe hung loose about my shoulders as I approached the doorway that opened into the Garden arena. I worked my arms to loosen them, tapped my gloves together, and paused at the door. The house lights were down. The crowd was hushed, sitting in darkness, waiting.

I felt my heart pounding.

Suddenly, the spotlight hit me, and I started briskly down the aisle. The crowd was cheering. In that moment, as before, the nervousness left me. The spotlight was shining on me all the way down the aisle, and as I climbed through the ropes and into the ring. I was ready.

Then the spotlight lit big Bill Gilliam as he came down the aisle and climbed into the ring. The house lights came up, and we went to the center of the ring to get our instructions from the referee. Gilliam looked strong, weighing about 215 to my 185. His arm was as big as my thigh.

Years later, Lolly Kent recalled watching us being instructed by the referee:

When they walked to the center of the ring, Gersh looked like a flyweight compared to Gilliam! When Eddie came back to our corner, I told him, "Listen, if you don't box, I'm going to stop the fight!"

Eddie said, "Don't stop the fight!"

I told him, "If you go out and start swinging, I'm going to stop the fight!"

"Don't stop the fight!"

As the bell rang, Kent pushed the mouthpiece into my mouth and yelled, "Then box!"

Gilliam and I sprang up.

And I boxed.

Keeping moving, moving all the time, jabbing with my left, ducking Gilliam's overhand rights – which would have laid me low – and landing that left hook solidly to the body, again and again. Boxing, scoring points by connecting with inside punches and avoiding getting hit. Kent said:

Gersh tore the Garden down that night! There wasn't anybody sitting in their seats. He was giving that guy a boxing lesson like you wouldn't believe!

The crowd's roars were deafening.

As I fought, my Uncle Bill was so excited, yelling and throwing elbows, hitting the guy next to him until the guy finally said, "Hey, take it easy!"

"I can't," said Uncle Bill, "he's my nephew."

The guy took a long look at me and then at big Bill Gilliam and asked, "Which one?"

Kent, at ringside, was momentarily interrupted:

In the middle of the fight, Mike Jacobs, the Garden's top promoter and a friend of mine, came running down to the ring.

"Who's got that guy?" Jacobs said, meaning, who's Gersh's promoter?

The New York Daily News *poses Gersh studying for his NYU finals after winning the Golden Gloves heavyweight championship; a book on boxing is at the bottom of a pile of English literature.*

I said, "You got him, Mike, he's yours."

"That's all I want to know," Jacobs said, and he ran back up the aisle again.

He wanted Gersh.

Mike Jacobs was the promoter for none other than Joe Louis, the world heavyweight champion.

The Gersh-Gilliam fight went the full three rounds, and the

crowd loved it. Two heavyweights moving and punching, battering each other relentlessly, pressing each other nonstop, made for a great, exciting fight.

I worked inside Gilliam's longer reach, taking a good deal of punches, but never getting caught by one that staggered me. My aggressiveness, and the accuracy of my punches, gave me a points advantage over Gilliam in the second and third rounds. Gilliam, whose own conditioning was excellent, never backed off.

When the final bell clanged, the crowd roared its approval. I returned to my corner and slumped down onto the stool, where Kent took out the mouthpiece, wiped my face with a wet cloth, and gave me a swig of water. It was all up to the three judges now. Kent was sure we had won on the points I earned in the second and third rounds.

After a few moments, the announcer was at the center of the ring, reading the judges' scores, one by one, over the public address system. . . . It was close – then, suddenly Eddie Irwin was declared the winner. I was the new Eastern Golden Gloves Heavyweight Open Champion, my hand raised by the referee as the crowd cheered. There had been so many successful Jewish boxers over the years, but Edward Irwin Gersh was the one and only Jewish Golden Gloves Open heavyweight champion.

Larry Kent recalled watching his 1943 heavyweight champion at center ring:

Eddie had nothing to his name when he started in boxing – he had nothing, he had no money, nothing, but then he did this! . . . He did this.

Afterwards, I was sitting in the dressing room, when Sugar Ray Robinson came in to congratulate me. I shook his hand, thanked him and said, "Ray, it won't be long before you're a champion, too."

The fighter, Eddie Irwin, soon after winning the Eastern Regional Golden Gloves heavyweight championship in 1943.

Chapter 6

'PRO TIMBER, BUT IT'S WAR'

THE FOLLOWING DAY, A NEW YORK PAPER wrote that "Erwin [sic], the violent Violet," was an "aggressive athlete who used short, driving punches with telling effect." The writer added: "The going was rough for Erwin at times, but there was no doubt of his right to the verdict."

The *New York Times* called the heavyweight title bout a "slambang affair in which the violent student won as the result of a heavy barrage of blows in the last two sessions of their three rounder."

The *New York Post* ran a dramatic picture of me getting under a right cross from the towering Gilliam, with the caption: "It pays to duck – Ed Irwin, NYU student, ducked just in time to miss a hefty swing by Bill Gilliam."

The *Daily News* wanted to come and take a picture of me in James Monroe, teaching in front of the class, but the principal wouldn't allow them to because he thought it would be too disruptive. So they came over to the house and took the picture there. The *News* set up a photograph of me, wearing a dark suit and tie, looking studious in my glasses, and reading intently while sitting behind a tall stack of books.

"A Champ?" asked the caption's headline.

Don't let that pile of book larnin' fool you. Edward Irwin, student-teacher at James Monroe High School, Bronx, won the Golden Gloves heavyweight championship. He'll start training for the Inter-City matches in Chicago, March 31.

Almost hidden at the bottom of the pile of books – they were on Shakespeare, language studies, and literature – was a single volume, entitled *Boxing*.

One New York reporter called me the "Evergreen Avenue battler," and said I was expected soon to turn pro and have a few fights before being inducted into the army. In fact, there wouldn't be much time for professional boxing, since the military wanted the Enlisted Reserves who were finishing college to go right into the service. We learned that the rumors were true: the NYU senior class would be graduated a couple of months early, around the end of March, without taking final exams. The students would have to cram, however, to complete their course work. We would be called up some time in April.

This meant my studies were in direct conflict with the East-West Intercity Golden Gloves competition in Chicago. I had my required final work to do, but I couldn't do it if I went to Chicago. A difficult decision faced me. I wanted to compete, but I also wanted that NYU degree firmly in hand before I was inducted into the service. Who knew whether I'd ever again have the chance to earn a degree?

In an article headlined, "NYU Boxer Pro Timber, But It's War," a reporter wrote about my potential as a professional boxer:

Any New York collegian with a fair amount of boxing ability – this one is Ed Irwin, Eastern heavyweight Golden Gloves champion – now would be getting flattering invitations from pro fight managers were these ordinary times. But the NYU student, who soon leaves with his teammates for the Intercity matches in Chicago March 31, is in the army reserve and may not be around long enough for professional fighting.

Unfortunately, the tournament in Chicago might not be possible for me, either. Not only did I have my NYU work to do, but I was also expected to continue my student teaching at Monroe, where I'd been an assistant football coach the previous fall, and now was the idol of the students because of the Golden Gloves championship. The high school newspaper featured me with the headline, "Gloves Champ is at Monroe," and the subhead, "Eddie Gersh Trained Six Months in Rain and Snow on Pelham Park Track." It opened with a reference to the photograph in the *Daily News*:

Glorified in print on March 19, a picture of the new Atlantic Seaboard Golden Gloves champ surrounded by Shakespeare and Will Durant's book on philosophy, heralded a change in Monroe's activities.

The English office suddenly seethed with fight fans and less spitballs were thrown in the classes he entered. It wasn't a miracle that wrought this change, it wasn't a gun . . . it was just 5 feet 11 inches of muscle named Edward Irwin Gersh.

Mr. Gersh is an English student-teacher here at Monroe and when he isn't studying Shakespeare and verbs and nouns, he's running around the Pelham Bay track, snow, rain, or sun, six in the morning. At 9 he's at school, and at night he takes extra courses toward becoming an English teacher. . . .

Now that the Champ has tasted the sweets of fame, he is contemplating the finals, which will determine the national heavy-weight champ. . . .

The Eastern Golden Gloves Intercity team had never beaten the West in Chicago during the 17 years of competition. We'd won the previous year, when the tournament was held at the Garden. New York sports reporters called us "one of best teams ever assembled," and I was the top heavyweight. I had to make a quick decision whether to go to Chicago or stick with my studies and student teaching. By now, I was working out at Stillman's Gym, but I couldn't put in the long hours there that I really needed to put in. I was a schoolteacher until noon, a boxer during the afternoon, and in the evening a college student with two classes, one at 4:30 p.m. the other at 7:30 p.m. Then there was the studying late into the night.

The *Daily News* soon featured me again, this time in a photograph of me working out with a punching bag:

In the basket! Employing a heavy bag and a lot of imagination, Heavyweight Ed Irvin [sic] drives home a left uppercut to some Westerner's solar plexus as he trains for the Intercity Golden Gloves championships to be held at Chicago a week from today.

In this same time, Lolly Kent went by train to Chicago to scout the tournament's leading heavyweight opponent. Kent immediately saw the fighter was exceptional and considered him to be a "ringer" – an experienced boxer who didn't belong in the Golden Gloves. A ringer is a seasoned athlete whose abilities are much higher than that of other athletes in a competition with a speci-fic level of ability. Apparently, some manager or promoter had set up this boxer to build his reputation by winning the national Gloves championship, which was a springboard for a professional career.

Kent was troubled, worried about the safety of his fighter, who was far less experienced than the western heavyweight and might be seriously injured. On the train back to New York, Kent sat with the *Daily News* executive who was in charge of promoting the Golden Gloves tournament. Kent described that moment:

I bluntly told the guy that it wasn't fair to put Eddie up against a ringer.

"What do you mean, he's a 'ringer?'" the guy asked, annoyed, and denied the fighter was a ringer.

"He's a ringer," I said. "He's too good, he hits too hard – my fighter's not going up against him."

Lolly knew I'd willingly go up against anyone, but he was the manager, and the safety of his fighter was foremost. I didn't know about it at the time, but he'd decided not to let me fight in Chicago, and he told the executive as much. Unfortunately for Lolly, he was at the time on salary with the *Daily News* as a boxing consultant. The *News* executive gave Lolly a warning.

He said I'd be fired by the *News* if Gersh didn't fight the guy in Chicago. He said to me, "You'll lose your job." I told him, "Fine, pay me off," – and they did, and I lost a big opportunity there, but my fighter's safety came first.

Kent told nothing of this to me at the time. I didn't know about that situation. I had my own concerns about taking the time off from school to go to Chicago, which would require at least 10 days, including the train trip. I wouldn't be able to finish my course work if I fought in the Gloves. After all my struggles, I'd lose the NYU degree. For different reasons than Kent had, I reluctantly came to the decision not to go to Chicago. Better to graduate, get my degree, and then enter the military service.

I was disappointed, but gave up my spot on the East team, which was filled by Cornelius Young, a Coast Guardsman, who'd won the serviceman's heavyweight title at Madison Square

Garden the same night I won the Golden Gloves Open title. Coincidentally, Young was from Chicago.

Taking the top heavyweight spot on the team roster was Newark's Bill Gilliam. As it turned out, the East team lost the tournament 13-2, and Gilliam was defeated in a close fight.

❧

BEFORE I HAD TO GO INTO THE SERVICE, I had a few more fights, including a rematch with Bill Gilliam. By then, however, I'd been mostly studying and student-teaching and wasn't training enough. Gilliam, on the other hand, had been in the thick of training and fighting. He'd competed in both the Golden Gloves East-West championships in Chicago and in the national tournament sponsored by the Amateur Athletic Union (AAU).

The *Home News* previewed the Irwin-Gilliam bout, set for the St. Nicholas Arena on April 17th and sponsored by the local Post Office Clerks Association, Branch 1. The fight was a fund-raiser for the union's Sick and Death Benefit Fund. The paper said the "rank and file of fight promoters are sure to cast their eagle eyes" on Gersh and Gilliam, who were fighting their last bouts as amateurs. Another heavyweight fight on the card that night also offered a pair of up-and-coming young boxers, including Eddie White, whom I'd beaten in the Golden Gloves.

The *Home News* featured me in its headline: "Ed Irwin Makes Last Appearance as Amateur at P.O. Clerks' Bouts." The article predicted the quality of the heavyweight double card, "Both contests promise to be real punching parties." It went on to say:

Much of the interest will center upon Irwin, who finishes his course at New York University today. Irwin has been ordered into the service next week and will report at an Army base. The New York University student passed his examination for the service some time ago as a member of the Reserves. Since he is reported to be suffering from a perforated ear drum, there is a likelihood that he may be rejected.

By now, I'd fought 16 bouts in my one-year amateur career, with four losses, two of which I'd reversed in return fights. As a pro prospect, I was of special interest to both New York fans and the newspaper reporters. One paper said that boxing promoter "Nat Rogers, 20th Century matchmaker, already has asked for his services in May." In fact, the military had the first claim on my services. Still, Larry Kent hoped his fighter would be able to get a professional career off the ground.

"A few more amateur bouts under his belt and Gersh is going to make his pro debut," Kent told a reporter. "He is really the best young heavyweight making the rounds today, and I'm aiming high with him."

One reporter wrote that the Irwin-Gilliam match "has boxing observers agog," saying it was "a return engagement and was made by popular request when followers of the two fighters clamored for another bout." The writer went on to tell about Gilliam's last two fights, the Golden Gloves and AAU:

Though he dropped close decisions, ringwise fans believed the experience he gained in both tournaments may give him an edge in their clash tomorrow.

Among Irwin's followers tomorrow night will be a delegation of N.Y.U. professors who will root for him. Irwin majored in English at college and conversing with him leaves one with the impression if he scales the heights, he will make boxing followers forget about Gene Tunney, the Shakespearian scholar. Irwin for some time has been a student teacher at James Monroe H.S. where he quickly became one of the most popular members of the faculty. Because of his entrance into the service next week, Irwin received his diploma Wednesday.

Gersh in training, photographed by the Daily News,
but soon to enter the U.S. Army.

Several topnotch young boxers were on the card of nine fights
that night, including other Golden Gloves national finalists about
to turn professional. Eddie White, too, was expected to become a
pro. It was a sellout, with 4,000 boxing fans in the audience. Eddie
Irwin and Bill Gilliam were the main attraction.

This time, Gilliam's additional experience from his two recent tournaments did indeed make a difference. Gilliam didn't let me duck those crashing right hands, but I was able to shake off the blows and fight right through the final round. One reporter described the battle:

> Reversing a setback suffered in the Eastern Golden Gloves finals in Madison Square Garden several weeks ago, William Gilliam, Newark heavyweight, floored the Bronx's Ed Irwin three times to gain a five-round decision over the former New York University student in the feature fracas. . . .
>
> A capacity crowd . . . saw Gilliam outbox and outpunch the Army-bound Bronxite . . . and floored his rival for nine-counts in the second, fourth, and fifth rounds, crossing rights each time to accomplish the feat.

I regretted that I'd not better prepared for the bout and ended my amateur days with a victory. Gilliam would go on to have a professional career that ended in 1953, when he lost a non-title fight, a 10-round decision, to Ezzard Charles, then the reigning world heavyweight champion.

Eddie Irwin's amateur career was over. One week later, Edward Gersh reported for duty to begin his military service.

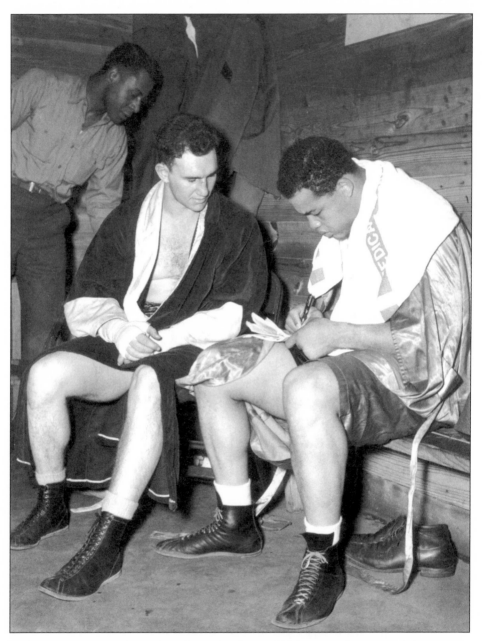

A moment to remember: Edward Gersh asks world heavyweight champion Joe Louis for his autograph before an exhibition match for the soldiers at Fort Bragg in 1944.

Chapter 7

THE ARMY BOXING INSTRUCTOR

I FOUND MYSELF IN THE 4TH BATTALION, 4th Field Artillery Regiment, stationed at enormous Fort Bragg in Charlotte, North Carolina. Gertrude moved down there to be with me, renting a small apartment near the base, which we shared with another couple. We spent our weekends together when I got a pass. Many married enlisted men had similar arrangements, since there was no room on the base for their wives to stay. Gertrude got a secretarial job on the base.

Soon after basic training, I became a boxing instructor at Fort Bragg's Infantry Replacement Training Center. Boxing was part of the soldier's physical fitness regimen, and since my reputation had followed me, I was welcomed as an instructor. There were generally several hundred soldiers taking boxing lessons at the camp at any one time. My friend from the NYU football team, Irv Kintisch, was in the same platoon. Irv had been the national shot-put champion in college. We often worked out together.

I did my best to keep fit. When we went on marches, I got permission to run when the others walked. I used to run around and around the company as it marched. For the first nine months in the service I didn't have any fights. Boxing matches are the best kind of conditioning there is, and a boxer needs them.

I had good sparring partners in this time because there were several accomplished boxers at Fort Bragg, including two professionals. One was New York heavyweight Enzo Avondoglio, who'd won the Golden Gloves championship at Madison Square Garden a few years earlier. At 28, the big, good-natured Avondoglio was six years older than me, and had fought more than 100 times, many as a professional. A native of Italy, he'd been brought up in Manhattan, and had briefly entered a seminary to become a priest. Boxing suited him better, and he fought under the name Enzo Avon. He was good enough to be a sparring partner for heavyweight contender Billy Conn, who twice lost to Joe Louis for the world championship.

Avondoglio and I were both boxing instructors and good friends. Like me, military service had cut his fighting career short The more experienced Avondoglio sparred with me and became my trainer. Avondoglio had taken part in a number of exhibition fights to entertain the troops, and he was well-regarded on the base. An article in *The Military News* told of Avondoglio's youth as a tough street fighter, which supposedly had led him to taking up boxing. The title was, "They Annoyed Cpl. Avon, So He KO'd 'em – That's How He Became New York's Top Heavyweight." The article went on:

> Avon won bouts from [several] . . . ranking glove-swingers, receiving raves from the best of New York's sports scribes.
>
> Then – as he stood on the peak of his career – came another kind of fight, this one preceded by "Greetings" from the commander-in-chief. Uncle Sam wanted to borrow Avon's fighting talents for the all-time card between the Allies and Axis. . . .
>
> Avon is now managing and training Pvt. Erwin E. [sic] Gersh, Center Headquarters Company, but his active ring career is past. He desires now to help swing the haymaker that will knock out Hitler, Hirohito and their partners.

"After that," he grinned, "no more for me. I do something else after the war."

In mid-January 1944, Avondoglio and I got the good news that none other than reigning world heavyweight champ, Joe Louis, was coming to Fort Bragg for an exhibition fight. Louis had suspended his professional career and enlisted in the army, and his duties included touring military bases around the country. He and an accomplished pro – in this case George Nicholson – would put on a show for the troops, the highlight to a night of exhibition boxing that would include bouts between servicemen. Avondoglio and I were asked to fight in a preliminary to the Louis match.

Joe Louis had been the undefeated world champion since 1937, and I had great admiration for him. It was a thrill to meet him, let alone be on the same card with him. Joe was nicknamed the "Brown Bomber," and he dominated boxing. Just about every boxing fan around the world admired him and considered him the best heavyweight ever. He won most of his fights by knockouts, with that terrific left hand of his. He had the modest, gentle character that was so respected in great athletes in those days. Fighters tried to live up to the standards established for them, with good manners and grace. Joe epitomized that ideal.

Nicholson was black, but all the opponents Louis had fought for the championship until then had been white. In those days, the boxing card was a black fighter against a white fighter, or two white fighters against each other. Because of prejudice, it was thought that nobody would come to see two black fighters in the ring. Few promoters would put on two black fighters then, although blacks did fight each other in the Golden Gloves and in exhibitions.

The Joe Louis exhibition was held at Fort Bragg's Field House, which was packed with thousands of soldiers that night. The event was to serve as a fund-raiser for the Fresh Air Fund, which benefited city children, helping them spend summer days in the country.

Before the fight, Enzo and I made an agreement that we would put on a good show, but if one of us got hit hard, got staggered, as we termed it, then the other guy would step in and we'd clinch – hold on to each other – and give the guy who got staggered a chance to recover, and then we'd fight on. We didn't want to hurt each other. There'd be no decision, just an exhibition.

The fighters, including Joe Louis, got dressed in the same locker room, and a newspaper photographer took our pictures posing with the champ. My top sergeant had asked me to do him the favor of getting Joe Louis's autograph, and I sat down on a bench beside Joe while he signed the fight program for me. I didn't collect autographs myself, but it looked like he was signing for me, and the photographer snapped a picture of us together. That picture went out everywhere, to the military paper, *Stars and Stripes*, and even to new York City and the *Daily News* rotogravure section – a photograph section that ran on Sundays. In the *News*, it ran under the headline, "A Couple of Champs." That visit by Joe Louis was a high point of my boxing career.

The picture of Louis and me wouldn't be the only well-traveled photograph from the night's boxing show. In our three-round heavyweight preliminary, Avondoglio and I showed our stuff and were in good form. The crowd was enjoying it, but of course they were anticipating the feature match, with Joe Louis. Then at one point I caught Enzo with a hard punch, and he felt it – I could see he was staggered. So, as we'd planned, I stepped in to clinch with him, and of course, I dropped my hands as I did so. Well, he hit me, and I never saw it coming. The next thing I knew I was on my back, and the crowd was cheering. It was a misunderstanding between us, but I was furious – and maybe he was, too, because I'd hit him harder than he'd expected. I took the nine-count and got up and we went at it! Well, we had those soldiers on their feet. They were standing on their chairs and roaring! It was a great fight. More exciting than the Joe Louis exhibition, that's for sure. At the instant Avondoglio had hit me, a photographer had caught the moment, with me flat out, stiff as a board, but in mid-air. It was an amazing picture, and it was published around the world, becoming a well-known boxing photograph of the era. Unfortunately, I've lost my own copy.

ॐ

FOR ALL THE ENJOYMENT OF CONTINUING to box and instruct in the army, I still didn't have time for the strict workout regimen needed by a fighter in training, which requires regular bouts that improve sharpness and conditioning. One soldier at Fort Bragg who was trying to maintain his career as a professional boxer was Joey Maxim, a leading contender for the light heavyweight championship, and an athlete who was in superb condition. Maxim asked me to spar with him, and I agreed to, even though I wasn't in shape. He had a big fight coming up in Washington, D.C., and needed the work. I said, okay, and he agreed to take it easy. We began to box. Then some girls came into the gym, and all of a sudden he came at me with a two-fisted attack, with everything he had, obviously trying to knock me down. Well, he didn't knock me down, but he kept throwing a lot of leather.

After it was over, I asked him, "What the hell happened to you?"

He answered, "Gee, I don't know, I guess I lost my head and started showing off in front of those girls."

I told him, "Joey, not only did you lose your head, but you lost your sparring partner."

Maxim went on to become the light heavyweight champion by defeating Sugar Ray Robinson at Yankee Stadium a year later. Robinson was too exhausted to answer the bell in the 13th round.

As for me, I decided to enter the annual Golden Gloves tournament of the Carolinas, scheduled for mid-February. When I'd won the Gloves championship the previous year, I'd made friends with several of the Carolina fighters who'd been in New York for the tournament. Those connections and my performance in the exhibition with Enzo Avon had made local boxing officials and reporters well-disposed toward me. The *Charlotte Observer's* headline was, "New York Champion Enters Gloves," with the subhead: "Fort Bragg Heavy, Kingpin in 1943 Tournament of Champions, Ready to Go." The newspaper wrote about my hopes for a shot at the national title.

> Gersh's entry was the big news at Golden Gloves headquarters yesterday, and if the heavyweight field fills out as expected, the same fine competition should result that came off last year. . . . The Carolinas tournament has turned out some first-rate heavyweight scrappers, and Gersh will be one in a long parade.

If I became the next Carolina Golden Gloves heavyweight champion, I'd be heading back to New York and the Garden to defend my title and perhaps get a shot at the national championship. In a letter of introduction that accompanied my Gloves entry form, I told the local committee that I looked forward to the "opportunity to make up for last year and help the East avenge the 13–2 defeat [in Chicago]."

The *Observer* considered me "The most interesting individual entry so far." The Fort Bragg paper, *The Observation Post*, published a lengthy article about the upcoming tournament.

> When the 12th annual Carolinas Golden Gloves tournament takes place in Charlotte Feb. 17, 18 and 19, a hard-hitting heavyweight from New York may step into the ring to battle for the title. And if given permission to compete, his chances of winning it look excellent. . . .
>
> There's an old saying in sport circles that "experience gives class and class is what makes a winner." If that holds true, Gersh should have things pretty much his own way. . . . Gersh has one consuming ambition: he would like to be a

physical instructor in the Army. And few men are better qualified. When the war is over, he hopes to enter the professional ranks of boxers.

Interest in athletics was overtaking my interest in teaching English, the career for which my NYU degree had prepared me. The upcoming Carolinas tournament was a good stimulation for me. I knew I'd have some formidable opposition, including a finalist from the previous year's AAU national championship. With the Carolinas Golden Gloves tournament also serving as a fund-raiser for the Fresh Air Fund, the sponsoring *Charlotte Observer* gave me good publicity in order to drum up interest in the fights. A few days before the tournament was to take place, the picture of Joe Louis signing a program for me ran in the newspaper under the headline, "Gloves Entry, Joe – In Good Company!" It went on to say that Gersh,

> the most talked about individual entry . . . is training hard in hopes of winning here and going on to New York and duplicating his triumph of last year.

Indeed, I thought this could be the chance to put my boxing career back on track, and the army was cooperating, assigning an officer to organize the boxing team at the Infantry Replacement Training Center and drive me to the tournament in Charlotte. Matters wouldn't be so simple, however. First of all, I could only get a pass for a three-day leave, meaning I had to wait until the last moment to go to Charlotte.

The story of what happened next was told by *Charlotte Observer* sports columnist Jake Wade, as excerpted below:

> [Gersh] filed his Golden Gloves entry some time ago and had been training for weeks to box here, hoping he would be able to win out, make the trip to New York, and defend his

title in "the tournament of champions."

Our boys here were personally interested in his entry because they knew him in New York, and also his name added much to the tournament.

But when the weigh-in came off Wednesday, neither Gersh nor his teammates on the Reception [sic] Center team showed up. The deadline was 6 o'clock and the draw was made immediately afterward. There were four open division heavyweights in the field. Officials assumed that for some reason Gersh and his mates couldn't get there. They were left out.

Later, after the draw, tournament officials received a telegram from the officer in charge of my team, advising that they would come to Charlotte Friday. It had been delivered to *The Observer* office. Officials agreed that it was too late to do anything about it, and wired the Fort Bragg party that the draw had been made and my team would have to be left out.

Gersh Shows Up, Heartbroken.

Nevertheless, on Friday, Gersh and his officer showed up in Charlotte. They said they did not receive the wire and had no idea that Gersh, since he was a heavyweight and a weigh-in was not compulsory, would not be able to compete. They did not understand the rigidity of the rule that contestants had to be on hand Wednesday and felt it might be waived.

Since Gersh was the defending New York champion and there were only four heavyweights in the field, none of whom had fought, they were hopeful he might still be put into the draw. It was also pointed out that Gersh had been able to arrange only a three-day leave.

Officials decided that if the four heavyweights enrolled, or their handlers, would agree to his post-entry, he would be permitted to fight. A unanimous agreement, however, could not be obtained from this group. They felt that Gersh should have been here with the others, and that it was unfair to their men for him to report a day late. So Eddie Gersh, a rather heartbroken young man, has been only a spectator at this tournament.

There were hopes that the "unusual circumstances surrounding his inability to compete" in the Carolinas tournament would prepare the way for me to compete in New York as an unattached contestant. It didn't work out that way, however, and once again I lost my opportunity to fight for the national championship. Indeed, I was heartbroken.

Soon afterwards, I was transferred to Camp Robinson in Arkansas, as was Avondoglio, who continued to train me. (We would meet again many years later, in New York City, when I got into a cab and found the driver was Enzo.)

Gertrude followed me to Arkansas, driving the whole way out by herself because I had to travel with my company. Once again, we found an apartment to share with another couple, this time in off-base family housing provided by the military. I lived in camp during the week and with Gertrude on weekends. This time, Gertrude didn't work on the base, as she had at Fort Bragg.

At Camp Robinson, I continued to be a boxing instructor, and when it came time for a fund-raising benefit, my reputation made me a prime candidate for another exhibition.

I only had one real fight in the service, and that was at the Little Rock Boys' Club in the spring of 1944, just after I got to Camp Robinson. A couple of Arkansas A&M student athletes had been seriously injured in a car crash, and the college boxing team and the army arranged for a boxing event that would raise money for their benefit. In my fight, I just wanted to take it easy and put on a nice exhibition. My opponent was Jack Bales, a Marine studying at the college, and the state of Arkansas AAU heavyweight champion that year. He was a little heavier and quite a bit taller than I was. The wives of the two injured students were in the crowd, as were many servicemen, including high-ranking army officers such as the general who commanded Camp Robinson.

Bales came out with a big flurry in the first round and hit me a couple of times. The exhibition turned into a real battle, as a sell-out crowd of 1,200 saw me knock Bales down twice in that first round, with left hooks. Little Rock's *Arkansas Gazette* reported:

> Bales was down for eight counts twice in the opening round from hard lefts to the jaw. The lanky marine got the best of a hard exchange early in the second, but Gersh stayed and stuck in two lefts that staggered Bales.

When I sat down in my corner after the second round, Enzo said, "Knock him out!"

I answered, "No, I don't want to."

The trainer insisted, "You gotta knock him out!"

I was up against a tough and fast fighter, and it was best not to hold back, in case the determined Bales recovered the initiative.

The Gazette described the next round:

> The third was all Gersh as he twice drove Bales to the ropes with blows to the face and body, the match ending when Bales became too groggy to continue.

My left hook "draped Bales over the ropes, and his seconds called it a day," wrote the *Arkansas Democrat* reporter, who commended the Arkansas A&M college team's gameness, adding that Bales "took a pretty severe lacing." The reporter went on:

> Gersh was the epitome of sportsmanship in the ring. He seemed sort of embarrassed by the necessity of having to knock his opponent out, but eventually did it in an extremely efficient manner.

The New Yorker has a terrific left and under wise coaching and good management could go a long way in the pro ranks. But he probably never will fight as a pro. Eddie is well educated, a thorough gentleman, and is not too interested in a pro career. Besides, he has a job to do for Uncle Sam, and by the time that is finished he may not be as keen in the ring as he was last night.

The *Democrat's* reporter was insightful. A full-time soldier had little chance to hone the skills needed for a professional boxing career. I, however, didn't agree. I still wanted a chance for a professional career. When my perforated ear drum finally excused me from military service in mid-1944, I thought I now had the chance to catch up for lost time.

Just after leaving the army, I underwent surgery to straighten out my boxer's flattened nose. As I sat in the operating chair, numbed by local anesthetic, two doctors took turns working on my nose. Fully conscious, I sat there for hours, as the doctors hacked away with a hammer and chisel at the cartilage of my nose. I can still hear the sounds of the whacks. The doctors were trying to put a piece of bone in place to straighten the nose, but they both became exhausted. They weren't finished and still hadn't replaced the bone, but they finally had to stop, and they told me to come back another day for yet another operation of several hours.

I'd had enough and never went back.

ॐ

IN THE LATE SUMMER OF 1944, Gertrude and I were again in New York City, starting civilian life over. We found a small apartment on 112th Street, between Broadway and Amsterdam Avenue. I wanted to teach, and to earn my master's degree in English, so I registered at Columbia University Teacher's College. I also wanted to box, so I looked up Larry Kent once again.

CCNY boxing coaches Edward Gersh, left, and Yustin Sirutis.
(Photo: Jackson Pokress)

Chapter 8

A WATCH FOR THE COACH

GERTRUDE AND I WERE GLAD TO GET BACK to New York City after my discharge from the army. I studied at Columbia Teachers College for my masters in History, with the government's G.I. Bill paying tuition and a small stipend. We eventually moved from 112th Street to the second floor of the converted garage at Gertrude's parents' home in the Bronx.

Ambitious to earn an income, and driven by the urge to get into the ring as a pro, I took up boxing again. I trained with Lolly at Stillman's Gym on Eighth Avenue between 53rd–54th. There, the best pros in the city were established, including welterweight contender Rocky Graziano.

I had classes from ten to two, then went to the gym; I went back to school between four and six for more classes. It wasn't easy. I tried to study hard, and to train hard. But because of my studies, I couldn't train as hard or as much as necessary – and because of my training I couldn't study as much either – and I always had aches and pains from boxing. I soon had my fighting career restarted.

My first pro bout was a four-rounder against Tony Gillio of New Haven, Connecticut. It was a brutal fight and ended in a draw, the fighters sharing a $50 purse. By now, I was one of a declining number of Jewish fighters competing professionally. The wave of Jewish boxers from the first part of the century had passed, the last notable stars being brothers Maxie and Buddy Baer. One Jewish fighter who still had a presence in the fight game – but as a referee – was the legendary welterweight Benny Leonard. When he retired from the ring in the Thirties, Leonard had won 85 fights, 69 by knockout, and had 5 losses and one draw. In the Forties, he was still remembered and respected by boxing fans.

Sportswriter Al Lurie wrote:

When Leonard was accepted and admired by the entire fair-minded American community, the Jews of America felt they, themselves, were being accepted and admired. Leonard, therefore, symbolized all Jewry.

Once one of the richest men in the country, Leonard, a son of Orthodox Jews, had earned more than $1 million as a fighter. He had first retired from fighting in the mid-Twenties, then lost his fortune in the 1929 stock market crash. He returned to the ring, winning 19 consecutive bouts before retiring after a loss in 1932. Leonard next taught boxing and became a referee. He was a role model for young men like me. I wanted to stay in boxing after my own ring career was over, perhaps as a trainer or manager or referee.

Other famous Jewish fighters ended their careers in the mid-Forties. Heavyweight Abe Simon had recently finished after two losses to champion Joe Louis. Simon won 38 fights, 27 by knockout, in 49 professional bouts. Polish-Canadian Maxie Berger's fighting career had ended by now. A former Canadian lightweight champion, Berger had vacated that title and moved up to welterweight. The closest he came to a title fight was in 1942, when he was knocked out by Sugar Ray Robinson, who was on his way to winning the crown. Berger would retire in 1946. Although he won 99 fights, he never had a shot at the welterweight crown, perhaps because he was a troublesome opponent who could end an up-and-coming young fighter's career by beating him.

Georgie Abrams was an outstanding middleweight, who was soon to retire. Abrams had lost a decision and the world title fight to Tony Zale in 1941. To reach the title match, Abrams had defeated former champion Billy Zoose. Abrams couldn't get another shot at the middleweight title, though he kept fighting. It was said he was too good, too dangerous an opponent. Abrams was still in the ring in the mid-Forties, winning his share of fights and facing some of the best young boxers in his division. In May of 1945, he met Sugar Ray Robinson, who'd won the world welterweight championship the previous December. Abrams lost a 10-round decision, and Robinson would later say this was the toughest bout he ever fought. Abrams would retire in 1948, with a professional record of 48 wins in 61 bouts.

Another Jewish pro still boxing then was Natie Brown, who lost to Joe Louis just months before Louis took the world heavyweight title. Brown would fight until 1949, also becoming a professional wrestler, a spectator's sport rising in popularity in the late 1940s. He retired with 56 victories in 84 professional bouts.

One top Jewish boxer still active was Al "Bummy" Davis, the fiery and controversial young welterweight who'd been briefly banned because of his temper in the ring. Still in his mid-twenties, the Brooklyn-born Davis had returned to the ring early in 1945, winning his first four fights.

I, too, was winning at the start of 1945. After the Gillio fight, I fought three more times, winning them all, two by knockout. I was off to a good beginning, but the strain of studying and training combined with the full-tilt battles in the ring were wearing me down. The easy-going Larry Kent made things more uncertain for me by seeming less committed to me as a fighter. I wasn't happy with the way things were going. I felt I wasn't as good as I should be. Those pro bouts were tough. Kent was always playing jokes and fooling around during training; I thought he wasn't training me the way I wanted to be trained. He wasn't serious enough.

That April of 1945, in my fifth pro fight over a half-year period, I again faced the rough Tony Gillio in a six-round preliminary at Madison Square Garden. A newspaper reporter described the results: "Lacking in skill but long on punching power and aggressiveness, Eddie Irwin . . . just nosed out Tony Gillio. . . ." I took a lot of blows that night. Afterwards I questioned what I should do with my life.

Boxing meant a lot to me, but a teaching career was soon to open up, and I had the inner determination to find a way to become successful financially. I had affection for Larry Kent, but wasn't confident that I could ever become a heavyweight contender with him handling me. Rather than get another trainer – I was too loyal to Kent – I just said the hell with it. I decided right then and there to stop boxing and not go on as pro.

Years later, Kent remembered some other aspects of the end to my professional boxing career. Kent said Gertrude came to him at the gym one day and in so many words made it clear she thought her husband should be teaching instead of fighting. Kent agreed.

I said to Eddie, "You're gonna be a History teacher!" He had a college education. Look what he'd done. He came from a very poor family, and now he had the opportunity to teach. Eddie could've made it as a boxer, but he made it as a teacher instead.

Just what that teaching career would be was very uncertain in 1945, however, because I wasn't doing well at Columbia Teachers College. I failed key exams and was at risk of having my candidacy terminated. I wasn't the only promising young Jewish fighter who ended his career in the spring of 1945.

Bummy Davis was knocked out that May by Rocky Graziano. Davis gave up training and decided to enjoy his earnings from the ring. Unfortunately, he was a fast-liver and quickly spent or lost it all. He signed up for yet another fight, another payday, for late in 1945. Instead, he died that autumn, killed in an armed robbery attempt at a bar he was visiting. Davis had gone after the robbers, who turned and shot him as they fled. He was only 25 years of age.

In April of 1947, Benny Leonard had a heart attack while refereeing in the ring and died instantly. With Leonard gone, an era that had seen so many great Jewish boxers drew to a close.

ALTHOUGH STUDYING AT COLUMBIA Teachers College was difficult, other things improved for me by September of 1945. New York University had recently restarted its football program, which had closed up during the war, and I was hired as an assistant line coach by head coach John Weinheimer.

Coach Weinheimer had been a star running back for NYU in the Twenties, and he was a wonderful guy, but he had a difficult job because we didn't have enough time for practice. So many players commuted to NYU all the way from places like Hempstead, Long Island, or Coney Island, or New Jersey, and it took them an hour just to come uptown from Washington Square for practice. Then they had to go home afterwards and study. Coach Weinheimer worked hard. Sometimes he'd sleep in an old house next to the practice field if he'd been working late.

I was still well known at NYU, where my Golden Gloves success had been closely followed. The school newspaper featured the new assistant line coach and his "colorful career," as the headline writer put it. I was credited for helping develop the NYU team's offensive line, or as the reporter named it: "the stalwart forward wall of the Hall of Fame gridders." The tongue-in-cheek "Hall of Famers" nickname – one that had been used for some years – was especially ironic because the NYU team was out-manned by almost every opponent it faced. In the article on me, the reporter wrote:

> Besides being a football player and a boxer, Gersh is an excellent ice skater, a powerful swimmer, and an adept horseman. Ed is now working for his M.A. When asked about his future, he stated that he liked coaching and would definitely continue with it. He expressed the wish that a boxing team could be inaugurated at NYU because, "Since it is so important for one to know how to defend oneself box-ing should be put into the educational program."

Boxing wouldn't come to pass as a team sport at NYU, nor would my football coaching last very long, either. Coach Weinheimer resigned after two seasons, and his staff – including me – were all released. Around this same time, I was unable to continue at Columbia. My candidacy was terminated after I failed an important exam for the third time. These were bitter disap-pointments, but I shook them off, pushed on, and was accepted at NYU to take my masters in physical education.

Though I was still studying, I also took on stints as a substitute teacher at several city high schools. These included Benjamin Franklin High School and the all-black New York Vocational High School. A full-time sub was paid $12 per diem then, with no bene-fits. Even with summer work, it wasn't nearly enough for me.

By now, there was new happiness as daughter Ellynn was born in 1946. As for the marriage, itself, I came to realize I didn't love Gertrude. We were drifting apart. Gertrude was content to stay at home, care for the baby and play mahjong with friends. I was hun-gry to get ahead, always looking for opportunity, working as much as I could. By now, the momentum of the early years of our marriage had settled down into what I considered a humdrum life. In the summers, our family returned to the southern Catskills, where I was employed on hotel staffs, as I had been since my youth. The family would settle into a cottage for the summer while I worked. I had various positions, from maitre d' to athletic director and public relations. I had to work from 7 a.m. to 9 p.m. seven days a week. The hotels were the Falls View in Ellenville, my former home town, and the Lash Hotel in Parksville.

Pro fighters regularly came to the Catskill hotels to train for upcoming bouts. At the Lash, I ran a boxing program for the guests that often had working pros as featured instructors. One notable fighter was my friend, the Cuban-born "Kid" Gavilan, who was preparing for a title fight with Sugar Ray Robinson. I arranged training sessions and drummed up lots of publicity for both Gavilan and the hotel. Gavilan lost that fight to Robinson, but remained a popular figure with New Yorkers.

I kept fit by teaching boxing to hotel patrons, and also by sparring with Gavilan's stable mate, Omelia Egremonte, also a Cuban. We would go at it for three-round sparring sessions. This was when I first thought I could seriously begin training and managing my own fighters. I took on a black middleweight, Albert Fisher, of Jamaica, whom I'd met while we were both training at Stillman's Gym. I began to train "Jamaica," as he was nicknamed, for the Golden Gloves. Jamaica had promise, winning the New York City Gloves championship in 1948 .

Afterwards, I turned him pro, and he had a few fights. I thought he was pretty good, and I arranged to have him be the sparring partner for Rocky Graziano, who was training at the Neville Hotel in Ellenville. This was a great opportunity for Jamaica, but after he came back from that Graziano session, Jamaica disappeared, and I never heard from him again. But I now had the taste of managing my own fighter, and I liked it. Still, I wasn't ready to become involved in full-time training. I had my studies and my family and my work as a substitute teacher and in summertimes in the Catskills.

At the Falls View, I had a passing flirtation with Rosemarie Halbig, the teenage daughter of the hotel security chief. It was apparent that Rosemarie had a crush on me. Her father and I were good friends. Although I was discontented in my marriage, nothing developed then between Rosemarie and me, but we liked each other.

In 1949, a second daughter, Laurie, was born. I adored my children, but I was increasingly restless in my relationship with Gertrude. It was a marriage of convenience, and not happy. The summer work began to bore me, too, and I was growing tired of being at the beck and call of tourists and hotel managers. I began to consider it too demeaning.

The work I loved most was coaching boxing.

ح

IN 1947, I WAS HIRED AS ONE OF TWO BOXING coaches at City College of New York (CCNY), where I was also an instructor in the Hygiene Department. I'd already earned my masters degree in Physical Education at NYU and was a candidate for a doctorate in Physical Education. Teaching at CCNY was a good step for me. I was paid $2,700 a year salary, which was a lot better than the $1,700 I made for ten months' work as a high school substitute. And at CCNY I got to coach the boxing team – for no extra pay, of course.

At CCNY, my co-coach, Yustin Sirutis, and I had to reestablish the college boxing team, which had been inactive for five years. I trained team members who attended CCNY's uptown campus on 143rd Street, and Yustin coached the students from the downtown campus. When it came time for a match, we would get together and choose who would box competitively for CCNY. We knew who were the better fighters and always agreed on the team.

Yustin and I became very close friends. The boxing brought us together, and at the same time we were both working for our NYU doctorates. We collaborated on the topic, "The Teaching of Boxing," doing our research together. I eventually completed all the doctoral course requirements, but I never finished my final dissertation. Yustin didn't finish his, either.

The CCNY student-boxers were enthusiastic and eager to learn what Yustin and I could teach them. As with athletes at NYU, athletes at CCNY had little opportunity to put enough hours into working out. Some had part-time jobs and others had long commutes to school. In those years, CCNY was highly regarded for the caliber of its students. Although it was a public city college with low tuition, CCNY had very high academic standards, and its students could compare with the best anywhere in the nation. Though athletic facilities were limited, CCNY had its share of fine athletes and even fielded a football team then, with traditions going back to the 1880s.

CCNY's boxers on our newly reorganized team made up in determination for what they lacked in athletic ability and facilities. Training sessions were brief: noon–1 p.m. on Mondays and Wednesdays, and 1–2 p.m. on Tuesdays and Thursdays. The most intense sessions were on Friday, lasting from 1–5 p.m. At least the team had its own boxing room, with a ring, heavy bags and speed bags, and weights.

I got along well with the team. I later helped one athlete, Roger Dorian, get into officer's candidate school. I knew a recruiting officer and recommended Dorian, who became a career officer in the Marine Corps; we've kept up a lifelong correspondence. I loved being at CCNY and had a really good time. But after the second year, in 1950, New York City was in financial difficulty, and Mayor William O'Dwyer cut a thousand positions from the city colleges. The cuts were based on seniority, and since I was one of the newest on the staff, my job went.

The boys on the team fought to keep me on staff, writing letters to the chairman of the department, but there was no chance of my staying. It was another real disappointment.

Near the end, we had a team meeting, and to my surprise they presented me with a watch. It was engraved: "To Ed Gersh, with appreciation, from your boys at CCNY." So there it was: I'd started boxing because I wanted a watch, but never did get it from fighting. I finally earned that watch as boxing coach at City College.

I still treasure it.

Working with young boxers in the CCNY training room, Gersh guides team member Roger Dorian at the punching bag; Dorian, who made a career in the military , remained a lifelong correspondent with his college boxing coach.

Gersh's written proposal for a television boxing show had this sketch as its cover.

Chapter 9

COMING OUT FIGHTING

M Y STUDIES FOR A DOCTORAL DEGREE in physical education involved research into scholastic and college boxing. I found that the sport I loved was coming under fierce attack from educators who wanted it kept out of high schools and colleges.

I believed those kinds of critics didn't understand or appreciate boxing. I considered the sport, when properly taught and supervised, to be healthy and beneficial like none other for young men. The social trends were against me, however, as educators increasingly condemned boxing as a violent and dangerous sport that stimulated savage behavior. I didn't – and still don't – agree. Boxing has the potential to bring out the young athlete's very best – physically, mentally, and emotionally. Back in the late Forties, I wanted to see it develop in schools, and see it grow, but opposition was mounting, and scholastic boxing programs were being dropped around the country. They said it was too dangerous, and that it brought out the worst in both boxers and spectators. Boxing doesn't have to be that way.

Certainly, professional boxing was corrupt and dirty, just like politics, but professional boxing had nothing to do with boxing programs in schools and colleges. In 1950, I wrote a lengthy article for *Scholastic Coach* magazine, titled: "The Case for School Boxing." The article opened with:

> Thanks to the extreme unsavoriness of the professional game, boxing is generally persona non grata on the high school level. Educators attempting to justify it have met with some virulent opposition.

I went on to critique leading opponents of scholastic boxing. I faulted them for relying too much on the bitter experiences of unhappy former professionals. "This is a long way from the high school," I said, adding that anti-boxing studies made broad generalities, some of which could hold for any contact sport. I said critics should be more specific about what aspect of boxing was supposedly detrimental to young athletes.

> [One critic] states that most of the strength and endurance developed by a boxing program is not the result of the actual boxing, but is produced by the rope-skipping, roadwork, and other body-building exercises incidental to boxing, and which can be developed by engaging in other activities as well.
>
> Theoretically, this is true, but actually what other sport or activity will provide the motivation for these body-building exercises?

Paraphrasing a Navy aviation training manual that included boxing, I wrote:

> Boxing develops endurance and stamina, a highly trained nervous system capable of instant reflexive action, the ability to make quick and accurate judgments, the ability to

relax, to keep calm and poised under pressure, thus allaying the possibility of emotional blocks. It develops aggressiveness, courage, and finally self-confidence and self-reliance, in spite of the fact that the wearing of protective gear is compulsory in all Aviation Training drills.

I quoted a critic of boxing for youngsters who asserted that there is no proof boxing "is a particularly valuable method of developing character, determination, and personality." The critic went on to say that spectators are negatively influenced by attending a match: "Even watching a fight may elicit an unparalleled emotional response so powerful that it may carry the spectator away and cloud his judgments."

Answering this point, I didn't deny the passions stirred by watching a bout, but I explained that scholastic and college standards weren't those of the professional fight game.

As for the unparalleled emotional response, the collegiate code of ethics requires a dignified applause to be the only sign of approval voiced by the audience. It is the referee's duty to stop a bout whenever the audience response reaches an excessive emotional pitch. I conceded that audiences at collegiate boxing matches often did get worked up by the excitement, but "there is still no record of ring posts being carried away, as have the goal posts at many collegiate football games." I addressed the critics' assertions that boxing resulted in brain damage, the worst of which was termed "dementia puglistia," commonly known as "punch-drunk."

Injury to the brain may be incurred in many activities involving body contact, such as football, basketball, hockey, diving, and soccer. If the physical educator justifies body contact sports to any extent, then he must justify boxing to the same degree.

I went on to quote statistics that showed boxing rated below dancing (including modern) in danger. There were .16 accidents per thousand exposure in boxing, as compared to 8.7 accidents per thousand exposure for football, and 5.7 per thousand for wrestling. Scholastic and college boxing coaches were quoted confirming the low rate of serious injury to boxers. Regarding "dementia pugilistia," I wrote:

In no possible way can the punishment taken by a high school boxer be compared to that [of] a professional fighter."

I pressed my case further, with statistics from amateur bouts:

In 61 attempted blows, the average amateur boxer only landed 29. Fifteen of these blows were lefts to the face, which are the lightest blows in boxing.

Common sense and experienced, responsible coaching provided the best environment for youth boxing, I said. In the case of injuries, I added, a study should be made to determine: "Was it the activity, or was it the supervision which caused the accidents?" Necessary precautions included a well-padded floor, head gear, and competent supervision.

This writer is opposed to boxing unless the [appropriate] precautions are observed. Boxing, unlike most other sports, is an activity about which our physical educators know little. Few physical directors know more than a smattering of the fundamentals, and even fewer have ever competed on an intercollegiate level. When somebody is unfamiliar with an activity, he naturally is doubtful about its usefulness.

On the other side of the coin:

Men who have the boxing background seldom have the educational requirements needed to teach, and men who do meet the educational requirements do not have the boxing experience.

The physical education institutions have sadly fallen down in this respect. The men they turn out, although well trained in almost every sport, do not receive enough boxing to conduct a program with any hope of success. If an institution can find a man who has both the educational requirements and an adequate boxing background, it can be assured of the success of a very healthful physical activity.

I had both the boxing experience and the educational background. The theoretical and educational aspects of boxing interested me so much in this time that I further developed an idea for a television show explaining and analyzing boxing matches. It was titled "Come Out Fighting!" the admonition referees give fighters as they meet at center ring before the bout.

❧

AMONG THE MOST POPULAR PROGRAMS in these early days of television were the Friday night fights broadcast from Madison Square Garden and sponsored by Gillette safety razors. I came up with a concept to appeal to the enormous television audience that followed these fights, which were shown on video tape. My plan was for a 15-minute program that explained boxing, its techniques and strategies, and did so with famous ring personalities – fighters, managers, and trainers.

By now, I'd broadened my own status in the sport by qualifying for a New York State license as a professional boxing manager and trainer. I'd also acquired my professional referee's license for boxing and wrestling, which supplemented my income as a teacher and a Catskill hotel staffer. You got a referee's license by going to your local political leaders and asking them to start the application process by recommending you to the New York State Athletic Commission. The commission was asked to consider you the next time there was an opening for a referee.

Politicians had – and continue into the 21st century to have – great influence on the New York State Athletic Commission, which governs professional boxing. This influence results from the sitting governor appointing the Commission chairman, who in turn appoints the members. Those who are appointed are generally of the same political persuasion as the governor, or are owed favors by the governor's party. Since there's considerable social status in hobnobbing with famous sports personalities, a place on the Athletic Commission is a desirable reward for political cronies and financial backers of the New York governor. Thus, politicians run the Athletic Commission.

After I got my license, a friend of mine from my NYU days asked me how to go about it, and I told him what to do. He was Arthur Mercante, who'd refereed City College matches. Artie went on to become the foremost boxing official in the country over the next 25 years. For my part, I found it challenging as a boxing referee to keep score round by round while at the same time officiating the fight itself. Though I'd had little time to learn the finer points, I soon found myself assigned to referee pro fights in Madison Square Garden.

In those days, at the end of the bout the referee cast one of three votes for the winner. But it was very difficult to referee the fight and at the same time try to keep score – there's just too much to do when you're in the ring with the fighters. Artie Mercante, though, could do it very well. He was probably the best referee I've ever seen. In one important bout I was officiating, I gave my vote to one fighter as winner while the two judges voted for the other. After that, I was no longer assigned to boxing, and I was permanently made a wrestling referee. I believe the boxing commission felt I wasn't a good judge, and I think they were right. I don't think I could really judge the score of each round while I was refereeing. Later, the Athletic Commission took the duty of judging away from the referee, adding a third judge and letting the referee concentrate on his job in the ring.

My reputation as an athlete, coach, and college instructor bolstered my efforts to establish the television program, "Come out Fighting! . . . with Ed Gersh." I prepared a prospectus explaining the potential appeal of the show:

As television grows, so grows the popularity of boxing – in fact, today, as one well-known columnist put it, "The ringside has become the fireside."

Since the arena has given way to the armchair, more and more people want to know more and more about the techniques and terms of the prize fight ring.

"Come out Fighting!" introduces its program material, not as a commentary, but in action – combining actual explanation and demonstration of positions, blows, and strategy, with an opportunity to meet a top-flight fighting star as well as prominent sports celebrities each week.

This weekly 15-minute show is designed to appeal to: sports fans in general; boxing fans in particular; youngsters eager to learn ring techniques; women spectators who have become fans via video.

In short, "Come out Fighting!" is a "natural" for all the members of the TV family.

In my prospectus, I wrote a sample script for a typical show, detailing how the various punches, stances, and blocks were used. Of course, I featured my own best punch – that short left hook.

This is used when the opponent is rushing. All you do is step aside and hook. I will never forget the first time I won by a knockout. It was the short left hook that did it. I was boxing a six-foot-three fellow by the name of Phil Brady in Jamaica Arena. During the first round I moved in after him [This is demonstrated] until I got him in a corner and then, boom, boom, boom, he came out punching. I figured I better get out of there, so I moved away. Then I started moving after him again. I worked him into a corner, and again I was sorry. He came out hitting me with everything but the ring post. This continued . . . I would chase him until I got him trapped in a corner, then he would beat the daylights out of me. . . . [Between rounds] his second must have told him I was ready to be knocked out because when the bell rang for the [next] round, he came leaping from his corner and ran across the ring to get to me. As he rushed at me, I stepped aside and hooked – To my amazement this huge mass of flesh hit the canvas with a thud that made the roof shake. To this day, I do not know who was more surprised – Brady or Gersh.

Around this time, I'd been a special guest on "Kid Boxing," a television program presenting five exhibition bouts with boys between the ages of three and eight. The children were chosen from boxing programs sponsored by metropolitan-area Police Athletic League (PAL) clubs and Boys' Clubs. The program, said a press release from WATV-13 of Newark, which aired it, had "the blessing" of the New Jersey Boxing Commission, police departments, and other top civic groups. The boxers used oversize gloves which prevented serious blows from connecting. The press release explained:

Handlers are fathers of the boys, working in their corners. Ringside, in addition to the press, are members of the PAL or participating organization and invited guests. Winners of bouts receive a set of boxing gloves. Best boxer of the afternoon receives a $75 bike.

Such high stakes indicated the value sponsors put on boxing as a youth sport that should be supported. So, "Kid Boxing" went directly contrary to the educators I'd disagreed with in my *Scholastic Coach* article of 1950. Youth boxing was clearly safe, sportsmanlike, and wholesome when managed by responsible parents and organizations that were vigilant regarding the well-being of participants. Boxing was family fun in those days, and "Kid Boxing" got excellent newspaper reviews: A woman columnist from the *New York World Telegram* called the program, "A must-see," and the *Newark News* said it was "A knockout – delightful."

I'd also been the guest on radio talk shows, one of them on my favorite subject: "The Beneficial Aspects of Scholastic and Collegiate Boxing." One commentator said I was coming on the show to address "the prodigious amount of adverse publicity heaped upon the boxing profession."

Despite the pro- and anti-boxing controversy, the sport's undeniable popularity made the time seem ripe for "Come Out Fighting!" To further reinforce the qualifications for the show, I collected signed promises from dozens of well-known boxing personalities, who agreed to come on. These included fighters such as light-heavyweight champion Archie Moore, retired heavyweight contender Joe Baksi, Kid Gavilan, and world light-weight champion Beau Jack. There were also top trainers and managers: Whitey Bimstein, Charley Goldman (Rocky Marciano's trainer), Chris Dundee, Jimmy White, and Irving Cohen (Rocky Graziano's manager). Bobby Gleason also agreed to be on the show, as did Stillman's Gym manager Jack Curley and gym owner Artie Curley, himself a noted trainer. Many of the fighters sent along their best publicity photographs to supplement my pitch to the stations.

Regardless of my qualifications, or the fame and charisma of my prospective guests, and the popularity of boxing on television, I was unable to sell the idea for "Come Out Fighting." Yet

Under Gersh's close supervision, kids box with oversized gloves in a televised youth program designed to teach the sport of boxing. (Photo Moe Zuckerman)

my driving ambition to make something more of myself compelled me to keep on trying new avenues – as I had when I ran for the New York State Assembly in the fall of 1950. I ran as a Liberal Republican for the 6th Assembly District in the Bronx.

"Let me Fight for You!" was my campaign slogan. I was 30 years old then, and well-known in the Bronx. The *New York Times* interviewed me and explained why I'd decided to run:

Time and again, young Gersh complained to his neighbors about the lack of traffic lights, public libraries, recreational facilities for adults and children, and public housing for mid-dle-income groups in the Hunts Point and Westchester Avenue areas.

"Well, my neighbors replied: 'Do something about it.' I did. I got myself the nomination for the Assembly," he says. The Sixth Assembly District in the Bronx is a Democratic stronghold, he admits, but he promises that "win, lose, or draw, I'll be throwing punches with both hands."

If elected, he will take a leave of absence from his teaching career. "If not," he adds, "I'll still be in there punching for civic improvements."

As it turned out, I lost the election to the incumbent Democrat. Well, any future civic improvement I'd be fighting for would no longer be in the Bronx. Gertrude and I soon bought a home out in the fast-growing suburbs of Franklin Square, Long Island. I was about to become a workaday commuter to the city because I'd accepted a full-time teaching position at Galvani Junior High School (PS 83) in East Harlem. This was an all-boys school, and one of the city's toughest public schools.

There, during my next 17 years, everything I knew about youngsters, discipline, and hard work, would come into play.

Referee Gersh at the side of Argentine native, Antonino Rocca,
perennial favorite of the pro-wrestling crowd in the 1950s.

Chapter 10

GALVANI

IN THE SPRING OF 1950, I walked into an East Harlem all-boys school, hoping to get regular work as a substitute teacher. Galvani Junior High, P.S. 83, was an old, five-story brick building on East 109th Street between Second and Third Avenues, with 800–1,000 boys in the seventh, eighth, and ninth grades.

There were just three days left in the school year, and the students had already taken their final examinations. Needless to say, they were eager to get out, and classroom discipline was a problem.

As soon as he met me, Principal Israel Flax said, "Mr. Gersh, I have a class – it's a ninth-grade graduating class."

He told me this particular group already had their graduation pictures taken and didn't care much about school at that point. They were halfway out the building as far as they were concerned. It would be a difficult group of boys.

"Do you think you'll be able to do that?" Mr. Flax asked.

I smiled and said, "Sure, I can."

"Okay," he said, handing me the keys for the classroom.

"They're on the fifth floor."

I knew these boys had been put up there to keep them separate from the rest of the school so they wouldn't readily cause a disturbance. As I climbed the stairs, I could hear them yelling and shouting.

At that time, the Galvani population was 60 per cent Puerto Rican, 25 per cent Italians, and 10 per cent black, with a few other white families mixed in. Third Avenue was a border between the different neighborhoods. West of Third, it was Hispanic and it could be was dangerous for a non-Hispanic to go there. East of Third it was Italian, home of the Mafia. Blacks lived mostly to the west. Whites were moving out steadily, and successive waves of Puerto Ricans were moving in, along with more black families. The neighborhood around Galvani had a lot of small shops, mostly owned by first-generation Italians, who once had been the majority in the neighborhood. The school had been named for the famous Italian inventor, Luigi Galvani. By now, the Italian shop owners had pretty much moved their homes out of the neighborhood, but they kept their businesses going.

Most of the buildings were three-storey walk-ups with stores at the ground level: candy stores, vegetable stores, cleaners, food stores, clothing stores – Malfatano's, on Third Avenue, had very nice clothing. Though the Italian residents were leaving, most people still knew each other and knew the kids. The neighborhood could be rough at times, with ethnic street gangs who fought over turf and committed a good deal of crime.

When I got to the fifth floor I found the boys walking around the hall. There were about 20 of them, and they had their hats on, a sign of disrespect. I unlocked the classroom door and stood a moment in the doorway, watching as they milled around in front of me. They were saying things like, "Should we cut? Nah, we got a new sub – let's see what he's like!"

So they decided they'd see what I was like, and they came filing in. I closed the door behind them and went to the front of the room. They still had their hats on and were walking up and down the aisles between the desks, yelling and screaming. I let that go on for maybe a minute, and then spoke in a very high-pitched tone of voice.

"Now, boys, I want you to sit down and shut up." I paused, then said, "And if you don't sit down, I'm going to knock you down."

Well, that completely surprised them. And for about 10 seconds there was absolute silence.

Then I said, "Now, is there anybody in this class that knows how to fight?"

They all pointed to one boy, a strong-looking kid.

"Okay, you come up here!"

As that boy came to the front of the room, I said, "Now I want you other boys to sit down!"

So, I had their attention, and I was talking about fighting, which was their cup of tea. So, they all sat down, and I turned to face the boy who'd come to the front of the room.

I said, "Now if you were going to have a fight with somebody, how would you hit him?"

I squared my shoulder for him to hit it. After a moment of hesitation, he punched my shoulder moderately hard.

"Well, okay," I said, and took off my glasses, took off my wristwatch, took off my jacket, and turned to face him.

"Now if, if you were going to have a fight with me – I want you to show me how you would hit me. Hit me on the shoulder again, the way you would hit if you were going to fight somebody."

This time he hit me with a solid shot.

"Oh come on," I said, "you can do better than that! You wouldn't hit me that easy, would you?"

He was surprised. Then he punched my shoulder harder. The class was watching, absolutely silent. They didn't understand what was happening. The boy was reluctant to hit me again, but

I urged him to do it, and finally he hit me fairly hard on the shoulder.

"Now, you see the way he did that?" I said to the class. "He didn't do it right. This is the way you're supposed to do it – "

Boom! I hit him on his shoulder with a right hand, and he flew back against the blackboard, bounced against the door, and into a corner before staggering forward, shocked.

"Now, that's the way you're supposed to throw a right hand," I said. "The way you're supposed to hit somebody if you're having a fight with him."

He was rubbing his shoulder and said nothing.

"Now, I want you to sit down," I continued, "and I want you boys to take off your hats, and I don't want to hear a sound out of you."

He sat down, and they all took their hats off.

"We're going to be talking about boxing, and I'm going to give you some lessons on boxing. And if you want to ask a question, you've got to raise your hand, and when I call on you, I want you to stand up and ask your question."

Everyone was listening.

"Otherwise, I'm going to ask you to come up here, and I'll teach you how to throw a right hand."

They got the message.

I put on my glasses, watch, and jacket and sat on the corner of the desk. I passed around my Golden Gloves key chain, which title winners receive. I also had that picture of Joe Louis and me together at Fort Bragg in 1944, and I passed that around. They were eating it up, thrilled to see those things and to know I'd been with Joe Louis, who was an idol in those days. They asked me questions about boxing, but I made them raise their hands first. If they didn't raise their hands, I wouldn't call on them.

Then I realized Mr. Flax had come up to check on what I was doing. The door had a glass pane about three quarters of the way up, and he was standing on his tiptoes, peering into the room. He

108

couldn't believe what he saw. Everybody was seated. Nobody had a hat on. He opened the door and came into the room to find the boys were raising their hands.

At the end of the day, he said to me, "Mr. Gersh, would you like to work here permanently, full-time?"

I said, "I sure would!"

And I did, for the next 17 years.

❧

IN MY NEXT YEAR AT GALVANI I became the disciplinary dean – a "behavioral counselor," handling the most disruptive and troubled boys. The students quickly came to know me as a strict disciplinarian, but also as someone who cared about them.

Coming from my background as a fighter, I believed in corporal punishment, provided it was done with understanding – not in anger – as a measure, as one technique of disciplining. Properly applied corporal punishment can do a child a lot of good. Although it was legally not allowed, we used corporal punishment when necessary. This was the case in many of the tougher city schools, but few schools had someone with my experience, someone who could provide the physical discipline some children needed.

At first, Galvani didn't actually have a budgeted position with my responsibilities, and I was officially a health teacher who was expected to instruct a certain number of classes. The way Mr. Flax arranged for me to have the required number of classes and still have time to be the disciplinarian was by giving me one period in the auditorium with ten classes of children all at the same time. The rest of the day I was free to be the disciplinary dean. I loved my job right from the start. When I came into school in the morning, I never knew where I'd be that day – in a classroom, in a child's home, the father's store, the police station, court, morgue, or a funeral home. I often had to be decisive, had to take action on the spot, especially in that first year, when students would challenge me. One of those tests came in front of a couple of hundred students who were sitting in the auditorium during the performance of a play. While the program was going on, teachers were supposed to supervise, so I was walking up and down the aisle. I started at the back of the auditorium and slowly walked down to the front, then turned and walked back to the rear. While I was walking down, I noticed a boy reading a comic book.

I leaned over and whispered, "Please put the comic book away."

He looked up at me, looked back at his comic book, and continued reading. He was a big kid, almost as big as I was. I walked down to the end of the aisle and came back to find him still reading. So, I leaned over and said, more firmly this time, "Please put your comic book away."

Again he glanced up, then continued reading. I walked to the back of the auditorium, thinking what I should do next. I came down, took him by the shoulder, and squeezed, saying, "Now put that comic book away!"

He jumped up and yelled, "Don't you put your hands on me!" so that the entire auditorium heard him.

I slapped him across the face with my left hand, keeping my right up in case he came back at me. Everybody gaped at us, including the people on stage, who stopped their performance.

"Hit me again!" the boy shouted. "Hit me again!"

I said, "I'm not gonna hit you again unless you're fresh with me."

He said, "Hit me again, and I'll get a gun and blow your brains out!"

Whack! I hit him with the other hand and grabbed him by the collar and said, "Come with me."

I marched him out the door of the auditorium, everybody staring at us, and brought him down the hall to a back stairway. Then I took off my glasses, took off my wrist watch, and put them in my coat pocket. Then I took off my coat, set it aside, and went up to him. All of a sudden, he started crying like a baby, hysterically crying.

After a moment, I said to him, "Now, aren't you ashamed of making me so angry?"

He sobbed, "Yes, Mr. Gersh."

"Are you going to do this again?"

"No, Mr. Gersh."

"Okay, done," I said. "Let's go back."

And we returned to the auditorium. I never had any problems with that boy again.

ॐ

A HARD SLAP USUALLY WAS ENOUGH to straighten a student out and put him in his place. At times I had to face them down, ready to fight them. They almost always backed off. One method of corporal punishment was to whack a troublemaker's open palm with a ruler, but sometimes the ruler broke. One day, a boy came in from shop class with a ruler some of them had made for me. It was two inches thick.

"Now, when you hit us, it'll never break," he said.

Another disciplinary solution that invariably worked when two boys had got into a fight was to take them to the gym, put boxing gloves on them, and tell them to go ahead and slug it out. By that time, they didn't want to fight anymore.

I did much more than discipline the children, however. Mr. Flax and I were constantly working with relief organizations and social services, finding them clothes, coming up with a little money to buy them shoes or eye glasses or get them a haircut – even a bath, if the child had no home life. The school had a small fund for this, but it wasn't much. Often, we'd loan the parents our own cash to help get their kids what they needed. We were usually paid back in time, maybe at a rate of 25 cents a week.

I also tried to give children a broader life experience, show them something of the world outside their neighborhood, which most of them had never seen. Sometimes I'd take a whole class – as many as 14 kids – piling them into my car and driving them to my house in Franklin Square for frankfurters. We didn't need written permission to take a trip in those days. It would be a big surprise for Gertrude when we showed up at the door, but she'd laugh and pitch in, and we had a good time for a few hours. I took them to the beach sometimes, or to the airport to walk through the terminal and see planes landing and taking off. I had very few problems with the children then, even though some were known roughnecks. For example, if we took the subway, the boys were always polite to people, getting up to let ladies and older folk sit down, and so on.

Before long, I earned a reputation throughout East Harlem. People knew that if I hit a kid, then there had to be a reason for it. And if he went home and told his parents that I'd hit him, they'd often give him a real beating for being so bad that Mr. Gersh had to hit him. One father came in to complain that a teacher had struck his son. When I told him what the boy had done, the father exploded in rage and went after the boy, and I had to pull the man off him.

The community around Galvani changed as the Italians moved out. Then Urban Renewal demolished many of the three-storey walkups and built high-rise projects, which were so impersonal that people didn't know each other the way they once did. The population changed, too, with new waves of Puerto Rican families. Often, there were too few parents and too little parental control in these new families, who suffered from grinding poverty. Many children only had grandmothers or aunts or older sisters taking care of them, and they often had no discipline other than what I – and the police – gave them.

When there were problems, family members were requested to come in to see me or I visited families to discuss their boys or encourage them to come in and meet with Mr. Flax. Usually, there was the understood threat that if the family didn't come in for a meeting, the boys would face juvenile court. I soon found out that I had to make the request for a meeting in a certain way. In those days, it was very difficult if I asked a child to bring in his mother or father and there was no mother or father. The child would be absolutely embarrassed and shamed if they didn't have a parent to bring in. So, instead, I'd say, "Bring in someone from your home." That way the child wouldn't lose face.

The Italian families had strong ties. If I had a problem with an Italian boy and there was no father in the home, I'd often go to an older brother. As the years passed, a lot of those older brothers had graduated from Galvani and knew me. They became furious if a younger brother made trouble. They could be tougher on a boy than I ever would be. The Italian families had great respect for education and for the teachers. They treated me like a prince, because I was the "maestro," the teacher, and they'd put out fruit and cheese and wine when I came to visit. They couldn't do enough for me.

Across from the school was an Italian candy store, and a lot of the children went there at lunchtime. Every day, I'd go out when the bell rang to end lunch period, and I'd tell the students who were loitering there to go back to school. In good weather, the children would play out in the street at lunchtime – stickball or handball. One day I joined in a stickball game, and when I swung the bat I accidentally hit a boy on the head. He was bleeding, and I had to take him to the hospital. I felt terrible. After he was stitched up and bandaged, I brought him home. He was an Italian boy, and when his mother saw the bandage over his eye, over his face, she started yelling at him, assuming he'd been in a fight.

"You bum, what were you doing?"

I interrupted and said I'd done it, explaining that I'd hit him by accident with the stickball bat. She calmed down immediately.

"Oh, you did it, maestro – oh, well it's all right then."

She gave me a cup of coffee and I visited for a while.

At Galvani, the relationship between most teachers and students was one of friendship, and the majority of teachers felt they could do something with their kids. The wiseguy students often called us "Teach," but it was a term of affection and regard. And if you did help them, they loved you for it. Number one was to be fair. The kid usually thought: if I do something wrong and you punish me, then I deserve it and accept the consequences. If you punish me unfairly, though, you'll never have my respect, and I'll cause trouble every chance I get.

In school, the discipline that really worked came out of the personality of the teacher, and that required earning the respect of the boys. It was very interesting that even the worst of the so-called "bad" boys responded to women they respected. We had an unmarried older lady named Emma Beck, who had a quiet dignity that seemed to awe the boys. They knew she was a complete lady and a wonderful person. You could walk into Miss Beck's classroom, and every child was busy working. No talking, perfect classroom decorum. And she did it just with the force of her gentle personality. The students adored her. The same boys in another class could be just the opposite, causing all kinds of trouble.

≷

IN THIS TIME, GERTRUDE, THE GIRLS, and I had a nice home in Franklin Square, Long Island. It was a very modest house, but compared to how we'd been living in a converted garage at Gert's parents in the Bronx, it was like a palace to us. It had two bathrooms, two bedrooms, a den, living room, dining room, and kitchen, and was on a 60-by-100 lot. I car-pooled with other teachers, and we drove into East Harlem every day with hardly any problems, no traffic jams.

In the summers our family went to the Catskill Mountains, where I worked as a maitre d' at one of the hotels. We took a room in a nearby bungalow colony, and Gertrude and the girls enjoyed it, but I worked extremely hard, seven days a week, from 7 a.m. to 9 p.m. It was grueling, but I intended to make enough money to start my own business on the side.

During the school year I kept on refereeing professional wrestling matches, which provided much-needed cash. I was then paid $25 for a bout in the smaller venues such as Broadway Arena, Ridgewood Grove, and Saint Nick's. If I had a main event at Madison Square Garden, I'd be paid $100. It was fun to refer-ee wrestling – which was a staged exhibition of athleticism and strength more than a true competition. I also kept my involve-ment in boxing. When I was at the Lash Hotel in the Catskills I handled promotions for them, arranging to have fighters come up and train before their upcoming matches. The hotel got lots of good publicity, press photos, and news articles when we had one of these celebrity athletes training there.

As previously mentioned, one fighter who came up to train was Kid Gavilan, a terrific young Cuban who'd challenged for the welterweight crown in 1949, losing to Sugar Ray Robinson. In 1951, Robinson moved to the middleweight division, and Gavilan won the welterweight championship in a decision over Johnny Bratton. Gavilan, whose name was Gerardo Gonzales, was a pop-ular and exciting fighter. He made seven successful title defenses until losing to Johnny Saxton in one of boxing's most notorious decisions. At the bell, 20 of the 22 ringside reporters considered Gavilan the winner. Gavilan is credited with inventing the "bolo punch," half hook and half uppercut. He claimed to have devel-oped it after years of cutting sugar cane with a machete back in Cuba.

One of the great benefits of knowing big-name wrestlers and fighters was that I could invite them to school to give talks, either in class or in the auditorium. The kids loved it, because these ath-letes were famous personalities. You had to give those youngsters something to look forward to in their lives, and seeing the stars

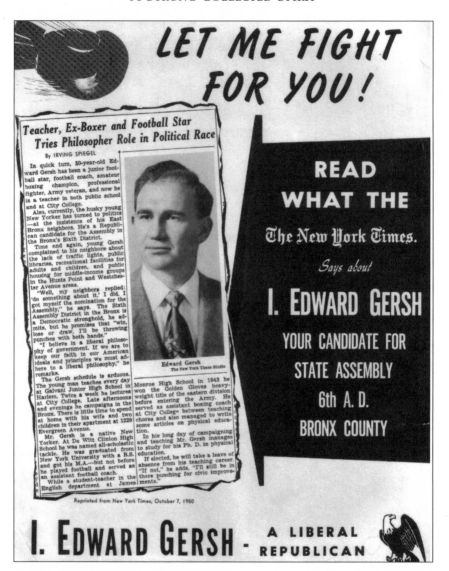

Gersh's brief foray into politics was
heralded by this election poster in 1950.

in person did just that. Israel Flax loved it, too, because the message the kids heard from the athletes was a very fine one – about the importance of good character, of common courtesy, encouraging them to better themselves. One of the most popular athletes who came to Galvani was the Argentine wrestler Antonino Rocca – one of the nicest men you can imagine outside the ring, where he played a rough, tough character who wrestled barefoot.

Antonino came to school several times at my request, and it was something special to see how the kids had the highest respect for him. Everyone he spoke to benefited from what he said. Kid Gavilan also came to Galvani. He was an inspiration to the Hispanic students, and he was especially kind to my little daughters when I introduced him to them. Kid Gavilan won 107 fights, 28 by knockout, and lost 30. He was inducted into the Boxing Hall of Fame in 1990.

Although I thoroughly enjoyed my work at Galvani, I was ambitious, always trying to better myself, trying to find the route to success. I usually had more than one job going at a time – refereeing, working at the hotels – but despite my aspirations and efforts, I never missed a day at school in a teaching career of 17 years.

Boxing star Kid Gavilan caused a stir whenever he visited Galvani,
where he signed autographs for the students. (Photo Jackson Pokress)

Chapter 11

'CALL MR. GERSH'

IN 1951, I WANTED to get more involved with professional boxing, either in promotion or in producing boxing-related entertainment, or maybe even managing fighters. I was working on the idea of making a documentary film about fighters, and I got together with a camera crew. Following up on earlier ideas, I planned to ask some of the top boxers I knew if I could film them during training. First off, I went to Sugar Ray Robinson's bar in Harlem and approached him.

"Ray," I said, "I'd like to take some footage of you, while you're training."

When he asked why, I explained I was making a film on boxing.

"We won't disturb you," I said. "We'll take some shots of you hitting the bag or jumping rope, and it won't disturb your training at all."

Then Ray asked, "Eddie, what's in it for me?"

"Ray, I can't tell you that, because I don't know yet – I don't even know if there'll be anything in it for me in doing a film."

I told him I couldn't guarantee anything, and certainly wasn't able to pay him to be one of our subjects for the film.

"Well, then, I can't do it," he said.

Sugar Ray's flat refusal was a real disappointment, but I didn't want to give up. Next, I got in touch with Joe Louis, who was training for his upcoming fight with Rocky Marciano. Joe was trying to make a comeback after retiring in 1949 as the heavy-weight champion. He'd returned to the ring in 1950 to fight Ezzard Charles, who'd succeeded him as champion. Joe had put on weight then and was in no condition to meet Charles, but he needed money badly. He owed IRS more than half a million in back taxes, so he went back into the ring and lost by unanimous decision to Charles, who inflicted a severe beating. Afterwards, Joe said he'd never fight again, but he did go back into the ring because he desperately needed the money. As it turned out, he began to win fights again, but he'd become slow.

Al Weill was managing the up-and-coming Rocky Marciano, who was described then as a young tiger ready for the bigtime. Marciano's trainer was Charley Goldman. Marciano had a terri-fic left hook, too, just like Joe Louis. Goldman had taught Marciano that punch. This fight would be a big payday, but Joe refused to take anything less than 45 per cent of the gate receipts, leaving Marciano only 15 per cent – the fighters' combined shares being 60 per cent of the total gate. Marciano agreed to take less because he needed the fight to build his reputation and to get a shot at the latest heavyweight champion, Jersey Joe Walcott. The winner of the Louis-Marciano bout would likely get a title fight the following year.

When the camera crew and I went out to Joe's training camp in Pompton Lakes, New Jersey, I found him working hard to get ready for the fight. It was set for a few weeks later, at the end of October. I was glad to see Joe had worked himself into such great shape, and those of us who were his fans believed he was on the way to regaining the championship. When I made the same request of him that I'd made of Sugar Ray Robinson, Joe didn't hesitate, saying we could take any footage we wanted.

"I'm going to be punching the heavy bag for three or four rounds, so you can stand over here and take some good pictures," he said. "Then I'll be hitting the light bag, and you can set up your cameras over there."

Joe Louis was the most magnificent and generous person you'd ever want to meet. I cried when Marciano beat him. Marciano did it with that left hook, setting Joe up for an overhand right that knocked him out, right through the ropes, ending his career. There was never any other champ like Joe Louis. Without him, professional boxing would never be the same.

❧

THIS BOXING FILM WAS MADE AND PLAYED on television several times. Still, I was always looking for the opportunity to get ahead. My position at Galvani took a tremendous amount of energy and time, but I kept on refereeing pro wrestling and worked summers in the Catskills. Our family was comfortable in Franklin Square, but I wanted to start a business and tried to save for it.

Gert was a full-time mother and housewife. She didn't go out to work, preferring instead to take care of the household and to socialize. She still enjoyed playing mah jong.

I became good friends with Norman Schnittman, another Galvani teacher, who was ambitious, like me. Norman was a couple of years older, tall, very handsome, and an athletic type. He was so handsome that women would turn to look at him when he passed them on the street. He and I often talked about pooling our resources and starting some business endeavor that would make us a good extra income. We planned to be partners as soon as we found the right business. We thought about vending machines, but that business was run by gangsters, so we dropped the idea. Then we considered hairpieces, but that wasn't so good either.

Meanwhile, I continued at Galvani, which was immensely rewarding in many ways for me, although not enough financially. I was making about $3,000 a year, and it was a hard-earned salary.

ॐ

Galvani was an old building, in very poor condition – so bad that we couldn't close all the windows. They were on a slant, and made the building cold in winter. On some mornings, science teachers used Bunsen burners to warm up their coffee to start the day, sitting in their overcoats because they were cold. Andy Moskowitz, a math teacher and my good friend, once was so cold that he used newspapers to light a fire in a wastebasket in our teacher's room.

In spite of having so little, most of the teachers loved being there. We were friends, we were colleagues, comrades who thought we could make a difference with the kids. We were there because we wanted to be, and we had the highest respect for one another. We were very social after school and got together for parties. Our families made for a very close-knit group. There were many terrific teachers at Galvani, and Israel Flax was an excellent principal and a wonderful man. He was an ordained rabbi, a licensed attorney, a humanitarian, and he had the greatest love for his job. He was in his late-40's then, about 15 years older than I, and was like a father to me, although he considered himself more as an older brother. He and my mother were the most influential people in my life. From Mr. Flax I learned how to have more understanding, more patience. He taught me so much of what I know about children and how to take care of them. If we could handle a problem ourselves in school, we tried to avoid bringing in the police. We wanted to give a boy another chance to do the right thing. In one particular case, we suspected a boy had stolen a master key to the teachers' rooms and was slipping in to rob purses. Mr. Flax and I tricked him, pretending we were playing at mugging him and stealing his money. I got a hand in his pocket, where I found the key. We could have prosecuted him, but instead we gave him a chance to go straight, and he did. There were no more robberies in the teachers' rooms, and this boy came to believe that if you do something wrong you'll always be caught.

Although Mr. Flax was a devout Jew, he never proselytized or tried to influence me in any way. He lived in the Bronx and spent every summer upstate in Pine Plains, where there was no phone. You had to go up there if you wanted to get in touch with him. He was, himself, a superior teacher and enjoyed coming into a class to help, giving a great lesson, mixing in humor. He would show teachers how it was done, yet he never insulted or threatened them – did it all very subtly. He was a great psychologist with a tremendously good heart, and he loved people, loved the children, and we loved him. When teachers needed Mr. Flax, they often said, "Let's go see the rabbi."

In the neighborhood around Galvani, there was a certain amount of senseless violence. One especially horrible crime was the murder of an elderly Jewish man who had a second-hand magazine store near the school. An Irish kid drove an ice pick into the poor fellow's head and stole some magazines. The kid was sent to reformatory for two years, and when he got out the courts put him back in our school again, into ninth grade. Nowadays, a kid would get 20 years in prison for what he did, but back then they hoped to rehabilitate young criminals, not just lock them up. We didn't like having him back in the school, but we did what we could to keep him in line, and had no difficulty with him in the time he was with us. He was an example of some of the worst of the young people we had to deal with each day.

As time went on, Galvani earned a reputation in the New York City school system for being able to handle difficult kids. So, when a school in East Harlem had a serious problem with a child, its administrators would ask Mr. Flax to take that child – a "disciplinary transfer," it was termed. He usually agreed to do it, because he had me to discipline the student. This meant that Galvani had far more than its share of problem children.

Unfortunately, the teachers weren't always up to the task. That resulted in the "bad" children becoming worse discipline problems. Weak or irresponsible teachers would send a difficult student out of the room, and I'd soon hear about that boy wandering the halls, usually causing trouble. "Call Mr. Gersh!" the cry went out, and I rushed away to deal with it. Then there'd be another crisis in the lunchroom. "Call Mr. Gersh!" Next, it would be on the playground. I'd have to take care of difficult situations again and again every school day, but the teachers should have been doing the job in the classrooms.

I finally asked Mr. Flax not to keep accepting transfers of difficult children.

I said, "Boss, we can't keep taking these bad children unless we also get our weak teachers to do their jobs."

Mr. Flax was too kind, though, and didn't have the heart to really admonish weak teachers, and certainly not to fire anybody. That would lead to problems in the future because the burden on me to handle so many troublesome children just became too great. At the same time, crime in the streets was increasing, as New York City became burdened with worsening criminality. This trouble found its way into Galvani many times in those years.

And when it did, the cry went out to "Call Mr. Gersh."

༄

In my first year at Galvani, Mr. Flax came in and said, "Eddie, I have a boy that I'd like to transfer to your class, because his teacher can't control him."

"Sure," I said, "put him in my class."

No teacher in the school could control Wilfred Avellez, who was about 12 years old and the biggest boy in the seventh grade. I could tell Wilfred was a very bright person, but he'd never learned to read or write – part of the reason for much of his being difficult and for his antisocial behavior with the rest of the kids. Wherever he was, he had to be the boss – except with me, that is. I was a strict mentor. When he was bad, he would be punished quite severely, often with that thick paddle the boys had made in shop for me. Wilfred got smacked by it more times than anybody else, because he was cocky at first until he realized I was bigger and stronger. Strength was all that some children at Galvani accepted and respected. If they respected you, that was the first step in getting them to accept your authority. It wasn't long before I was like a substitute father to Wilfred. For the full year I had his seventh-grade class, he pretty much behaved himself for me, and I began to really appreciate him. When I ran for assembly, Wilfred went with me to help hammer election posters onto telephone poles. At one point I even saved his life: I'd taken the class to Orchard Beach, where he went in over his head while jumping for a ball. Wilfred couldn't swim, and I had to pull him out. There was a kind of chemistry between us that's difficult to put into words, and I liked him better than all the other children. Perhaps he was the son I didn't yet have, and I was a father figure to him. Wilfred had a father, whom I met, but the man just couldn't handle his son and pretty much had given up trying.

I worked hard to teach Wilfred the basics of the alphabet. In fact, lots of kids at Galvani were illiterate, both in English and Spanish. Some of them had been abandoned by parents who'd gone back to Puerto Rico and left them behind to fend for themselves. Other parents were in hospitals or prison, and more than one in a mental institution. Some well-meaning parents sent their boys out to school every morning, unaware that they were truant every day. One boy played basketball in the projects on good days, and on rainy or snowy days he rode the train for hours.

Some good kids cut school because they had to stay home and take care of younger siblings when parents weren't around. At least one boy didn't come to school for a while because his brother had just been killed, a homicide. Mr. Flax counseled him and got him to come back. Students were promoted to the next grade on the basis of their size and their age, not academic achievement. That was unofficial city-wide policy in those days.

There were plenty of poor families that couldn't afford decent clothing, so their kids were too embarrassed to come to school. Others had no shoes. We arranged assistance for them from charity groups, especially Catholic Charities. Our small fund at the school to help out was never enough. We also had a closet full of donated articles of clothing to give away. Mr. Flax and I often loaned parents some money for clothing and even for personal hygiene. We'd give them 15 cents for a bath and a dollar for a haircut. Mr. Flax gave a boy five dollars for glasses, and the mother repaid him a little each week.

When I became disciplinary dean in my second year at Galvani, Wilfred went to another teacher. Now that he wasn't with me, he often caused trouble, and since he was one of the biggest boys in the school, he frightened the other children. In fact, he got to be very bad and was brought in to me for discipline I beat him up more than once. I'm probably the only person who ever hit Wilfred and he didn't fight back.

One day a boy came to say, "Mr. Gersh, Wilfred took my lunch money!"

I called Wilfred in and told him, "I know you took this boy's lunch money, and I don't want you to do it again."

So he said, "Okay, okay, okay."

A couple of weeks later, another boy came and said Wilfred had taken his money.

Again I called Wilfred in.

"Wilfred, this is the second time I'm telling you: I don't want you to take another boy's money. The next time you do it, I'm going to send you to the Youth House."

This was the reformatory – known as the New York State Training School for Boys.

Wilfred said, "All right, all right."

I'd given him a grave warning, but he stole a third time, and I confronted him. He admitted it, so I called the police. He went to youth court, and was sent upstate to the reformatory. While he was there, Wilfred began to teach himself how to read and write – a tremendous personal achievement – and he corresponded with me, telling me he was now a weightlifter, and that when he came out of the reformatory, he wanted to be a fighter. Well, he was impossible for the reformatory to handle. He might have been released after a few months, but he was so difficult that he was kept there for the full three years, until he was 16.

I regretted it had turned out this way, but hoped Wilfred would eventually benefit from such harsh experiences. A lot of youngsters from Galvani and East Harlem never had any opportunities for advancement, but Wilfred had the strength of character to make the most of his chances when they came his way. First, however, he had to overcome a truly rough youth and learn how to avoid making more serious mistakes.

❧

IN 1952, GALVANI WON THE DUBIOUS REPUTATION of being the first school in the country where a dope sale was made to an undercover narcotics agent inside the school building. A narc saw a kid in the schoolyard with dope, asked to buy some, and the boy gave

him a price. The narc said they should go into the school to complete the deal, and that's where he arrested the boy. Even though
the boy was persuaded to go into the school, and the sale didn't
need to have transpired there, newspapers carried it as a lead
story – "Dope-dealing inside East Harlem school!"

Street gangs were a major problem, with lots of petty crime,
and sometimes serious crimes. If a gang leader shot someone,
he'd pass the gun to another gang member, who was under 16,

Mugging for the camera, Kid Gavilan and Edward Gersh are kept apart by Galvani principal Israel Flax. (Photo Jackson Pokress)

the age at which they could be charged with a capital offense. The younger boy would plead guilty and would be sent away to a youth home for a few months, or if the victim died, to a reformatory for a couple of years.

We knew who all the gangs were and which students belonged to them. I had a box of file cards with the names of the gangs, their members, and descriptions of their colors, their ethnic backgrounds, and how troublesome they were. I understand that the Broadway show, "West Side Story," was originally conceived as "East Side Story." In fact, Galvani is the school seen in the opening scenes of the movie version, showing a side wall of the school building covered by graffiti and gang names. The Copians, Dragons, Viceroys, Conservatives (formerly the Enchanters), and Latin Gents – all Puerto Rican; the Redwings and Harlem Hawks were Italian; the Hellbinders, Yorkville Dukes, Norsemen, and Charmers were made up of various white groups, and the Sportsmen were a black gang. These and many more gangs were active in the neighborhood over the years.

Street gangs fought with knives and with zip guns – homemade weapons that used elastic and a makeshift trigger to fire a single bullet. I confiscated many zip guns in school. In my office I had a large cardboard Kotex box filled with zip guns and switchblade knives. The police would come and take away any real guns we confiscated, but they never bothered with the zip guns. When I took a zip gun away, I didn't call the police, not unless the boy was involved in some kind of gang fight. Boys often surreptitiously made their zip guns right in shop class, when the teacher wasn't looking. So, I accumulated quite a collection of zip guns. Then, one day somebody broke into my office and made off with every switchblade and zip gun in the box.

If there came word of a big gang-fight brewing, I'd send out gang members from school to bring in the leaders. I'd have a sit-down with the two leaders and many times was able to resolve the argument and stop a fight from taking place. We also often had to defuse gang conflicts right in school. Eventually, the gangs began to work out their hostility by appointing a warlord, their best fighter. Instead of 15 gang members fighting 15 gang members, one warlord took on the other – as portrayed in "West Side Story" – and the result of this single-combat settled things.

Gangs took the place of parental supervision in many cases, but discipline in the schools was also essential to many a boy's survival. Yet, many were eager to learn, to study, and they did learn, and many of them became outstanding adults.

Sometimes, real guns were brought to school, and I could find myself confronting outsiders, older guys who came to make trouble. One day, I was sitting in my office at Galvani when the cleaning lady rushed in and said, "Mr. Gersh, I think there's going to be a fight downstairs."

I hurried down and saw four fellows standing there, two on one side and two on the other. Two were outsiders who'd graduated several years before. I told them all to come upstairs to the principal's office, where we found Mr. Flax at his desk. The first thing I did with outsiders was to search them. When I put my hand inside the pocket of one guy's jacket, I felt the handle of a gun that was tucked into his belt.

I threw a head lock on him and yelled, "He's got a gun!"

Mr. Flax jumped up from behind his desk, pulled the gun out of the belt and started hitting the guy over the head with it. In the meantime, the office secretaries phoned the police, telling them a boy in school had a loaded gun. It was a .22 automatic – a very potent weapon. Within minutes, police cars converged on the school, sirens wailing and red lights flashing. As the police came running along the hall, guns drawn, a secretary met them.

"It's safe now!" she gasped. "You can go inside."

After it was all over, I asked Mr. Flax, "Why did you hit him on the head with the gun?"

"I don't know," he answered, flustered. "I guess I saw it in the movies!"

*Principal Flax, left center, and Gersh at his side, join a Galvani
ninth-grade class for its yearly photograph. The teacher of this
class always declined to be photographed – perhaps not happy
with seeing herself age from year to year.*

Chapter 12

SELF-RESPECT AND DISCIPLINE

FOR ALL THE CORPORAL PUNISHMENT and tough discipline that was meted out at Galvani, I firmly believed that giving children a sense of importance was most essential to their educational development. Imparting belief in their self-importance was very effective in winning their respect. So many of those nondescript children had nothing, with little to look forward to in their futures, so making them feel they mattered was my objective as a teacher.

A very simple tool was my envelope of nails. I kept this envelope full of nails by my desk, and sometimes when I had an agitated kid in the office for disciplinary reasons, I'd give him the envelope and tell him it was important that he take it up to the shop teacher and come right back. Rather than go head-to-head with the boy right then, I avoided trouble by giving him something to do that seemed important to him – something I trusted him to do. The boy had a real sense of responsibility in taking those nails to the shop, and he felt better about himself.

I also had a policy of letting children do me a favor, letting them do something for me. If they did a favor for me, that meant I was obligated to them, and if somebody is obligated to you, then you like them better. I learned that from reading Benjamin Franklin's wisdom. Often, I had the children in my class do things for me – for example, helping me put on my coat. Also, I kept a shoeshine box in my closet, and the children would battle with each other to shine my shoes.

"It's my turn, Mr. Gersh," they'd say, "it's my turn, because he did it yesterday!"

I never paid them, which was part of the psychology I used. Shining the teacher's shoes was something that you wouldn't expect children to do in a classroom, of course, but when they did that for me I was then obligated to them, and they liked me for it. Of course, some of the things we did as teachers in those days wouldn't be acceptable at all today, but we believed it was good for those children in that time and place. Our years of grueling experience with difficult problems brought us to some solutions that were practical, direct, and effective, even if they wouldn't be politically correct by modern standards.

We had some unconventional ways of dealing with problem children. There was a young boy who caused the teachers a great deal of difficulty. He'd go completely crazy if he were denied something or if a teacher told him to do something he didn't want to do. He'd kick up a tantrum, throw books, throw chalk, erasers, chairs – would go completely crazy. He'd start all this by hyperventilating – and then he'd explode into violence. One day, a teacher wanted to send him down to me, but he refused to come. I had to go up and get him. I knew about his background, his mode of operation. I brought him down to my office and asked him what he'd done wrong. He started to give me some surly answers, and then he began to hold his breath, about to hyperventilate. Right then, I held my own breath, as if starting to hyperventilate myself. He gaped to see I was turning blue. He was shocked to see this six-foot, 200-pound, former prize fighter and disciplinary dean of the school hyperventilating.

He suddenly blurted out, "Oh, I'm sorry, Mr. Gersh, I'm sorry!"

I took a breath and relaxed.

From that day on, this boy never hyperventilated in school again.

There was a boy in seventh grade who was impossible to control. His name was Petie, and I was called many times to take him out of the classroom. One time I brought him down to the office, and he was struggling and fighting so that Mr. Flax and I tied him into a chair. He screamed and yelled and tried to get out, spitting at us and finally throwing the chair over onto the floor. We had to hold him down with physical force. Another day, Petie was in the office and starting to carry on, getting worked up. Trouble was coming. Sure enough, he started to fuss and spit at Mr. Flax and me. All of a sudden, Mr. Flax grabbed an army jacket from the closet and put it over Petie's head. I grabbed Petie, so he couldn't take it off, and after a brief struggle, he went limp.

"Oh, oh, oh, oh – I'll be good," he whimpered. "I'll be good – but take it off, take it off, please, please, take it off, I'll be good, I'll be good."

We took the hood off, and from then on, if Petie ever started to act up, I'd say, "I'll get the hood," and he'd settle down immediately. I believed his response to the hood was the result of having been put in a dark room by his parents when he was younger, left there all by himself. Well, Petie went out into the world after Galvani and committed many crimes. In the end, he mugged somebody in the subway and was running down the tracks when he was hit by a train and killed.

Often, we had to do unconventional things in order to protect the students or ourselves from violence. During changes of periods, the teachers would be in the hall, patrolling, and watching the kids. There was one little blonde-haired Puerto Rican kid, Willie, who was as crazy as could be. Willie decided to play handball in the hall. A teacher named Dave went to stop him.

"Hey Willie, cut it out!" Dave said, and tried to get the boy into the classroom.

Willie resisted, took a pencil, and stabbed Dave in the neck, twice. Dave lost his temper and yanked the kid into the bathroom, grabbed his head, and put it into the toilet. I was nearby, but didn't interfere. After a few seconds of dunking, Willie calmed right down, and he wasn't a problem after that.

Then there was the time when a student came into the principal's office and said someone had a rifle in the basement bathroom. I went running out of the office, with Frank Goldman, the assistant principal, running behind me, and Mr. Flax running behind him. We rushed into the bathroom to find two small boys at the urinals and one big boy just standing there. I knew this boy was a troublemaker, so I went up to him, took a close look, then turned him around and put him up against the wall to frisk him. He had no gun, but I didn't stop there. I looked into all the cubicles and, sure enough, a jacket was standing up in one as if by itself, leaning against the wall. Underneath I found a loaded .22 rifle with a bullet in the chamber. We brought the boy to the office and called the police.

Actually, I carried a gun myself at times. The school lunchroom would collect a thousand dollars a day, and I was responsible for going to the bank with all that cash a couple of times a week. It was a lot safer carrying thousands of dollars through East Harlem if I had a firearm. The police agreed with me, and I received a permit to carry a gun in New York City. Not many people were given carry permits in the city in those days.

Sometimes, we administrators had to protect the teachers from superintendent office hassles. For one thing: whenever the deputy superintendent arrived on a surprise inspection I'd hurry through the school and alert every teacher to make sure they were doing the right thing when he got to their classrooms. I'd just appear at their doors and say the last name of the deputy superintendent, and the teacher would be at his or her best.

On one occasion, students tried to prove that some of the teachers weren't doing their jobs properly. We had two Irish boys in Galvani – the only Irish among the Puerto Ricans, Italians, and blacks. Their names were O'Neill, and they were twins. The O'Neill boys were always on the verge of misbehaving, but were never really bad. One day, I saw one of them with a camera, and I found out he'd been taking pictures of teachers doing things they shouldn't be doing in school – such as smoking in the classroom, or reading a newspaper as the children worked away, or maybe loitering together outside when they should be in class, whatever the case may be. This O'Neill was taking as many compromising pictures of teachers as he could, so I called him down.

"That's a nice camera," I said. "Would you let me see it?"

I admired the camera and, since he was going to phys-ed class, offered to keep it safe for him.

"I'll hold it here, and then you come back and I'll give it to you."

He agreed and left for class. I then took the camera into the bathroom, exposed the film, and put it back. Needless to say, there were no further candid camera episodes at our school.

There were situations where I had to curb my own emotions and anger.

I always had a student monitor or two in my office, ready to be sent on an errand, such as escorting a problem boy down from a classroom. The monitors were there because they were being disciplined for doing something wrong, generally for being out of control. Usually, boys the teachers couldn't control were the toughest kids in the school, so they would be obeyed by boys they escorted. Across from my desk was a bench where monitors sat, awaiting instructions. When a student had to be brought down, I'd give the monitor a note and tell him to go and fetch him. One day, a monitor who'd been sent to get a troublemaker named Knight came back empty-handed. I didn't notice at first, because I was working at my desk, busy with paperwork. When I looked up to see my monitor sitting on the bench but no Knight, I asked what was going on.

"I thought I told you to go get Knight," I said.

"You did, Mr. Gersh, but he wouldn't come."

"What do you mean he wouldn't come?"

"He wouldn't come, Mr. Gersh."

"Did you tell him that I wanted him?"

"Yes."

"And what did he say?"

"I can't tell you."

The monitor was uneasy, hardly able to look at me.

"What do you mean you can't tell me?"

I was getting annoyed now.

"I can't tell you what he said, Mr. Gersh."

"You tell me what he said!"

"All right," the boy began hesitantly, then exclaimed, "'Tell Gersh to go to hell and kiss my ass!'"

I didn't show my anger, but I was steaming.

"Is that what he said?"

"Yeah."

Well, I was busy with something more important, and I let it go for the moment. A couple of days later, I saw Knight in the hall. I grabbed him by the shoulder.

"Come with me," I said and took him into a bathroom which only the principal and I had the key to.

I closed the door, took off my glasses, took off my wristwatch, put my glasses in my breast pocket, put my wristwatch in my coat pocket, hung up my coat, and then went up to him. In the meantime, he'd backed into a corner, knowing what was coming.

I said, "Did you tell Gersh to go to hell and kiss your ass?"

"Mr. Gersh," he said quickly, "I never told you to go to hell."

I stood there for a moment, staring, and then I burst out laughing. I just broke up. It was impossible to stop laughing, and in the meantime he was looking at me with such confusion and fear.

Then I said, "All right."

I put on my jacket, put on my glasses, put on my wristwatch, and told Knight to go to class. For years afterward, he'd come back to school to visit, and whenever he'd see me at the far end of the hall, he'd yell, "Hey, Mr. Gersh, I never told you to go to hell!"

❧

WE HAD CHILDREN WHO WERE in a Class of Retarded Mental Development – CRMD. This was the precursor to what eventually became special education. Ironically, some of these children had powerful mental abilities. One Italian boy in CRMD used to be a numbers-runner on the street – that is he worked for the gamblers and took bets from people who picked a number, usually tied to the next day's horse-racing results. This boy would remember the numbers he was given, and placed their bets with the gamblers. He even brought the cash to pay them off if they won. Remembering the numbers required a tremendous amount of brainpower, but otherwise he was mentally deficient and had to be in the CRMD group.

My colleague Andy Moskowitz recalled some of his experiences educating these children:

> As part of teaching children in the CRMD classes, we helped them adjust to what they had, to make use of what they had. We would teach them in the shop class to make shoeshine boxes. Then, we allowed them to go around the neighborhood to shine shoes for money. Next door to our school was an empty lot that was covered with ashes, because ours was a coal-burning school. We taught them to clean the lot up. Sure, this was not completely legal, but they used to do all sorts of work like this, sometimes polishing cars for teachers, and we paid them for it. We also would take CRMD children around the neighborhood and show them how to shop, say

in the local A&P supermarket. This was part of their essential education, and it was of great value to them.

Then there were those challenging children, like Wilfred Avellez, who were such extraordinary people despite their tough lives. They walked the line between criminality and normality, and for Wilfred, the criminal world could seem more normal than the straight world.

ε�

WILFRED HAD CONTINUED CORRESPONDING with me from prison. He got out of jail in 1954 at the age of 16 and came to school to see me even before he went home! He told me he wanted to be a fighter, and he'd built himself up beautifully by weight-lifting. He was extremely strong and athletic. That good chemistry was still there between us, and I agreed to help him become a fighter.

I got Wilfred a job as a dishwasher at a little diner on 50th Street and Broadway, a place owned by my longtime friend, Frankie Ganger. A "ham-and-eggery," we called those diners. Then I hired a trainer at Gleason's Gym, paid Wilfred's gym dues and so forth, and he started training. He soon was looking pretty good, and was doing well, learning to box and winning fights. I thought he had a real future in the ring, but then he met a girl, Jenny, who was 10 or 15 years older than him. Jenny was a prostitute and a heroine addict. They fell in love, she started supporting him. Being supported by his woman was a lot easier than fighting, so Wilfred started missing days at the job, and the trainer at the gym said he wasn't training as he once had been.

Frankie called me and said, "Ed, I'm depending on Wilfred to work, but he's missing so many days."

"Well then you'll have to fire him," I said reluctantly.

So Wilfred got fired, also stopped going to the gym, and we lost contact. Less than a year went by and I got a call from him from the Tombs, the notorious New York City prison. He'd been arrested and was in serious trouble. I went down there and spoke to him on a telephone through the glass partition.

"What happened, Wilfred?" I asked.

"Well, they accused me of mugging somebody."

"Did you do it?"

"Yes."

"Then tell the judge what you did, and tell him you're sorry, and take your medicine. And when you come out of jail, I'll help you again."

I later found out that Wilfred had been mugging clients of Jenny's. As he recalled it:

I used to hang out in this bar with Jenny, and she would go and attract a trick, a John, and take him into the hallway. Then I would go into the hallway and boom! One punch, one shot, and he's knocked out. We'd take his money and keep on stepping. Well this one time it didn't happen that way – I got busted. The cops came after me, I ran, and they fired – and pffffffffffft, the bullet went right over my head. I felt it go past, and I stopped running. The guy didn't shoot no more, and I was lucky to be alive.

Wilfred pleaded guilty, and they sent him away to Comstock State Prison for a sentence described as "zip to five." In other words, he could get out almost any time for good behavior, but if he didn't behave, he'd have to serve the full five years. Well, Wilfred served the full five years. He was the toughest guy in the whole place, king of the prison. He was 185 pounds of muscle, and tough, tough, tough.

Years later, Wilfred recalled those five years in New York prisons:

I wanted to get onto the football team they had at Comstock, but I had to prove I was the roughest, so I put on a helmet and showed how I could run at top speed into the prison wall. I got the job on the team.

I might have been out in 19 months, but I misbehaved – I was in a prison riot, and that automatically made me have to finish my whole sentence – 60 months. The riot was about food. They were closing the dining hall too early for us guys who were playing ball to get there in time. We were missing a meal, so we finally rioted about it – about that and the poor quality of the food. I led the riot, so as a result they sent me up to Dannemora, a maximum security prison near the Canadian border. The coldest place. You get up at seven, by eight you're in the mess hall, by nine you're working, by three, you're out, by four you're in the yard, then back to the cell.

At Dannemora you either had to make it or you'd go berserk and they'd take you right over over the wall – meaning next door to the prison was the mental hospital. I never got to the mental hospital, but I sure came close to it.

For the last two weeks of his five-year sentence, Wilfred was kept in solitary at Dannemora because the guards couldn't control him, and they couldn't extend his sentence. They didn't trust him in the general population, so they kept him in solitary confinement.

In solitary, they'd give you three slices of bread with your meals, so what I used to do is take one slice of bread and roll it into marbles. I'd play marbles, because there was nothing else to do in solitary. So I wouldn't go out of my mind, I played marbles. Then, when I got tired of playing marbles, I'd eat the bread.

Wilfred and I stayed in contact, and he improved his literacy as well as built up his body. He said he still wanted to be a fighter. Although the years passed – he didn't get out until 1959 – I was prepared to give him another chance when he was ready. Why did he still write to me after I'd put him in prison once and then had persuaded him to confess for another sentence? In Wilfred's words:

Aside from the fact that he put me in jail, I had this feeling that the man was all right. The man was all right. I put myself in the position that I was in, and if I would have listened to him, I wouldn't have been there. And this is why I kept in touch with him all the time. One thing in particular he put in my mind when I went back to prison was "Read a lot!" He told me, "Read a lot!"

And I did.

I never imagined it then, but Wilfred Avellez eventually would become one of the most important people in my life.

West Hill campers in the 1950s take swimming instructions from Ed Gersh in one of the newly built swimming pools.

Chapter 13

WEST HILLS

A ROUND 1953, MY COLLEAGUE and friend, Norman Schnittman, and I were employed part-time by a former Galvani teacher who ran a private school called Sky Top, on 72nd Street in Manhattan. We worked from three to five in the afternoon, taking care of little children in an after-school program. It was a new experience to be working with such young children One day, near the end of the regular school year, Norman brought the astonishing news that he'd been offered $5,000 to run a Brooklyn day camp during the summer. That was much more than we were paid for a whole school year, and I found it hard to believe. Furthermore, the job was only five days a week.

In the Catskill hotels I had to work 14 hours a day, all week long, and made only $1,500 for the entire season. I was eager to look into the day-camp business and soon became convinced it was for me. Norman and I could teach during the year and run the camp in summer. Both of us were athletes, so we knew that side of the business, and we were willing and able to work hard, building fields and facilities, maintaining the grounds, managing a staff. . . . We were enthusiastic as we started looking for a site out on Long Island, where there were lots of wonderful old estates for sale.

Long Island was a perfect location for a day camp, because it was becoming increasingly built-up, with thousands of suburban families needing somewhere to send their kids in summertime. Norman and I went out every Saturday and Sunday, looking for a site, visiting mansions that were on the market – and it seemed most of the mansions were available then. We still had to find the necessary funds, but we believed if everything was arranged properly we'd be able to borrow from relatives and friends.

Finally, in early 1953, after a great deal of intensive looking, we found a place in the West Hills section of Huntington. It was a big, beautiful mansion, plus 12 acres and a pond. The estate was run-down, and the family was living only in a part of the house. We saw it in the springtime, and the Christmas decorations still were up. The estate was available for $75,000, which meant $15,000 down and the balance on a mortgage that Norman and I would sign for personally. We also needed enough funds to build the camp, so we required a total of $45,000 dollars for the down payment and development. The most Norman could raise was $2,500, and the most I could raise was $2,500, so that left $40,000 dollars that we had to find. We began to ask everyone we knew for loans.

That summer I found myself at a reunion of half a dozen Dewitt Clinton high school friends. We were in a beautiful Central Park West apartment owned by an extremely wealthy fellow who worked for his father in the garment industry. At the party was my old pal Bernie Gladstone, the one who'd persuaded me to go out for football and who'd told me about boxing for a watch. Bernie had been an important influence on me, stimulating me to do things that completely changed my life. He was a successful lawyer now, and very well off – like everyone in the room but me. I was undoubtedly the least prosperous person there.

I took the opportunity to tell Bernie about my plans for a day camp. Then I asked if he would consider providing a loan of $500 to help me get started. Well, Bernie shocked me with his response, which was unexpectedly sharp. He said that if I needed money for food, he'd let me have it, but he wouldn't give me anything to invest in a gamble like a day camp. Things got a bit testy between us, and I became annoyed.

Then he said, "You know what the trouble with you is, Ed? You're a failure. For the first time in your life, you're a failure. You're a failure because you're broke. You're a failure, and you're bitter about it."

I was growing more angry, but I kept my self-control and told him that I hoped what I was doing at Galvani "contributed to the lives of a lot of children."

He ignored that and went on: "All your life you've been top dog – an all-scholastic football player, a champion boxer – but today we measure success by the amount of money a person has, and you don't have a penny to your name!"

We argued for a while, and I was upset, but when I got home, I realized he was right: I subconsciously envied my rich friends. Right then and there, I decided I was going to become a millionaire by the time I was 50. I didn't know how, of course, but I was determined, just as I'd been determined when I first stepped into the ring.

Here I was, 32 years old, with the most exciting business concept I'd ever envisioned, and didn't have the money needed to get started.

Gert and I were living in Franklin Square at the time. She played mah jong with a group of women whose husbands were mostly prosperous tradespeople – one was a butcher, another a bread man, two others were pocketbook makers, and so on. When Gert told the wives about what I was trying to do, they indicated an interest and said their husbands might like to invest in a venture of this kind. So, we got 10 people, who put in a total of

$40,000 among them. They were to be silent partners, and Norman and I were to run the camp. It was an exciting moment in our lives, but now we had to make the camp succeed.

We bought the Huntington estate and started building the facilities, clearing land and making ball fields and tennis courts, and we built a swimming pool. Much of the work we did ourselves, working long, hard hours with shovels and picks and rakes. We named it West Hills Day Camp, and started that first season, 1954, with 169 children. It was a great beginning, but as the summer progressed it seemed that every one of the partners thought they knew how to run a camp better than we did. They constantly phoned me about it, because they all lived in my housing development. Somebody would call me every night to get a report on the camp.

Norman and I began to get very tired of interference from people who were supposed to be silent investors. They had no educational experience at all, but they were telling two very experienced educators how to handle children and run a day camp. One evening I got home, exhausted, at about eight o'clock, and I'd just started dinner when I got a phone call from one of the investors.

This lady said, "Ed, my son told me that such-and-such happened at the camp today. Would you tell me everything about it?"

"Are you calling me as an investor," I replied, "or are you calling me as a parent?"

Now, as a parent she was completely entitled to a full, detailed description of everything that happened. But she said she was calling me as an investor.

So I said, "Call a stockholders' meeting!" and hung up.

From that point on, our relationship with our investors went steadily downhill. Finally, at the end of the summer, Norman and I decided we'd no longer be partners with them. We left West Hills Day Camp to them, and went looking for another site to start up again. We found a former estate on Round Swamp Road in Huntington, about five miles from West Hills.

I asked several other friends if they wanted to invest in a day camp, and a fellow whom I'd taught with at City College said he would. This was Dave Polanski, who'd been the CCNY basketball coach after the great Nat Holman. (Holman compiled a 423-190 record in 37 seasons at CCNY, which in 1950 became the only college team in history to win both the NCAA and NIT tournaments.) Dave went into partnership with us, and we all put in $7,500 each.

Most of the money Norman and I put in was borrowed from friends and relatives. Several loaned me a few hundred each, but to get my $7,500 I was very fortunate in being able to borrow $5,000 from my friend Emma Beck. Emma was the elderly unmarried teacher at Galvani whom the students and staff loved so much. As I've said earlier, Emma was a wonderful woman and a wonderful teacher. She liked me very much, and her loan was given just on the strength of my signature on a piece of paper that stated I promised to repay her – which I did within a year. I'll never forget Emma Beck as long as I live. She gave me the opportunity that led to everything else in my business career.

So, with less than $25,000 we started a new day camp called Crestwood Country Day School. Again, we all worked long and hard to build and prepare the facilities. Most of the children from that first summer at West Hills decided to come with us to Crestwood. As a result, West Hills had a great deal of difficulty filling its enrollment. They'd hired another director, also a schoolteacher, and ran it in competition with Crestwood, but they had other troubles of their own making. Right after we'd left West Hills, the partners immediately started fighting among themselves. Then I got a call from one of them, who asked whether I'd like to buy his interest in West Hills. At this point, I was no longer a stupid schoolteacher, who sold a majority of his stock to other people.

I said, "We'll buy your stock if we can get the majority of the West Hills Day Camp stock."

"With the stock you already have," he said, "and the stock I can assemble for you, you'll have the majority control of West Hills."

"If that's the case, we'll buy it."

He assembled the shares, and Norman, Dave and I bought majority control. The investors who were operating the camp didn't know their partners had sold out from under them. Norman and I went to the home of the ones who had the corporate books and who'd been conducting the business of West Hills. We said they no longer had majority control, and that we did. We requested the books and all the records, which they very reluctantly gave up. The minority partners stayed for one more year and then sold their stock to us at the price they paid for it – so they recouped their money. We now owned both camps: West Hills Day Camp and Crestwood Country Day School.

After lengthy discussions, it was decided that Norman and Dave would stay at Crestwood and work that camp together, and I would move to West Hills to take charge of the operation and management. West Hills became my full responsibility, and every year the enrollment increased and the camp became bigger and better, with a growing reputation. Of course, West Hills wasn't just a two-month summer commitment as I'd first thought, but required attention all through the year.

After working as the dean at Galvani until 3:30 p.m., I'd get into my car and ride out to Huntington to supervise the maintenance, the building, the development, the staff, the hiring – all the operations. For nine months of the year, I'd leave my house at 6:30 in the morning and not get home until 10-11 o'clock at night. It was hard, really hard, but I enjoyed it, and I enjoyed the fact that the business was growing and my income of course grew with it. West Hills Day Camp was very rewarding. It was perfectly positioned to benefit from Long Island's population-growth, with thousands of new homes being built for families with young children. Our location in increasingly prosperous Huntington made success that much easier.

In spite of all the work teaching and at camp, one of the real enjoyments in my life was refereeing pro wrestling – "shows," we called them, not "matches."

꙲

PRO WRESTLING WAS STEADILY RISING in popularity and had a huge television audience. It was a "show" because the outcome was predetermined, and the wrestlers were putting on an exhibition of athleticism, acrobatics, strength, and showmanship. It was true that many people who followed wrestling didn't realize they were watching an exhibition, not a genuine wrestling match, but it was all a lot of fun and quite exciting – especially for me, refereeing in front of 20,000 screaming and yelling fans in packed Madison Square Garden and with that television audience.

I'd usually referee every couple of weeks. I'd get a call at school from the New York State Athletic Commission to tell me I'd be working that coming Friday or Saturday. At first, I refereed shows at the Broadway Arena, Ridgewood Grove, and Saint Nick's – the same venues that put on the boxing matches. I'd also referee preliminaries at Madison Square Garden, and in time, I regularly refereed main events at the Garden. In the Fifties, I was paid $25 for the smaller arenas and $100 for the Garden. It helped out a lot to have that income. By the end of my career, in 1972, I was paid $350 for officiating at the Garden – a good fee for just an hour's work or less.

The wrestlers usually practiced their well-rehearsed moves in a session before the show. Sometimes I was told how it was going to end, but most of the time I could tell who was supposed to win by the way the wrestlers put on their exhibition. After refereeing a few years, you could pretty much tell what was going to happen next. I could anticipate their moves. They were faking it, but they still hit each other hard with those rehearsed punches and kicks, and it could be hazardous for me, too. Once, I was standing too close to a wrestler who unexpectedly reared back to punch an opponent, and I got hit on the nose by the backswing. I had to hold a handkerchief to my face to slow the bleeding, but I let them keep on wrestling.

I had to also be careful when they were both on the mat and I was in close looking for the pin, sliding a hand under the bottom guy's shoulder to see if it was on the mat. If the top man was suddenly thrown off, he could land on me, which did happen sometimes.

Once I declared a pin when a guy on the bottom didn't raise his shoulder quickly enough. He was supposed to win that night, but he was too thoughtless or too lazy, and afterwards in the locker room he was very upset.

"Why'd you do it?" he shouted. "Why'd you count me out?"

I said simply, "Why didn't you raise your shoulder?"

Next time out, he performed better.

There was one especially colorful and crowd-pleasing routine: a wrestler would have a concealed razor wrapped in tape, exposing only the edge of the blade. During a clinch, he'd use the razor to make a shallow slit on the opponent's forehead or eyebrows, making him bleed and stirring up the crowd, which would go crazy. There were other times when the wrestlers would do what was termed "a shooting," meaning they were really angry at one other and were trying to inflict injury. It was none of my business, but if one man pinned the other or knocked the other out, I'd count him out. If time ran out, I'd call it a draw.

I refereed wrestling for 20 years and thoroughly enjoyed it. For the most part, it was a lot of fun, but nowadays, what I see on television is just disgusting and vulgar.

&

IN THE MID-FIFTIES we were doing very well financially, and even though it was obvious there was more money in the camps than in teaching, I stayed at Galvani instead of retiring and turning full time to our own business. Although teaching was incredibly demanding while also running the day camp and refereeing, I continued at school because I loved the job – loved almost every minute of it. Teaching in East Harlem was the most exciting and interesting aspect of my life.

With the camps, school, and refereeing I was away from Gert a lot. In fact, our marriage was seriously failing, and I was not faithful to her. By the mid-Fifties, I was having an affair with Rosemarie Halbig, whose father had been a friend of mine at the Falls View Hotel in the Catskills. Rosemarie had come to live in New York and had contacted me. We fell in love and started a torrid affair. Our relationship became so serious that I eventually rented an apartment in Manhattan for her. I'd meet Rosemarie for dinner before I went to referee a wrestling match, then she'd come to the match, and afterwards we'd spend the evening together.

Life with Gert was separate from everything else I did. She wasn't part of it, and preferred the suburban family world. But I was still ambitious, and West Hills promised prosperity that could lead to even greater success if I were willing to work hard for it. Gert didn't share my ambitions, my drive, and we grew apart and were not in love – although I adored my two daughters, Ellyne and Laurie. After a year or so, Gertrude found out about the affair. We divorced, and I married Rosemarie.

Whereas Gert wasn't interested in working at the camp, Rosemarie was enthusiastic about it, and she was very good at the many facets of the business, from office work to handling campers to leading the staff and communicating with parents. Rosemarie and I had two children, Kevin and Roxanne, and we were happy, working hard during the day and drinking too much in the evening. But we were in love and very successful – and seemingly indestructible.

West Hills staff members in the mid-1970s join Ed and Rosemarie Gersh, at front, with Connie Continue at left and Harvey Geller at right; back row, l-r, Mike Moore, Dan Kalina, Evelyn Salmami, Stu Marks, Arthur Ilingsworth, and Bill Migren.

Wilfred Avellez, pictured here in the 1960s, especially enjoyed working with the riding horses at West Hills.

Chapter 14

JEFFERSON PARK

I N 1960, THE NEW YORK CITY Board of Education closed
Galvani and combined it with an all-girls junior high school.
Students and staff moved into a beautiful new building just
across 109th Street, named Jefferson Park Junior High School,
P.S. 117. Mr. Flax was appointed principal, and I was dean. Instead
of 900 students, there now were 1,700, with twice as many teachers on staff. That same year, I was given the Teacher of the Year
award by an East Harlem community group set up to help children. The group got to know me by their activities in the community and by coming to consult with me at school. I'm still very
proud of that award.

Of course, such honors didn't make the job easier when it came
to dealing with problem situations. I soon found that girls could
be very difficult to handle, and in many cases were rougher and
tougher than the boys. There was one girl who was causing a

great deal of trouble for the teachers of every class she was in. She was told to come down to me, but she didn't appear in my office. I went up there myself and found her walking through the halls. I started scolding her for her bad behavior and told her to come to my office. I was standing right in front of her, and suddenly she hit me on the face, knocking my glasses across the hall. I reacted instinctively, smacking her a couple of times, and hauled her to the office. Next, I pressed charges against her. In court, the judge asked what happened, and I told him she'd hit me. He looked at the girl, who had two black eyes.

"Well, who hit her?" he asked.

I said I didn't know.

The judge turned to the detective, who was nearby: "We'll hold this case over, and you investigate it. Come back in a week, and let us know who beat up this girl."

A few days later, the girl was murdered by her lover, a guy who'd just killed his wife and another girlfriend – killed all three women in the same week.

One afternoon, when Jefferson Park had closed and all the children had left, an older black girl was standing in the doorway. She was as big as I was, if not bigger, and heavy.

"Would you mind leaving please?" I said. "I have to close the doors."

She just scowled at me and stayed there.

"Would you please leave?" I pressed. "I have to close the school."

She used obscene language to tell me what to do, so I gave her a push to get her out, and she grabbed my shirt and ripped the front right off. I grabbed her and put her down on the ground, and she was fighting, trying to scratch and kick me. Finally, I gripped her by the hair and started dragging her down the hall to the principal's office. It was quite a sight, her flat on her back, me with my shirt ripped off, bare-chested, dragging her by the hair along the hallway as she kicked and screamed.

Mr. Flax appeared and asked, "What is it, Eddie?"

"She's an outsider, Mr. Flax."

"Oh, okay, Eddie, keep going."

We called the police and had her arrested. It so happened that I had a teacher's banquet that night, so I had to go into the neighborhood stores, shirt hanging half off, to look to buy a new one.

ॐ

OLDER OUTSIDERS COMING INTO SCHOOL were among the worst problems. In one case, a 26-year-old guy was molesting girls in the halls, and he took a swing at Mr. Flax. I broke the fellow's tooth with a punch, which took the steam out of him. Some outsiders were even more dangerous. One day a woman cafeteria worker came running up to my office, yelling.

"Mr. Gersh, they're beating up Mr. Moskowitz!"

I rushed to the cafeteria to find one fellow had his arm around Andy's neck, pulling him backward, while another one was swinging at Andy. I hit the fellow who was holding Andy with a left hook, right on the jaw, and he went down. Then I turned to the other fellow and hit him with a right hand and a couple of other punches and got him up against the wall. At that moment, Mr. Flax came in, saw me, and shouted in Yiddish:

"*Weiter mal!*" meaning, "Once again! Hit him again!"

I threw another right, but the fellow turned his head aside, and my hand hit the wall. We soon had them subdued and took them up to the office to wait for the police. My hand was a little bloody from punching the wall.

"Eddie," Mr. Flax said, "go to the nurse's office and take care of your hand."

One of the troublemakers, whose face was bleeding, said, "I want to go to the nurse too."

Mr. Flax agreed to let him go with me. I made a mistake then that I never made again in my career: as we went down the corridor I let him walk behind me. Next thing I knew, he was off and running down the stairs toward the exit. I went right after him. He ran out the front door with me behind and onto 109th Street. He dashed over to Third Avenue, me running after him, yelling, "Stop thief! Stop thief!" We ran down Third to 106th Street, me still yelling, "Stop thief!" as startled people watched us go by. On Lexington Avenue, a big dump truck was stopped at a red light, and he jumped into the back of it as the light turned green. The driver started pulling away.

"Stop thief," I yelled. "Stop thief!"

The driver jammed on his brakes.

Now this fellow was reaching down into the truck for something to hit me with. Just then, the truck driver jumped out of cab and saw him.

"Get out of there you sonofabitch!" the driver bellowed.

That did it. The guy gave up and came down meekly. I grabbed him, put one of his arms behind his back, and began marching him to school. He started to say something, but I hit him across the face.

"I don't want to hear one word out of you!"

"Mr. Gersh – " I smacked him again.

Hundreds of people were watching me march him along, whacking him every time he opened his mouth until he finally got the idea and shut up. The police were waiting at school when I got him there. We later found out he was on probation for car theft and for packing a gun. I'm glad to say he never came back to Galvani again.

In another case I was grateful to have Wilfred's help. After he got out of Dannemora, Wilfred came to see me, still wanting to be a fighter. Although our day camps were booming, and my teaching and refereeing wrestling were going strong, I decided to manage him. I soon found myself back in boxing – at the gym, then in Wilfred's corner during an important heavyweight fight, a roaring, eager crowd around us – and I loved it.

At first, Wilfred lived with my family in Franklin Square, but he didn't go back to school to study. He'd come to Jefferson Park with me every morning to sit in my office and be a monitor. If a teacher had a troublesome student who had to be removed from a class, I'd send Wilfred up, and he'd escort the child to my office. Nobody dared resist Wilfred. He stayed until three o'clock, when he'd go to Gleason's Gym. I'd either work there with him or would come by to pick him up later and take him home to Long Island. More than ever, it looked like his boxing career was about to flourish.

One day, a small boy came and said, "Mr. Gersh, the Capeman stole my money."

This fellow was known as "The Capeman" because he wore a cape and carried a cane. He was not the same notorious Capeman killer of another time in New York, but this Capeman frightened and bothered the children, and was a threat. I went out looking for him but didn't see him anywhere. Two or three days later, another boy came to tell me the Capeman had stolen his lunch money. I went out but still didn't see him. This continued for two or three weeks. I wanted to get the Capeman, but nobody knew where he was, although everybody in school knew I was looking for him. Then a boy came into my office to say the Capeman was in back of the school.

Jefferson Park ran for an entire city block, and in back was a high, chainlink fence, with a walkway between the school wall and the fence. The Capeman was likely lurking there.

So I said, "Wilfred, you go around to the right and I'll go around to the left, and we'll meet in the back of the school."

Wilfred went running one way, and I ran the other way. The Capeman was there and saw me coming first. He turned and started running the other way around the school. Then he saw Wilfred, and of course he knew who Wilfred was, so he turned around and came back at me instead. I grabbed him, put him down, and took his cane. When I yanked on the handle, out came a three-foot sword.

I was damn glad that we surprised him before he had a chance to pull it out. If he had drawn that sword, I wouldn't have been so fast to grab for him. We took this boy downtown to children's court, and after the judge heard the case, he pulled the sword out of the cane and asked:

"Who took this sword away from this young man?"

I said "I did, Judge."

He just looked at me and shook his head.

≈

If we could, we tried to protect teachers from their own mistakes or bad judgment. One day, a couple of detectives came to tell Israel Flax and me that the mother of a 15-year old girl had complained about a teacher having an affair with her daughter.

These detectives, who were good friends of ours said, "Listen do you want us to handle it, or can you take care of it?"

Mr. Flax replied, "Let us take care of it."

We found out it was, indeed, true. This girl was Puerto Rican, very good-looking, and very mature for her age. The teacher who was playing around with her – and she was all for it, it wasn't against her will – was married. We called him in and told him to grow up and behave himself. It was clear we didn't want to ruin his career, because otherwise he was a good teacher. We knew it was impulsive on his part. That cooled down the situation. He realized what the consequences would be if he didn't behave himself, so he stopped seeing this girl. Years later, he became a superintendent in the New York school system.

≈

WILFRED AVELLEZ WAS BECOMING PART OF MY FAMILY. He slept in the den, where he had a bed. He'd get up and run early in the morning, then go to school with me, first as my monitor and then I got him a job as a custodian. He was learning how to fight at Gleason's and getting to be very good. I taught him the left hook. He began to call me "Pappa."

Then Wilfred got back together with the prostitute, Jenny, but this time he helped her straighten out. First, he worked with her to kick the drugs, cold turkey. I saw him do it. Jenny was at Wilfred's father's apartment during the ordeal, and Wilfred nursed her through it. She was so sick, throwing up – but he stayed with her day and night, cleaning her and washing her and helping her struggle until she finally kicked the habit. Afterwards, they lived together for a while.

In the summer, Wilfred worked at West Hills, doing grounds work and construction and taking care of horses. He could work harder, longer and faster than any man I ever met in my life. He was very helpful in making West Hills the success it finally became. There was a certain warmth about Wilfred that the kids picked up. He used to teach them boxing and about horses. The children loved him and would run to him when they saw him coming.

The counselors adored Wilfred, too. He spent much of his time at the corral, helping a riding instructor, and they fell in love. She divorced her husband and married Wilfred, who got a job working in a meat factory in the city. They rented an apartment and had a baby they named Edward, after me. I carried the baby home from the hospital. Meanwhile, Wilfred's fighting career had peaked and ended.

Wilfred had 18 heavyweight fights, with only three losses. One victory was over Howard Davis, the father of future Olympic champion Howard Davis, Jr. At a crucial point we had the chance to get Wilfred up in the ratings by fighting an up-and-coming contender. Going into that match, Wilfred had a slight cut over one eye that we didn't tell anybody about. The cut opened up in the fourth or fifth round, however, and was bleeding so badly the referee had to stop the fight. Looking back, Wilfred should never have gone into that fight, and it was my mistake. I told him he could fight – he did anything I told him to do, but this time I was wrong. He fought once again and lost, then told me he had trouble seeing out of one eye. I took him to the doctor, who diagnosed a detached retina. That ended Wilfred's prize-fighting. In those days a detached retina meant that a boxer was finished. Of course he was very disappointed, and so was I. He eventually lost that eye.

Wilfred and his wife lived together for about five years, and I saw them from time to time. Then things went wrong, and they got divorced. Wilfred moved back into East Harlem. I didn't know it, but he began selling drugs to support himself and was feared all over Harlem as "Cowboy Al" – he wore cowboy boots. Then somebody didn't pay him. Wilfred put five bullets into the guy and took the next plane to Puerto Rico. Down there, he again sold drugs until six or seven narcotics agents broke down his hotel room door and pounced on him before he could get the gun hidden under his pillow.

Wilfred was back in jail, doing 9–15 years.

&

I CONTINUED TEACHING, BUT WAS TOO BUSY to take the exam for principal, which would have been the natural direction for my career. Anyway, I was earning much more with the camps than I ever could have earned even at the highest principal's salary – more than $100,000 in those days. And running West Hills was more challenging than being a principal. For one thing, we were constantly adding new features, such as swimming pools, handball courts, stables, tennis courts, pavilions – we improved the facilities for 20 years before I could say we were finished. At camp there were as many children as at school, and we had hundreds of staffers, all needing direction.

I could have retired from teaching at any time, but I continued at Jefferson Park until things began to change for the worse around 1965.

For years I'd left school at three or four or sometimes five o'clock in the afternoon, then went to work at the day camp or to referee wrestling. I usually came back the next day completely refreshed and ready for anything. If you like what you're doing, it doesn't tire you, and that's the way it had been for most of my career at school. By 1965, teaching and school and my enthusiasm weren't what they used to be.

At Jefferson Park we didn't have the close-knit group of teachers that we had at Galvani, and the cooperation I'd once known was long gone now that we had so many more teachers. Making things more problematic was that fact that instead of having a full-time, trained staff, we began to get inexperienced substitutes who worked every day but who couldn't handle the students. I resented that. Too many teachers at Jefferson Park weren't doing their jobs, which made things much more difficult for me and also for the responsible teachers who took their duties seriously. Things were getting very rough in school.

There were lots of problem children running around, and I was being called to chase them up and down all day long. I wasn't seated at my desk even for a minute during the school day. It was, "Mr. Gersh, on the third floor," "Mr. Gersh on the second floor," "Mr. Gersh in the auditorium," "in the lunchroom." There were just too many places to be, and I couldn't handle all the disciplinary problems. Well, at last I had to confront Israel Flax about it.

I said, "We have to do something about the school."

"What are you suggesting, Eddie?"

"Either we have to stop taking the bad children, or we have to get rid of some of our bad teachers – we can't have both."

Dancing directors, l-r, Gersh, Polanski, and Schnittman take part in the shenanigans of a masquerade day at West Hills.

After a moment, he said, "Well, I can't do it Eddie."

"Mr. Flax, you have to, we just can't exist this way."

"I can't do it," he said.

So I had to tell him: "If you can't do it, then I really can't do it either – I can't do all this, and I know I'm going to have to leave."

"Well, do what you have to do, Eddie."

At the end of that semester, I took a year's sabbatical, and they appointed another dean. I did not go back to Jefferson Park. Instead, I took a position teaching at the New York Institute of Technology. After 17 years, my public school teaching career was over. I never rejoined Mr. Flax, whom I admired so much. Two years after I left, his school got so bad and the parents complained so much about it that the board of education removed Mr. Flax as principal and transferred him. Hearing that, I never forgave myself for leaving him, but at the same time I knew he wasn't doing the right thing by taking in those bad children, and not getting rid of the poor teachers.

ॐ

MY CAREER WITH DAY CAMPS AND OUR COMPANY, Crestwood Country Day School, was steadily growing into a full-time job. Yet, even though it required so much from the three of us who were partners, it was extremely satisfying to see it develop, and we thoroughly enjoyed close participation in everything from joining in activities to handling administrative tasks. As my teaching career came to an end, my entrepreneurial ambitions began to lead to expanding our day-camping and day-school efforts and even to founding a new college, building it from the ground up.

In the late 1960s, this 40-room Woodbury, Long Island, mansion became Crestwood Country Day School's newest venture, the Woodland School and Day Camp; the mansion was built in 1917 in the style of a French country house.

Chapter 15

MILLIONAIRE AND MANAGER

A SLEEK, BLACK LIMOUSINE PULLS into the driveway of West Hills Day Camp in Huntington, Long Island, where late October leaves lie brown and windswept on the lawns. A Halloween "haunted house" with straw bales, pumpkins, and costumed mannequins has been set up in a building near the large former mansion that serves as the camp's main office. West Hills sprawls over 20 of some of the most valuable acres on Long Island. For generations, Huntington has been one of the wealthiest communities in New York's metropolitan area.

West Hills is quiet today. There are no campers at this time of year, and the Halloween celebration was a few days ago. Some groundskeeping staff are working at raking leaves, dismantling the haunted house, and maintaining walkways and athletic facilities. The camp's five swimming pools are empty, their water slides in winter storage. The limousine passes few people as it glides along the driveway and approaches the office building, which is painted red with white trim. The car stops at the entrance, and the driver gets out to open the door for Holli and Ed Gersh, married since 1987, and a writer who is their guest on this visit to West Hills. The Gershes and guest have driven in from Manhattan. It is 2001, a few weeks after the terrorist attack on the World Trade Center in Lower Manhattan. There is a certain gloominess, and it is not just from the chilly gray clouds of a raw autumn morning.

The gloom is felt by everyone in these sad days. Still, the Gershes are cheerfully welcomed as they enter their day camp's main building. The office staff is composed of employees with longstanding experience at West Hills. For example, camp director Mike Moore, who has a masters in English and Education from Adelphi University, has been employed at West Hills since 1972. Gersh comes to camp regularly to keep his hand in the operation, work at his desk, and address the latest tasks, large and small. On this day, however, Holli takes over his president's chair in order to cradle the newborn baby of Gersh's youngest daughter, Roxanne, who is also visiting camp. In the course of the morning all the Gersh offspring arrive to see their father and Holli: daughters Laurie and Esther (formerly Ellyne, but this is her chosen Hasidic name), and son Kevin, who looks just like his father when he was young. Here, too, is Wilfred Avellez, well-muscled and jovial, in his mid-60s, a well-spoken, gentle man with little outer trace of his rough-and-tumble youth.

The Gersh family members joke and chat in lively conversation in the president's office – an unpretentious space with plain furniture set along the walls, and oriented toward the desk, which is at the far end. The Gersh family members obviously enjoy having a few hours together at West Hills, where they all spent their younger years, working hard and helping to build the camp. Each has many personal memories of this place, and each has left a share of sweat and blood and tears in the West Hills earth. West Hills is Ed Gersh's most enduring life's work, the result of half a century of toil. From very the start, his family was an intimate part of it.

After handling some business with Moore and the administrative staff, Gersh takes his guest for a stroll around the camp.

"Swimming is one of our leading programs," Gersh says, gesturing to the complex of pools that, in the warmth of a Long Island summer, swarm with hundreds of excited youngsters. "Each pool is heated, and all of them are designed for specific age levels and skill levels of the campers.

As he walks along pathways that wind between wooden pavilions, tennis courts, and playgrounds, Gersh explains how West Hills grew from a simple beginning, with a swimming pool and a couple of new-made ball fields until now, when it offers everything a young Long Island day-camper could desire. Children can fish and boat at the West Hills pond, and in the pavilions and classrooms they can learn arts and crafts such as ceramics, jewelry-making, woodworking, and sand art. Other nonsport activities include learning computer skills, music, dance, and dramatics.

"We never were content with what we achieved the previous summer," Gersh says, "but we kept improving each year, kept on building new facilities, and at first my partners and I did a lot of the physical work ourselves."

Sports at West Hills include a dozen team activities, such as softball, soccer, handball, volleyball, street hockey, and basketball. The individual sports include tennis, wall-climbing, martial arts, gymnastics, and miniature golf.

"We place a lot of emphasis on athletics here," Gersh says. "but it's not about winning for its own sake."

The West Hills brochure sums up much of what Gersh believes is the deeper value of sports: "In our view, athletic competition is a means to an end, not an end in itself." Gersh continues: "Our main goal with athletics is to help each child achieve his or her optimum performance-level through teamwork, physical development, and improving coordination."

Echoing his own athletic code, acquired by experience in college football, in a boxing career, and by managing boxers, Gersh states a key West Hills precept: "What we try to achieve in athletics requires a lot of patience on the part of both the counselor and the child. And in the end, it's well worth it."

Lots of special events fill the West Hills summer calendar, such as talent shows, treasure hunts, a carnival, a masquerade, line dancing, pirate day, and folk music performances. In rainy weather, there's plenty to do in the covered areas and buildings – movies are shown and computers are available, campers work on arts and crafts or give performances in theater and music, and some write, direct, and produce their own videos on the spot.

There are also day trips to the seashore or to a Yankees or Mets game, or to popular tourist sites or amusement parks. Older campers make overnight trips to cities like Boston and Montreal, as well as to dude ranches and resorts, Disneyland, and Washington, D.C.

Heading back to the main building, Gersh indicates the haunted house.

"Every fall, West Hills puts on an open house for Halloween, and thousands of children from miles around come all dressed up to go through our Haunted House; it's a real treat for the whole community, and something the children here look forward to each autumn."

"After all these years," Gersh smiles. "I still look forward to it myself."

ॐ

WEST HILLS DAY CAMP CONTINUED TO BE THE FOCUS of my business life, although I stayed in education a while longer. Beginning in 1968, I worked two years at the New York Institute of Technology on Long Island, teaching history and serving as an assistant dean. The Institute's dean, Donald Ross, had the ambition to start his own college, and asked me if I'd be a partner with him. Like Ross, I had a strong ambition to start a college, and decided this would a challenging and interesting venture.

Ross had a couple of hundred acres in upstate New York near Lake George, where he wanted to start the college. I was opposed to that location, however, because up there you have nothing but woods around you, not enough population to acquire students. My thinking was that the college should be in a metropolis, where you can draw from a large population. We agreed to look in New Jersey, New York, Pennsylvania, and Maryland – that densely populated corridor between New York City and Washington, D.C. We finally found an old tourist house with a neighboring gas station in Wilmington, Delaware. We bought both properties and turned the tourist house into a college building and the gas station into our library. This was the start of Wilmington College, and I felt very good about being part of it.

Ross was president, and I was executive vice president. Ross was there seven days a week, and I would come down for Tuesday, Wednesday, and Thursday, and then go back up to New York, since I still had West Hills to run. Ross and I were trustees, and we each selected two additional members for the Board of Trustees. He selected his wife and an uncle to be on the board. I selected my wife, Rosemarie, and a longtime friend. My friend had to decline, however, so for the time being Ross had two members on the board to my one.

Wilmington was geared for a class of student that few if any colleges accepted at the time. It was very difficult for students with low high school grades to get into college, but we opened our doors to any graduate who wanted to attend. There were many thousands of young people who wanted a higher education. This was during the Vietnam War, and every college was filled to capacity because so many men wanted the student draft-deferment. Wilmington accepted students who had not done well in high school and gave them the opportunity to have a college career. This was a time before the community college movement which has since proven so valuable in providing further education to all high school graduates. From the start, Wilmington College was immensely successful as far as enrollment was concerned. I was pleased that Wilmington gave so many fine young people an opportunity to realize their potential.

Another educational institution appeared in my life around this same time. With my partners Norman Schnittman and Dave Polanski, I became co-founder of a Long Island private academy that we named the Woodland School and Day Camp.

ॐ

IN 1968, OUR COMPANY – Crestwood Country Day School – was a major force in the day-camp programs of Long Island, and we were looking to expand. When a real estate broker told us about a magnificent estate available in Woodbury, near Oyster Bay, it seemed a perfect place for a day camp and private school. We bought the estate, with its 1917 chateau-style mansion and 38 acres, for about $550,000, and started the Woodland School, for grades from early childhood through junior high school. We also established a day camp there. Woodland was a division of Crestwood Country Day School.

We were so confident in our future that we even established our own bus operation for transporting campers and school children. We'd been renting dozens of school buses at great expense each camping season, so we thought having buses of our own was a smart idea. Our company, Mid-Island Transit, was the largest bus transportation system on Long Island. That endeavor lasted only a few years, however, and we sold it. Camping was our expertise, not running a bus business. We had to concentrate on what we did best – day camps and education.

The Woodland School and Day Camp had about 150 students in small classes in a non-graded instructional setting. Along with basic elementary through junior high school courses, we offered specialized tutoring in the creative arts, languages, and horseback-riding. Woodland had that great mansion and beautiful grounds

– wonderful surroundings, with bridle paths, a formal garden, and an arboretum. Our promotional literature described Woodland as a school that offered "an atmosphere where children want to learn."

So, Norman and Dave were at Crestwood, Rosemarie ran West Hills, and I operated Woodland School and Day Camp. As it turned out, making Woodland profitable as a school was a slow and difficult process. We were learning fast, however, and one of the things we realized was that when children get into the fourth grade, they like to go to sleepaway camp. We had hundreds and hundreds of children in our three camps, but they were leaving when they were in fourth grade to go to sleepaway camps. Starting a sleepaway camp was the next move in our expansion, and we bought Camp Kent in Kent, Connecticut.

Dave took over Camp Kent, which became a very successful operation. We had three day camps feeding Camp Kent with children old enough to sleep away. By now, Crestwood Country Day School was one of the largest private camping companies in the country, with as many as 6,000 children in our four facilities.

As it turned out, Donald Ross of Wilmington College felt I should have made him a partner in the Woodland School. That was absolutely impossible, however. For one thing, Woodland was not a college, and for another, I was already committed to my original partners. As a result, Donald voted me off the Wilmington College board and out of the administration. He could do so because he had three trustee votes to my two, since I hadn't yet come up with another trustee.

I wasn't too upset, though, because I'd satisfied my desire to start a college. Wilmington went on to prosper and to educate thousands of students, and I consider that one of the crowning achievements of my life. I later was involved in higher education, serving 10 years as a trustee at Dowling College on Long Island. I also had Woodland to operate, and I continued to be involved in the Crestwood Country Day Camp organization.

Around this time, I met with a young man from a nearby town on Long Island who wanted a job as a camp counselor. He was only 16, though, not old enough. I told him he needed at least one year of college to be on our staff. He was Howard Davis, Jr., the son of the boxer Howard Davis, whom Wilfred Avellez had defeated some years earlier. I told the young man to come and see me if there were any other way I could help him. I didn't imagine then that he'd come back into my life a decade later as a world-class boxer.

৯

Through the mid-Seventies, life was going along well for Rosemarie and me, with our growing children, Kevin and Roxanne. Rosemarie and I worked hard, and in the evenings we usually polished off too much liquor. Neither of us admitted that we were in danger of alcoholism. We were enjoying ourselves too much.

The camps were doing very well, but as early as 1972 we had to admit that Woodland was a losing proposition. Another complication was the estate's skyrocketing potential value if it were on the market for multi-family development. Within three years of buying the Woodland property, a developer made us an offer for it – an offer in the millions. He wanted to build condominiums on the property, but the Huntington town board would have to change the zoning to permit multi-family dwellings. At first, we were unsuccessful in our request for that change, even though I was a staunch supporter of the Republican Party and had good connections among county and state officials. We faced fierce local opposition to rezoning Woodland for condominiums.

It took a few more years before my pull in high places made us successful. My influence and political connections won the day at the same time as Huntington was redoing its master plan, and town officials recommended that the land be used for multi-family dwellings. The property was rezoned, and we closed Woodland

School to put it on the market. After about three more years, we sold it to a developer. This was a very happy moment in my life, because I'd now achieved my ambition of becoming a millionaire by the time I was in my early fifties. Around this time, Norman, Dave, and I dissolved our business partnership and went on with our own careers. I kept West Hills, while Norman had Crestwood and Dave had Camp Kent. It was an amicable parting, and we all remained good friends. Norman was my best friend, and we socialized, playing golf regularly.

I didn't have to work hard anymore, but I did so anyway because West Hills remained a major part of my life. Further, I had to find a good investment for my share of the return on the sale of Woodland.

I was told about University Gardens, a large apartment complex for sale in Port Jefferson, Long Island. There were 376 garden apartments, available for approximately $5 million. I had no experience operating apartment complexes, but the fellow who introduced me to the project claimed to know how. He was supposed to be my partner and put up half the money, but things didn't go well right from the start. When we were preparing for the closing, he told me he had no money to contribute. Then he recommended that he run the complex and receive a salary. I agreed.

At first, it was a grim proposition. I hadn't known when I bought it, but University Gardens was just a terrible place, with the dregs of society living there – prostitutes and drug addicts everywhere. Graffiti was on the fences and buildings, and people would urinate in the entry halls. My manager ran the place for about two weeks until one Sunday there was a major flood as a septic system overflowed. Water and sewerage poured over the grounds, but my manager was nowhere to be found. After that, I told him I'd manage it myself and released him from his contract – for which he sued me, but he didn't win the case.

Fortunately, this was in the fall of the year, when West Hills was not active, so I devoted myself completely to University

Gardens for the next six months. I took over day-to-day management and learned very quickly how to operate an apartment complex. I was there every day, morning until night. I got rid of the bad tenants, one by one, and cleaned the place up. It could be dangerous with such tenants – let's call them undesirable neighbors. I had to carry a gun, although fortunately I never took it out. I did have to put a tenant or two physically on the ground, however. In one case, I stopped a young man from painting graffiti on a wall, wrestling him down to do it. When I was kneeling on his chest and telling him never to vandalize the complex again, he yelled that he'd get his father after me.

I said, "Good, and I'll do the same to him!"

The father never confronted me, however, and that was the end of the graffiti scrawling.

Such was the life of a newmade millionaire with a major investment in dilapidated garden apartments. I worked harder than ever, but finally turned University Gardens around and made it successful. I got the kind of tenants who not only paid their rent, but they were good, respectable neighbors. Many of them studied or were on the staff at nearby Stonybrook, a major campus of the State University of New York. Gradually, I renovated all the apartments and began to sell them as cooperatives, for $70-95,000 each. I eventually sold all but 59 apartments.

There were a number of other business ventures in this time, not all of them successful like University Gardens. Several lost quite a lot of money. In one case, I lost more than $200,000 to a swindler – a subject I don't like to recall. Then I lost a million dollars in the imported Italian clothing business, which I went into with a young fellow I wanted to help get started. After two years of steadily losing money, we finally gave it up. And there were some real estate ventures that didn't work out that taken together cost me another two million dollars. All the while, I kept an interest in boxing, but I'd stopped refereeing wrestling by now. As for my family life, it was increasingly unhappy.

ደ

ROSEMARIE AND I CONTINUED TO DRINK TOO MUCH, until one day I went for a doctor's physical and was told I was at risk of serious illness if I continued on the path I was following. I'd been healthy all my life, so to hear a doctor say I was at risk was a real shock.

When I discussed the situation with Rosemarie, she wasn't interested in trying to stop her alcohol consumption. I was determined to stop, however, and I did so – on the spot. I've never had a drink since. Because Rosemarie continued drinking, our relationship began falling apart. It's a very difficult thing to live with someone who drinks heavily when you do not drink at all. The one who is sober has an almost impossible task. It became impossible for me to go on together with Rosemarie.

At last, after much strife, Rosemarie and I separated, and I moved out. Rosemarie continued managing West Hills, but sadly her alcoholism worsened. It was a heartbreaking situation for me, and of course for Rosemarie and our two children. Things at home became so bad with Rosemarie that both Kevin and Roxanne eventually came to live with me. I tried to do the right thing as a single father, and my older daughters, Laurie and Ellyne, were a wonderful help with the younger children. Laurie was married by then.

In 1979 Rosemarie resigned as director of West Hills, having spent 10 years in charge there. In 1982, after a short illness, she passed away in Huntington Hospital. Rosemarie was just 49 years of age.

ደ

WHILE RAISING KEVIN AND ROXANNE and managing my businesses, I had a very active social and civic life. I was a board member of community organizations, including the Huntington Chamber of Commerce, and I was a member of educator associations and

of the New York State Athletic Association. I was also involved with local organizations that benefited youngsters.

I had a number of romances, some just passing flirtations, others more serious relationships, and I kept a separate apartment for that aspect of my life. I had real estate interests in the Caribbean and went there from time to time. On a trip to Puerto Rico in 1981, I again met Wilfred Avellez. Wilfred had been released from prison after doing seven years of his original 15-year sentence. It was good to see he was trying to make something of himself, and we still had that powerful bond. He still called me "Pappa."

Wilfred enthusiastically told me he was managing fighters and took me to a gym where he had a young pro and an amateur in

West Hills grew from one swimming pool to five pools—the heart of the Huntington, Long Island, day camp's summertime programs and activities.

training. When he asked me to manage them, I felt that familiar urge well up inside, that lifelong love of boxing.

"Okay, Wilfred," I said, "I'm interested in managing fighters, so let's bring them to New York."

Wilfred came back to Long Island and moved into one of my University Place apartments. I got him a job with the Huntington public works department, and we started training these two fighters. I paid for their apartment, got them cars, bought them clothing, set up a gym out on the South Shore of Long Island for their training, and prepared for their first fights. Wilfred soon became part of our family again. He had always been especially good with Kevin and taught him to take care of himself – with his fists if need be. While working at West Hills years earlier, Wilfred had shown Kevin by example how to work hard, and my son admired him. As a teenager, Kevin once went with Wilfred to a neighborhood club in Harlem, where everyone else was black.

"Wilfred introduced me as Mr. Gersh's son," Kevin recalled years later. "Immediately, I was warmly welcomed as part of them, and they began telling me stories about how Mr. Gersh beat them up when they caused trouble.

"After a while, Wilfred surprised me by telling me to go out to the car and get his phonebook for him. Well, it was dark out on the street, but I couldn't tell Wilfred I was too afraid to go out there, a lone white guy at night in Harlem.

"So, I did it and came back in with the phone book. I later found out that Wilfred had sent someone to watch out for me, so I hadn't been in any danger.

"He wanted me to show his friends at the club that Mr. Gersh's son had balls and wouldn't question anything Wilfred said."

છે.

As I began to work with Wilfred's fighters from Puerto Rico, I thoroughly enjoyed being in the gym again – teaching young men, boxing with them, feeling the whack of the gloves, sparring until my shoulders and arms and legs were exhausted, and sensing again that hungry ambition to win in the ring.

As my friend from NYU days, the writer Dave Metzger, once put it: "Dormant for years, the boxing blood of Gersh began once more to race through his veins."

That was no overstatement.

Unfortunately, my excitement about the Puerto Rican fighters was premature. We got them both on a card, but on the day of the fight the pro was seven pounds over the weight limit and wasn't allowed to fight. The amateur did fight, but was knocked out.

They were no good as fighters, so I immediately gave them their tickets home.

Yet this experience whetted my appetite to get back into the fight game, the sport that meant so much to me. By coincidence, that December of 1981 the same young man who'd asked for a job in 1972 came to see me again. Since then, Howard Davis, Jr., had become world-famous as the most valuable American boxer in the 1976 Olympics, winning the lightweight gold medal while not losing a single round in five fights. Davis had also won the admiration and the hearts of sports fans around the world by dedicating his championship to his mother, who'd passed away a few days before the Olympic tournament. By winning that medal, Davis had outshone the other great boxers from this U.S. Olympic team: "Sugar" Ray Charles Leonard, Leo Randolph, and Michael and Leon Spinks. In the following five years, however, Davis was the only top fighter from that team who'd not succeeded in a professional career.

Howard and his father, who was advising him, told me he needed a manager.

*Manager and fighter: Ed Gersh and former Olympics star
Howard Davis, Jr., prepare for a workout as Davis continues
with his dramatic comeback in the early 1980s.*

Chapter 16

BOXING: 35 YEARS LATER

A FTER THE 1976 OLYMPICS, DAVIS had started out hot, and soon was receiving $100,000 a fight. Trained by his father, he'd won all nine fights through 1978, but his performances had steadily declined. At the same time Sugar Ray Leonard's career had exploded to 17-0, and fighting as a welterweight he achieved international glory. Meanwhile, Davis was seldom fighting. He won a few more bouts, but was knocked down in two of them and seemed to be losing his determination, his will to win. He was also losing his money – supporting family and friends and making bad financial decisions. Steadily deteriorating personal situations and professional problems had weakened his fighting spirit by the time he came to me.

Howard later told a sports writer: "I had no idea what I was doing, no idea how to spend that much – it seemed like I was paying taxes every five minutes."

He said financial and professional stresses were bringing him to the brink of a nervous breakdown. In June 1980, he got the chance to fight Scotland's Jim Watt, holder of the World Boxing

Council lightweight title, but lost a 15-round decision. Critics said Davis just "went through the motions" in that fight. He, himself, admitted that he was mentally unprepared, as he told *K.O. Magazine*.

> I came into that fight so depressed . . . disgusted with the way things were going. Mentally, forget it. I was not there. And I didn't want to do it. I didn't want to win. I came in there defeated.

Such was Howard's state of mind when he began to discuss his future with me. He was living in Glen Cove, Long Island, and was bound by contract to the management team of Dennis Rappaport and Michael R. Jones, who also managed Gerry Cooney, another Long Islander and a leading heavyweight contender at the time. Howard said they were ignoring him in favor of Cooney and weren't getting him any more fights. He hadn't fought for more than a year, and his once-stellar career was going nowhere. A fighter at that stage of his career should fight a minimum of four to six times a year. I didn't know it then, but Howard's father had been vetoing the decisions of the management team, Rappaport and Jones, and this had caused the fighter's relationship with them to turn sour.

Howard didn't tell me that his father, Howard, Sr., was actually his closest advisor, not Rappaport and Jones.

Howard and I met several times, and he and his father asked me to take over managing him. I knew Howard had the potential to be one fantastic fighter. With his remarkably quick hands and feet, he'd been called "a lighting bolt in boxing gloves." Winning 125 of 130 amateur bouts – absolutely trouncing the best of the best – Howard was reputed to have been one of the finest amateur boxers of all time. He'd been sensational in his first pro fights, but mediocre in the rest. I calculated that with proper training and the right scheduling of opponents, Howard could become the world lightweight champion. This seemed the perfect opportunity for me to return to professional boxing in a serious way. Indeed, the idea of managing an athlete the likes of Howard Davis, Jr., made the boxing blood race through my veins.

زâ

I'D CLOSELY FOLLOWED PROFESSIONAL BOXING during the 35 years since I'd last fought. I'd studied the fighters and knew their records and their life stories. I'd been saddened by the death of heavyweight champion Rocky Marciano in a 1969 plane crash just before his 46th birthday. I'd watched Muhammad Ali rise to international fame in the 1960s and 1970s amid so much controversy. Then, in April 1981, when Joe Louis died at his home in Las Vegas, at the age of 66, I considered it the end of professional boxing's greatest era.

Things would never be the same in the sport that meant so much to me.

By now, Stillman's Gym had closed and been torn down for an apartment building after Lou Stillman retired in 1959. At Stillman's peak in the Forties, there had been guys lined up from 10 in the morning to eight at night to use the gym's three rings. Once there were 400 serious fighters in training there. Gleason's Gym was still operating successfully after Bobby Gleason had moved to Eighth Avenue and 30th Street in Manhattan in 1974. That address was close to Madison Square Garden, still the Mecca of American boxing – of world boxing, since most of the great pro fighters were Americans. Among the top heavyweights who'd trained at Gleason's over the last decades were Ali, Joe Frazier, Riddick Bowe, Larry Holmes, Vito Antuofermo, and Jerry Cooney – they would soon be joined by Mike Tyson.

By 1981, Gleason's had been sold, and Bobby had retired, but the gym kept operating. It was home for a new crop of talented fighters, such as Thomas Hearns, Leon Spinks, Julio Caesar

Chavez, Hector Camacho, Livingston Bramble, Roberto Duran, and Eddie Mustafa Muhammad. Hollywood script writers and actors liked to hang around the gym, getting close to the up-and-coming stars and collecting material for movies. Boxing still had the drama and power to appeal to a wide audience, and the 1970s had featured entertaining champions, such as Ali, Frazier, George Foreman, Ken Norton, and Larry Holmes.

The big fights were held in massive, packed arenas with a world-wide television audience, but such prosperity had faded from the lower tiers of the sport. The smaller neighborhood gyms and the mid-level boxing venues I once had known so well were going out of business. Places like Woodridge Grove and Jamaica Arena – the smoky dens that had nurtured young fighters – were closing down or had stopped putting on boxing shows. As neighborhoods changed and fight fans moved away, aged, or died, boxing audiences just weren't there for local arenas. Although the fight game had a vast following on television, with millions of dollars in purses, the small venues for serious young boxers to fight in were disappearing.

Another major change in this period was the coming of Hispanic fighters. Where the top boxers of the century once had been mainly Jews and Irish, then blacks and Italians, now Hispanics were coming to the fore – especially in the lighter-weight classes. While the rising stars of the welterweight and middleweight divisions included African-Americans such as Leonard, Hearns, and Marvin Hagler, the best lightweight in history was arguably Roberto Duran of Panama. Over his long career, Duran would hold the world titles to four different weight classes: lightweight (1972-79), welterweight (1980), junior middleweight (1983), and middleweight (1989-90).

In 1982, as I began to work with Howard Davis, Jr., I knew he needed first-rate promotion to realize his potential to be the future lightweight champion of the world. Perhaps one day he would meet Roberto Duran. To do that, Howard would have to perform extremely well – so well that the television networks, the major venues in Las Vegas and Atlantic City, and powerful boxing promoters like Bob Arum, Don King, and Lou Duva would have to offer him bouts against the fighters they controlled. We faced an uphill battle to get top-rated fighters in the ring with Howard, because we were not part of that in-crowd, that tight-knit fraternity of promoters and television broadcasters that was profiting so immensely from boxing while picking and choosing who fought in the spotlight and who remained in obscurity.

The world of boxing I had known had changed in many ways, and not always for the better. For one thing, an alphabet soup of professional boxing organizations had formed, and new ones were forming – all claiming to represent the legitimate, recognized champions. There was the World Boxing Association (WBA) which "sanctioned" fights in most of the United States; another was the North American Boxing Federation (NABF), which was affiliated with the World Boxing Council (WBC). The former National Boxing Association (NBA) would become the International Boxing Federation (IBF) in 1983, and the World Boxing Organization (WBO) was yet to come along. There were also a dozen more organizations aspiring to be legitimate sanctioning bodies.

To further complicate matters, these sanctioning organizations were establishing new weight classes, each with its own champion – making it impossible for boxing fans to follow who was fighting whom, for which sanctioning body, and who were genuine world champions or contenders at any given time. Nine new professional weight classes were established between the 1960s and early 1980s, including several "junior" divisions – Junior Welterweight, Junior Middleweight, and so on. Junior divisions were for fighters who were not heavy enough for the next weight class up but were at their best fighting at a weight higher than the next class down. For example, Junior Welterweight was between Lightweight and Welterweight.

As longtime boxing columnist Bert Sugar put it in a *USA Today* column:

> We once had eight divisions and eight world champions, with every kid worth his sports page able to name each and every. Today, we have as many as 17 weight divisions . . . and who knows how many champions?

Bert also objected to the appearance of new sanctioning groups, which he said too often cared more about making money for themselves than promoting the best interests of boxing or fighters.

When I stepped back into the boxing world in 1982, I was fully aware that a fighter's success required his manager to navigate the right course. There were more opportunities with so many weight classes and "sanctioned" championships to go after, but Bert was right when he said that, "with rare exceptions" too many sanctioning organizations were turning boxing "into a poor imitation of the jewel of a sport it once was." Along with a few powerful promoters tightly controlling who fought whom and where, the fight game was far more complex than it had been in my day. Yet, I knew what I was getting into when I took on Howard and had to restart his career almost from scratch.

❧

By 1982, MUCH OF BOXING'S RENEWED POPULARITY had been stimulated by exciting Olympic matches shown on television every four years. Future stars were showcased in the Olympics before they turned professional. One of the best, of course, was heavyweight Cassius Clay, who changed his name to Muhammad Ali. As a pro, Ali's flashy skills and international stardom appealed to the public in a way that no boxer had since Joe Louis. Ali's fights were worldwide events, and his media appearances were stage-managed performances. When his remarkable career ended in

1981, no other fighters could capture the imagination of the fans the way he did.

As for my personal opinion of Muhammad Ali, I had mixed feelings at best. Although he was immensely popular, I never liked him. He was a great fighter, of course, but I don't consider him a great champion – especially not when I compare him to Joe Louis. Ali and his over-the-top braggadocio changed the complexion of the entire sports world – his "I'm so pretty" and "Float like a butterfly, sting like bee." He brought out everything I dislike about the attitude of so many arrogant professional athletes today.

I witnessed personally one extremely unpleasant Ali incident – an incident that led to my dislike of him as a person. I was attending a sportswriter's dinner in New York to honor the retiring Bobby Gleason, and Joe Louis and Ali were sitting together at the head table. I was at a table nearby and could overhear their conversation. At this time, Joe was in his fifties, and Ali was the reigning heavyweight champion. During their conversation, Ali was very curt and nasty, very disrespectful to Joe. I was dismayed to hear Ali several times rudely tell Joe, "Aw, keep quiet!"

Then Joe accidentally knocked over a glass of water, and Ali sneered for everyone to hear, "What the hell's the matter with you?"

Joe handled it all with great dignity, and didn't say anything. At one point, I walked over and greeted him, saying, "Hi, Joe, how are you? How are you feeling?" He said he was fine. I didn't speak to Ali at all.

From the time I started out with Howard Davis, Jr., I was determined that any fighters I managed would live up to standards I set. This meant showing good manners and grace. Too many young boxers were braggarts and loudmouths, having learned from watching Ali. My fighters would carry themselves with dignity and modesty – let their fists do the talking, be athletes young people could admire. I looked for that attitude in a fighter, and I believed Howard Davis had it. He seemed an earnest, sincere, hardworking young man. I knew that one of the first things Howard needed was financial help so he could clear his mind and be allowed to do what he did best: fight. (He liked to joke it was singing he did best, but that wouldn't do him any good in the ring.)

Howard had blown about $1 million in earnings since starting as a pro in 1977. His record was 15-1, but he'd gone from being paid as much as $200,000 a fight to not being paid a cent for his last fight. That one had been on Long Island, arranged by his father, and the gate had been so poor that Howard came away empty-handed. I started by getting his financial situation in order. I paid his overdue bills – telephone, electric, a mortgage in danger of foreclosure, doctor's bills for his pregnant wife, food bills, and child-support for his first wife. In fact, Howard's second wife mailed their bills directly to my bookkeeper, who paid them. I had my accountants straighten out serious income tax problems that had resulted in Howard's bank account being frozen by the Internal Revenue Service. I even hired a manager for a couple of dilapidated houses he owned and was renting out to undesirables who were running them into the ground, not paying the rent.

I also arranged for sound legal advice that laid the groundwork for giving his contracted managers, Rappaport and Jones, a one-third cut of his earnings while he fought under my management. Over the first three months, I loaned Howard more than $36,000. At the same time, he began to train regularly and get in shape. With the agreement of Rappaport and Jones, I engaged the well-respected Jimmy Glenn to train Howard at the Times Square Gym in Manhattan. In those first few months, Howard and I traveled together in my car from Long Island to the gym, six days a week for training.

We became very close friends, and Howard was like family. It was very rewarding to see his enthusiasm for boxing steadily returning. I was also working with potential promoters and matchmakers to line up suitable fights for him.

ã·

THE FIRST OFFER HOWARD RECEIVED was for a bout in Atlantic City with purse of a mere $3,000, which we turned down. Imagine, Howard Davis, Jr., had once fought for $200,000 a bout, but now was offered so little. As it turned out, I did accept a match with Angel Cruz in Madison Square Garden for only $5,000 – but I liked the Garden as a venue to showcase Howard's newfound spirit. He won a 10-round decision and was on his way to a new career. Now, Bob Arum of Top Rank was promoting Howard's fights.

Howard fought five more times that year – four times in Atlantic City and once in Miami – and won them all. Three were 10-round decisions, and two were technical knockouts (his opponent could not continue to fight). That sixth victory of 1982 was a decision over former World Boxing Association lightweight champion Claude Noel, for a purse of $22,000. (I didn't take a penny from any of these fights.) The quality of our opponents, and the size of the purses were rapidly improving. Howard had risen from the depths of despair to being happier than ever before in his pro career.

"I want to win the championship, pay Ed back," he told a sports writer then. "I'm so thankful he's here."

ã·

THE INNER MACHINERY OF THE BOXING WORLD can be secretive and hard to fathom, often working in inscrutable ways that even managers can't discern. In the 1980s – as in most of the previous six decades of the century – there was a boxing network of unseen connections and operatives who could make things happen for a fighter – or not happen, as these operatives so chose, according to how it affected their own interests.

Early in my work with Howard, I wanted him to be matched against a specific fighter whom I believed would be just right for Howard's development. Beating this fighter would give Howard the chance to rise in the ratings. It turned out, however, that our promoter, Bob Arum, was unable to make the match. For some reason, hard as we tried, we couldn't get the television executives and this fighter's handlers to agree to the bout. It was understandable that this fighter might not want to risk going up against Howard, who was proving himself to be a tough opponent for anyone in his weight class. Yet, it would be a good fight, and if the television executives wanted to make the match, the other fighter would have had to accept.

I casually mentioned my problem to a friend and sometime business acquaintance, Tony Castellano, who surprised me by saying he'd look into it. A few days later, I was even more surprised when Castellano called to say the fight had been arranged. I was amazed and delighted. When I asked how he'd done it, Castellano was vague and would not reveal his influential connections. Years later, I learned Tony was a close family relation to Paul Castellano, a reputed leading New York mobster. I came to the obvious conclusion about who Tony's powerful connections likely had been – individuals who could, in a matter of hours, influence the boxing world, from the fighters at the bottom to the executives at the very top. However that fight came to be, I was glad for the opportunity it gave Howard, who won and kept on with his revitalized career.

Howard's contract with Rappaport and Jones expired in April 1983, and he signed with me. He fought for me three more times that year, winning two decisions – one over British lightweight champion George Feeney in Italy – and shocking the boxing world by stopping fourth-ranked Greg Coverson in the eighth round. Howard won $250,000 in this six-month period. I still took nothing, although I had a claim to a manager's fee of $9,500 for the Feeney fight.

Howard had won his last 11 fights and was a genuine contender, rated sixth by the WBA, but he deserved a higher rank-
ing. Our advancement was blocked by a corrupt combination:
dealmaking by sanctioning organizations in collusion with promoters who controlled leading fighters and had sweetheart contracts with television networks that orchestrated the scheduling
of matches. I was unhappy that Bob Arum's Top Rank seemed
unable to get us a title shot or to bring us highly ranked opponents. By now, Roberto Duran had moved up to the welterweight
division, but the next best opponent was Ray "Boom Boom"
Mancini. I made a handshake agreement with Mancini's manager for a bout in the near future.

❧

In this time, I built a second home in Fort Lauderdale, Florida,
renewing my friendship with Bill Gladstone, who had a place
nearby. I began spending time at Miami's famous Fifth Street
Gym, where so many great fighters had trained over the years.
There, I watched the young boxers and proceeded to select a few
to establish a stable of fighters called the "E. Gersh All-Stars."
This was exactly what I wanted to do with my life at this time.

I'd made my fortune, had enjoyed a fulfilling career in education, had established West Hills, had raised four wonderful children – achieving all the things that once had been my life's goals.
Now, my next goal was to manage a world boxing champion. I
would have unexpected help to achieve it.

While Howard was training for the Claude Noel fight in late
1982, who should walk into the Fifth Street Gym – looking the
same but sounding even worse – but my former trainer, Lolly
Kent. Lolly was as loud and rowdy as ever. We'd lost touch, not
seeing each other in 30 years. In fact, I'd heard somehow that he'd
died. We embraced, and he broke down in tears. Lolly, who was
74, was still driving a cab and sometimes selling insurance. He

Gersh specially designed this cushioned "Gersh-Vest" protection gear to give the fighter the opportunity to throw hard body blows without risking injury to his trainer or manager.

hadn't been active in boxing for more than 20 years, although he regularly haunted the Fifth Street Gym. It didn't take long for us to agree that he would join E. Gersh All-Stars as a trainer. When Lolly had trained me there was no written contract, just a handshake. Now, there was still no contract, just a handshake.

We hired highly regarded Miami trainer Sal Bunetta, whom Lolly once had taught the ropes. Together, and with the E. Gersh All-Stars also taking shape, we were eager to prepare Howard Davis, Jr., to fight for the world lightweight championship sometime this year. Little did we know that Howard had other plans, and those plans didn't include us.

Recently married, Holli and Ed Gersh join three victorious E. Gersh All-Stars after a 1987 boxing show in Atlantic City. The fighters, wearing the team's blue-and-gold jackets, are l-r Steve Frank, Alex Medel, and Freddie Pendleton.

Chapter 17

LIFE'S LESSONS

THE GERSH APARTMENT ON EAST 69TH STREET in Manhattan is in a mid-20th-century building that runs the length of the block. The entire back wall of the lobby is glass and looks out on a tranquil Japanese garden that transcends the bustle of the city beyond. Upon entering the Gersh apartment, which is on the 27th floor, guests are struck by the spectacular view of the city from large picture windows that fill a wall of the 40-ft. living room. The panorama, to the South and East, is unobstructed, since the building's owners control the air-space rights above Hunter College, far below. Mid-town Manhattan, Central Park, and the East River are in the middle distance, with Queens and Long Island as background.

In a remarkable boxing-world coincidence, this apartment formerly belonged to the well-known sportscaster, Howard Cosell, who made his name by closely following the career of heavyweight champion Muhammad Ali. During the 1960s and 1970s, Cosell was the sportscaster for every Ali fight as well as for most other major championship matches. Cosell's needling questions when interviewing Ali sparked some rough-and-ready verbal exchanges that gave the handsome Ali the opportunity to showcase his considerable wit.

Cosell (born Howard William Cohen) once said, "I have been called obnoxious, bombastic, sarcastic, confrontational, and a know-it-all. Of course, I am all of these things."

The International Jewish Sports Hall of Fame wrote that Cosell – also a commentator for professional football – "was arguably the most colorful and controversial national sports reporter and broadcast personality in American media."

A mid-1970s popularity poll concurred, finding Cosell was the most despised sportscaster in America while at the same time discovering that he headed the list of the most popular sportscasters. When Ali changed his name from Cassius Clay and converted to Islam, Cosell was one of the first to support him. This earned Cosell considerable criticism that was compounded in 1967 when he objected to the New York State Boxing Commission's stripping of Ali's title for refusing the military draft as a conscientious objector.

The staunchly anti-racist Cosell declared then, "Nobody says a damned word about the professional football players who dodged the draft. But Muhammad was different; he was black and he was boastful."

In his last years, Cosell broadcast directly from his apartment. Then, after several years in retirement – during which he became ill – he died in 1995 at the age of 77. Two years later, in 1997, when Ed and Holli Gersh purchased the apartment from the Cosell estate, they found it fitted with a confusion of wires and cables that had been used by television cameras and equipment – so much that the place seemed full of snakes. The wires and cables were removed as part of a complete renovation of the apartment.

East 69th Street is centrally located for the Gersh lifestyle when they're up North, being a relatively easy drive to the country house in Woodstock or to West Hills Day Camp in Huntington.

❧

EARLY 1984 WAS A GRATIFYING TIME FOR ME.

Not only was the career of Howard Davis, Jr., a rising success – and I loved being in the corner during his fights – but I was enjoying working as a volunteer to promote local youth boxing in Huntington. Although I'd built the house in Fort Lauderdale, much of my time was spent on Long Island. That May, I was honored with a Certificate of Recognition by the Youth Development Association of Huntington Village. I liked being appreciated by my own community.

Not all was going well with Howard's future, however. It was a frustrating disappointment to us when the World Boxing Council gave Roberto Elizondo a title fight against the current lightweight champion, Edwin Rosario. Bob Arum arranged that fight, and I was upset because Howard deserved that shot before anyone else. At least Arum and the WBC should have matched Howard and Elizondo to decide who would challenge for the title. That's typical of boxing politics and intrigues. The other match we'd wanted was against "Boom Boom" Mancini, World Boxing Association lightweight champion. Instead, Arum – who was extremely influential with the WBA – arranged a title fight between Mancini and Peruvian Orlando Romero. That left us out in the cold, so I went with Don King to promote Howard's next fights.

"King owns the title shots," I told *Newsday* in July. "There's no use blowing against the wind."

King and I signed an agreement in which he guaranteed Howard a title fight within eight months. I was considering moving Howard up a weight class to the 140-lb. junior welterweight level. That would position us to fight Aaron Pryor, whom Howard had twice defeated as an amateur. Another possible match was with Bruce Curry, who owned part of the junior welterweight title. Then Howard could come back down to light-weight and be a contender. Solid wins as a junior welterweight would have further enhanced his reputation, and a title fight with Mancini would have been a major boxing event. The possibilities being weighed by Don King and me were reported by *Newsday*, which said Howard might fight Curry, Mancini, and Pryor in the coming months.

Howard agreed with this plan, as was apparent in an interview he gave *K.O. Magazine:*

HD: We're looking for the junior welterweight title first, then I'll come down and fight Boom Boom Mancini, which I think will be attractive, something for the public to look at. It's white and black, and boxer and slugger. I think it would be interesting.

KO: If you could have one fight, would that be the one you'd want?

HD: Definitely.

KO: Does it concern you that since Mancini fights for Arum and you signed with King, that the fight might never come off.

HD: Look, it has to come off, the public would demand it. It's a good attraction, and he's been ducking me for a year and a half. The money's there, the attractiveness is there, it has all the ingredients of a fantastic fight. I think it would be a megabuck fight.

Well, I did have a handshake agreement with Mancini's people and the backing of Don King to bring a Davis-Mancini fight off in the near future. Howard said in the article that he believed we'd taken the right course in joining King. The interviewer asked whether he believed King would give him "a fair shake," meaning the opportunity to be a contender:

HD: Definitely. I know now that I will get a fair shake. . . . I believe he will put me in the place where I should have been a long time ago. I feel very confident with King.

KO: Why do you feel Arum wasn't able to do it for you?

HD: He just didn't do it. The relationship was amicable, but he didn't get me rated, didn't get me a title shot. . . . So we had to take another direction, and it was Don King.

The interviewer also asked Howard what was the "most gratifying" chapter of his career to that point.

HD: I think the most gratifying chapter so far is meeting Ed Gersh. He's been like a father, a confidant. He's been a motivating factor in easing up the road. He makes it easy for me to concentrate on what I do best, box. I've been through a lot of stuff, not only the boxing, but also with tax people. I owed a lot of back taxes to the government. That's been straightened out now. I owned some apartment buildings and they got burnt out and I didn't have the money to fix them up. He came in at the right time and I owe a lot to him. If I win the championship, it would be like paying him back.

I had the same kind sentiments for Howard because we'd become very close over the past 18 months. That spring of 1983, boxing managers, trainers, writers, promoters, and officials were congratulating me on resurrecting Howard's career. They compose a "Who's Who" of the boxing world then: Don Elbaum, Ted Menas, Teddy Brenner, Bruce Trampler, Don King, Bob Arum, Bob Waters, Dick Young, Randy Gordon, Arthur Mercante, Harold Lederman, Leon Washington, Artie Curley, and many others. Our decision to go with Don King was praised by leading boxing analysts, such as Gordon, who described Arum and the CBS television sports executives as "racketeers" who'd "refused to give Davis a . . . title shot."

Gordon also said Howard's career had been "incredibly turned 180-degrees around," and he described Howard's performance against Coverson as "brilliant boxing and combination punching." Of course, I felt very good hearing what the boxing world was saying about us. Then, to my surprise and dismay, matters between Howard and me became suddenly problematic. A couple of Long Island lawyers were courting him behind my back. They promised him things – gave him $50,000, according to the *New York Post* columnist Dick Young – and offered the use of a Rolls Royce. Howard was car-crazy. I'd never have given him a Rolls until he'd earned it. My philosophy is: if you've earned it and can afford it, great, but he was driving a Rolls Royce and hardly had the money to put gas in it. They wanted to manage him, and they finally turned his head.

Long before the article came out in *K.O. Magazine* that November, Howard was singing a different tune compared to what he'd said to the interviewer – how happy he was that I'd taken him on. That summer of 1983, he wrote to me stating he'd signed a fight contract without consulting me, and that I was "fired" as his manager. Of course, it was impossible for Howard to fire me, because that implied that I was working for him. Instead, we had a contractual relationship that could not be terminated by one or the other without sufficient grounds, good cause.

I filed for an injunction in New York State Supreme Court to prevent him fighting without my permission until our contract ran out in October 1984. In his declaration to the court, Howard claimed that his "good cause" for terminating our contract was that he objected to my signing up with Don King – even though *K.O. Magazine* quoted him to the contrary. My request for an injunction was denied, but an out-of-court settlement was agreed upon. I remained nominally Howard's manager until our contract expired, and my legal right to a share of his purses was confirmed. I wasn't in charge of Howard's boxing career, however. His trainer was now Angelo Dundee, who'd been Muhammad

Ali's trainer and had worked with Sugar Ray Leonard. In January 1984, CBS television scheduled Howard to meet leading contender Tyrone Crawley as a stepping stone to fighting for the WBA lightweight title. As it turned out, Howard fell ill just before the bout, which was canceled.

Eventually, his lawyer-managers personally apologized to me for what had happened. At the end of 1984, I even served as an advisor on their boxing card at Nassau Coliseum, with Howard as the headliner. That event was financially disastrous for them, though.

I'd been personally hurt by Howard Davis, Jr. It was one of the most painful lessons of my life. In the long run, however, it was Howard who suffered most. He'd been unbeaten when he was with me. If he'd stayed, he'd have been a world champion. That never did happen,. He fought in June 1984 against WBC lightweight champion Edwin Rosario, who won a 12-round decision. Howard "fired" his lawyer-managers immediately afterwards. He fought a few more years, showed flashes of his true ability at times, but his career went nowhere.

As for me, I soon was busier than ever with my up-and-coming E. Gersh All-Stars.

🙠

I'D ESTABLISHED A REPUTATION AS A MANAGER who knew what he was doing, and the All-Stars were making a mark. By November 1984, my record as a manager of professionals was 55-0. I had a wonderful lightweight in Adolfo Medel, a native of Nicaragua and a U.S. citizen. Adolfo had the talent and a great attitude, eminently trainable, and Larry Kent adored him. Adolfo won 21 straight, with 14 knockouts and was ranked in the top 20 in the world. I wanted him to fight Davis, and plans were under way to have them meet in April 1985. I estimated Adolfo would be ready for a title shot late that year.

Then he was playing sandlot soccer one day and got kicked in the head. It was a severe injury, and sadly I had to retire him. Adolfo became one of our trainers, but it was another great disappointment to me that his career ended so soon. I retired Adolfo in May 1985, at the very same time as I was being honored by the DeWitt Clinton Alumni Association. It was earlier in that same week of the banquet that I received the unhappy news of Adolfo's injury. That was certainly a time of mixed emotions for me. In many ways, Adolfo was a more bitter disappointment than Davis, since Adolfo was so good and so committed. His final record was 22-2-0, with one of his 1984 wins being a unanimous 10-round decision over Freddie Pendleton of Philadelphia. Freddie had not impressed me when first I saw him against Adolfo, but he soon would be an E. Gersh All-Star.

Some of our fighters made a mark, and others faded away. One good fighter we had was Juan Veloz, who in September 1984 won the junior featherweight Continental Boxing Association (CBA) championship in Puerto Rico. Juan was ranked in the WBC top ten. By 1985, I was known for taking fighters whose careers were failing, such as Howard Davis, Jr., and turning them into successes. *New York Times* boxing writer Michael Katz called me "boxing's rescuer of lost souls." He wrote this in a column after I took over Boston middleweight Vinnie Curto. Katz wrote that I was warned that Curto was "fickle with managers," but that I wasn't worried.

"Even if he cons me out of five, six thousand, it's not going to affect my standard of living," I told Katz. "I'm giving another human being a chance."

Well, Curto was fickle and did let me down. When I took him on, he was in line for a shot at the International Boxing Federation super middleweight title, but he'd been inactive so long that he was at risk of losing his status. I paid his manager $30,000 to release him from his contract, and he signed with me. The IBF fight was set for South Korea, where the opponent, Chong Pal-Park, lived. The Korean promoter caused so many problems and delays, however, that I registered a formal protest.

Among other things, they were unfairly trying to weaken Curto by blocking his airline tickets until the last minute and declining to provide prompt hotel accommodations. Vinnie would have been fighting with severe jet lag if I'd followed their process.

While I was negotiating with the IBF and the promoter, Curto ran off to South Korea without my knowledge and took the fight. He lost a 12-round decision to Park. So much for Vinnie Curto and my $30,000 spent to release him from his contract. Yet, losing money by having a fighter let me down wasn't a real problem for me. It made me all the better, all the more experienced, as a manager. I didn't need my fighters to win and earn me money. I cared about their success first and foremost, and I wanted to develop a champion.

In an interview with Associated Press sportswriter Ed Schuyler, Jr., I said, "I'll give somebody a chance – maybe I'll give them two chances, but if I see a pattern of behavior I don't agree with, I don't want anything to do with them. I'm in this for enjoyment, for fun."

As I told sportswriter Nigel Collins of *Ring Magazine*, "I always loved boxing and always wanted to be a champion. I couldn't do it myself, so now I sublimate my yearnings by managing fighters."

In one classic unsavory incident, Juan Veloz was scheduled for a bout in Puerto Rico, but just before the fight he complained there was something wrong with him. I sent him to a doctor who said Juan had a prostate infection.

"Can he fight?" I asked the doctor.

"No," was the answer.

So I got on the phone to the promoter and told him the situation. The promoter stood to lose a lot of money if the fight were canceled. He asked me who else knew about this. I said no one else knew about it yet. Then he offered me $10,000 in cash if I'd allow Juan to fight.

"You can go to hell!" I replied and took Juan back to New York.

I'd never put a fighter at risk like that. As it turned out Juan won a few good fights, but he stopped coming to the gym and I eventually dropped him. More than one fighter of mine was dropped because of lack of dedication or criminal activities on the street. More than one cost me money and didn't give their best effort in return, or broke our contract, and a few got involved with drugs. Managing fighters has been a learning experience, indeed. As sportswriter Dave Metzger, my old friend from NYU, once put it, I've been "thoroughly used and abused" by a number of fighters.

Ed says that they can only screw him once, and he's right, but put all these ingrates together and that's a lot of screwing.

Each case, each fighter, presented a unique set of problems and circumstances. I got cruiserweight Stanley Ross a shot at Boone Pultz's United States Boxing Association crown, and Stanley gave it his best showing ever. He won the title in a gutsy 12-round decision. Unfortunately, Stanley's post-fight urine test indicated marijuana, and the title reverted back to Pultz. The test results were overturned much later, but it was too late for Stanley.

Another fighter got into cocaine and disappeared a few days before a fight. I arranged for him to enter a rehabilitation program, and he kicked the habit. Then, just when we thought he had his act together, he did the same thing again.

One especially promising All-Stars fighter was light heavyweight Robert Folley, son of former champion Zora Folley. I had him signed for a fight in Atlantic City and was paying him $250 a week, but a few days before the date he claimed he'd hurt his hand and couldn't compete. I soon learned Robert had signed to fight in California for another manager. I was shocked and disappointed, but I worked out a deal to let him go and fight for whomever he wanted.

A good development in this time was being reunited with Dave

Metzger, who attended a prefight luncheon for Howard Davis, Jr., in New York. Dave had been working in Albany for a state assemblyman, but his love of boxing brought him back into the fight business, joining E. Gersh All-Stars as our publicist. Dave now handled our press affairs, arranged publicity, and wrote press releases on me and the fighters.

ॐ

OF COURSE, THE BEST DEVELOPMENT OF ALL was meeting Holli Greenberg in 1985. Holli was an interior design specialist advising me on decorating my University Gardens conversions into condos. For several months, she and I had a very good working relationship that developed into a genuine friendship, mutual admiration you could say. That warm relationship irresistibly turned into an affair.

Since we'd both been divorced, we weren't eager to have unnecessary complications, so we agreed to a few basic ground rules: first, we'd date other people; second, we wouldn't allow ourselves to fall in love with each other; and third, since I was never going to get married again, marriage would not be a consideration in our relationship.

From the start, it was right with Holli and me. We enjoyed the same music, went on wonderful trips together, and Holli even took an interest in boxing, coming to fights and accompanying the fighters and me on trips to the matches. I remember she was quite frightened the first time I took her to see a fight.

"I was scared I was going to get blood all over my dress!" she said, but soon found herself fascinated as she came to understand and appreciate the sport. "I'd never imagined how exciting boxing could be, especially when you get to know the fighters as we did and you're enthusiastically rooting for them."

Holli and I became ever closer, then broke all those ground rules, and in 1987 we were married.

Freddie Pendleton receives the USBA lightweight championship belt from association officials after defeating Livingston Bramble in 1988. Manager Gersh and trainer Larry Kent are in the background. (Photo Tom Casino)

Chapter 18

SHAPING A CHAMPION

FOR MUCH OF THE WINTER MONTHS, ED AND HOLLI GERSH live in Boca Raton, Florida, sheltered from the hubbub and traffic of southern Florida in the gated community of St. Andrews Country Club. The community has its own golf course, and there is a handsome clubhouse where resident families often have meals. After selling the house they had built in St. Andrews, the Gershes purchased this home in 2002.

A high-ceilinged contemporary, the Gersh house is airy and light, with a sunken living room and tan marble floors throughout. Holli designed the entryway's large double doors, made of carved cypress wood and overhung with a bronze and crystal chandelier. She and her husband are comfortable here, enjoying their privacy and friends, often spending quiet time together on the shady patio beside the pool.

On a balmy December morning, Gersh, in shorts and sneakers, is just back from his daily bicycle ride. He sits on a couch next to Holli on the patio near the swimming pool. A brunette, tall and pretty, wearing casual slacks and blouse, Holli would be the perfect model for the elegant ladies of Boca and Manhattan – admired for her good looks and good taste. She has a ready laugh and a lively sense of humor, and anyone seeing Holli and Ed Gersh together can understand that they were good friends long before they were lovers. Their relationship has, in large part, been defined by their years in boxing together, and the stories they can tell about their experiences go beyond the boxing ring. Their involvement as managers and promoters often put them in contact with shady characters. At the Diplomat Hotel in nearby Hollywood, Florida, they met the worst character of all, now named "Joey the Swindler."

"The Diplomat was often a venue for boxing shows," Holli tells a guest seated across from them. "Promoters, television executives, managers, and potential financial backers could meet there and make deals.

"At one time, Ed was looking for a promoter for the All-Stars, and he was introduced to a young guy named Joey, who was ostensibly interested in promoting fights."

Gersh takes up the story: "Joey and I became friendly, and one day he discussed a business partnership, exporting motorcycles to Germany. Joey convinced me that I should invest in this plan, but Holli was dead set against it."

"That's right – I didn't like Joey or his father-in-law, who was his partner," Holli adds. "Almost from the beginning, I considered these guys to be scary, especially when Joey hinted obliquely that he had Mafia connections – which of course was not all that unusual in South Florida or New York."

"So Holli wanted nothing to do with them," says Gersh, leaning back on the couch. "But I believed it when they explained how we could make a fortune exporting motorcycles, so I decided to go in with them – without telling my wife."

Holli rolls her eyes, and Gersh continues the story. Joey called him in Aspen and said he wanted to come and visit, asking Gersh to arrange the best hotel for him. He asked Gersh to do him the favor of putting the bill on his own credit card, and they'd settle up after Joey arrived in Aspen.

Holli continues: "Well, Joey was there for two weeks, and I just felt miserable the whole time because I didn't want him around, and in fact I became sick and couldn't get out of bed. I just knew something was wrong. Then one day I noticed Ed's jacket, hanging on a chair in our bedroom – it was stuffed full of cash! I confronted Ed and asked what was going on."

"So I had to explain to Holli that I was going to go in with Joey after all, but I didn't talk specifically about the exact sum of money I was carrying around in cash." Gersh can't help smiling at Holli as he continues, and she tries to look away, but smiles, too. "Joey had come to me with 'investment funds' for our motorcycle business – $300,000 in the form of three bank checks, each for $100,000.

"He asked me to deposit them directly in my personal account, then keep $100,000 for myself and give him the balance of $200,000, in cash – which was to be his and his father-in-law's share – all this cash withdrawn from my account, of course."

"When Ed told me about bank checks and withdrawing thousands of dollars, I hit the roof!" Holli declares. "I was hysterical and furious, both."

"I tried to assure her that everything was legal and the business would be very profitable, but Holli remained furious, so in order to calm her down I promised on the spot to buy a ranch near Aspen that I knew she adored."

This would become the "K.O. Ranch" (ultimately a very good financial investment). Holli did calm down, but not for long because matters took a turn for the worse after Joey left and their credit-card company called to alert them that the card used to book his hotel had been overdrawn.

"We hadn't used the card for ourselves," Holli recalls, "but it was maxed-out, and the amount was considerable! For two weeks in Aspen, Joey had bought jewelry, dinners, clothes, and paid for the hotel – all on our card!"

Gersh: "When I telephoned him, he promised to cover everything; but, next, our bank called to tell us his three bank checks had been stolen from a bank in Boston."

Gersh soon confronted Joey in a meeting at a Fort Lauderdale restaurant. Joey arrived with an escort of several men, further worrying Holli, who was also there. Joey said the bank check situation was all a mistake, a misunderstanding, not his fault, and that he'd cover the $200,000 Gersh had withdrawn and given him.

Then matters became even more drastic, as Holli explains:

"An attorney we knew had been disbarred telephoned us to warn us that a mob contract was supposedly taken out on Ed's life. Whether it was true or not – or whether Joey was just pretending to be a mobster who could put a hit out on Ed – we were very upset. I sent my daughter, Heather, away to school, and Ed said he thought we might even have to get divorced, just to protect me!"

At last, Holli called a friend who was an attorney practicing criminal law, and it was fortunate she did. The attorney immediately went to the FBI with their story and learned that the FBI had both Joey and Gersh under close surveillance.

Holli says, "The FBI were relieved to hear that we'd been swindled and were innocent, and they were even happier that Ed was willing to testify before the grand jury about Joey."

"When I was sitting there in the witness stand," Gersh remembers, "the prosecutor asked me to tell the jury how much I'd lost to Joey, and I said, 'All right, I'll tell you if you don't tell my wife.' That broke up the grand jury and the lawyers, too."

Joey was indicted, tried, and imprisoned, but the Gershes had lost more than $200,000 in the swindle, none of it ever recouped.

"We heard that somebody shot Joey in the knee while he was in prison," Holli says with a smile and a glance at her husband. "I just wish they'd aimed a little higher."

এ

IN ADDITION TO DEVELOPING THE E. GERSH ALL-STARS, who trained in Miami, I was busy with many other interests. University Gardens still took much of our attention as we converted the apartments into condominiums. My civic activities included serving on the board of the Huntington YMCA, and Holli and I were active with the Suffolk County Society for the Prevention of Cruelty to Children, where I was a board member.

In business, I was a leading stockholder in a development operation in the Dominican Republic and had property in Puerto Rico. Also, I financially supported pro boxing on the Caribbean island of Barbados. I felt the emergence of Barbados as a venue for pro fights would help that island's economy by stimulating the tourist trade. Out of Barbados came E. Gersh All-Star junior middleweight Edward Neblett, nicknamed "Yogi Bear" or the "Barbados Bomber." Neblett had a brief pro career, but he was immensely popular on Barbados, where he helped promote boxing after he retired.

The All-Stars included promising cruiserweight Scott Wheaton, a former tight end at the University of Miami. Showing the potential to move up a level to heavyweight eventually, Scott won his first three pro outings by knockouts and reached a record of 12-0-1. When he lost his next two fights, however, he retired.

By 1985, lightweight Freddie Pendleton also was an E. Gersh All-Star. Pendleton turned out to be a roller-coaster ride.

❧

FREDDIE HAD A WEALTH OF TALENT, but he needed discipline and management – and he needed to fight the right opponent at the right time. Choosing the right opponent is one of the most important responsibilities of a manager developing and guiding a fighter. Before Freddie signed with me, he'd lost as often as he'd won. In large part, this was because he'd had no manager, and he often accepted fights without training, without preparation. His talent had earned him 12 wins, including a first-round kayo of a top Detroit fighter, yet he'd lost the fight before that and the one after it. Many of his losses were because he was unwilling to produce that something extra needed to win. It's understandable that he took fights on short notice the way he did, because he had to make money for his family in Philadelphia.

Freddie was one of 12 children, and he left school early to help provide an income for them. Living in a rough Philly neighborhood infested with street gangs, Freddie chose boxing instead of crime and drugs. After a 1-5 amateur record, he turned pro in 1981. A young fighter needs dozens of amateur fights before he's ready, but Freddie became a professional at just 18 and, predictably, lost four of his first six fights.

"I needed money, so I would fight whenever they needed me," Freddie once told boxing writer Fran LaBelle of the *Boca Raton Sun-Sentinel*.

One of Freddie's defeats was a 10-round decision in 1984 to my fighter, Adolfo Medel – not a memorable performance by Pendleton as far as I could tell. Then in 1985 I was vacationing in Pennsylvania's Pocono Mountains, where I saw him sparring with junior welterweight titleholder Billy Costello. I watched Freddie carefully and saw tremendous potential. Some of the things he did were just great, reminiscent of top champs I'd seen. Costello couldn't hit him on the ass with a broomstick. Freddie had all the moves, but he also had this lousy record of 12-12-1 – and he'd just lost three in a row.

My successes in life have been a combination of hard work, luck, and the ability to take advantage of luck. I was never particularly good at close detail and organization – at things that require time and meticulous preparation. But I am effective in broadscale thinking and in evaluating things as being good or bad. I can evaluate potential, and I saw Freddie's untapped potential. Also, I utilize people whose judgment I can depend on. This included our legendary cornerman, Larry Golub, who was 86 and still active with the All-Stars. Another reliable person and a fine judge of boxers was a friend, Ken Hissner, who scouted for me. Ken recommended Pendleton, explaining that he "was not being taught how to punch [and] has a tendency of being lazy [and does not] take the blame when he loses – if you listen to him he could beat anyone."

Hissner said Freddie had good boxing skills, and encouraged me to invite him to Florida for a tryout with the All-Stars. I followed my instincts and Hissner's judgment and sent Freddie down to Lolly Kent for training.

"Find Pendleton a place to live and feed him until I get there," I said to Lolly on the phone.

Lolly hit the roof.

"What?" he screamed. "Don't send that bum down here to me!"

Lolly was prejudiced against fighters from Philly, as he later told the *Palm Beach Post:*

I don't like any fighter that comes from Philadelphia. They think they know it all. [Pendleton] was the same way when I got him . . . too cocky. I don't have the patience anymore to work with those guys.

Well, three days after Freddie got down there, Lolly called me, all excited: "Hey, Ed, you were right – that guy can fight like a sonofabitch!"

Lolly worked on Freddie's mechanics. Freddie had considered himself a good right-hand puncher, but he did everything wrong in his form, and he lacked real power. He couldn't set himself properly to throw the good punch. We taught him how to hit harder and how to develop a left hook. Later that year, Freddie won the Pennsylvania junior welterweight title, a good stepping stone for his career and his confidence.

The *Miami News* wrote about that fight:

"I put him out with a left hook," Pendleton said. "He went down cold. I looked at my fist and said to myself, 'Did I do that?'"

Kent remembered: "[Freddie] looked at me and screamed, 'It worked! It worked!' He had to be the most surprised person in the whole place."

Next I arranged a non-title match in November against IBF champion Jimmy Paul of Detroit, a good fighter who eventually had a career record of 33-6.

The fight was very close when the bell rang for the final round. Freddie was in control, but then Paul clinched and pushed him down – didn't punch him at all. I expected Freddie to jump back up, but instead he stayed down, and the referee began to count. To my dismay, Freddie took the full eight-count before getting up, and as a result, the push was considered a knockdown. Back in the corner, I asked Freddie why he took the count. He said he was tired. The decision came, and Paul was declared the winner. We'd lost that last round by two points – Paul won the fight by just one point. I was furious, shocked that Pendleton had quit like that, taking a count he'd no business to take.

"Okay, Freddie," I said. "Get showered and dressed and meet me at the hotel room."

I was ready to send him back to Philadelphia. Only Lolly kept me from sending him packing. When Freddie came into the room, I was steaming.

"You mean to say you stayed down just because you were tired?" I demanded. "Do you know that cost you the fight?"

Freddie mumbled something.

"You're goddam yellow!" I said.

Now he was shocked.

I grabbed him by the arm: "This isn't black, it's yellow!"

I grabbed his tit: "This isn't black, it's yellow!"

I grabbed the skin on his back: "This isn't black, it's yellow!"

I tapped his back and then his chest: "And it goes through there and comes out here."

Freddie had tears in his eyes.

"Give me another chance, Mr. Gersh," he pleaded.

Well, that's just what Lolly wanted me to do. I thought hard about it.

Finally, I said, "All right, but next time you better fight!"

And he did.

From that moment on, Freddie Pendleton was inspired. He won four of his next five fights, three of them knockouts. The other bout was a draw in a USBA title fight with Frankie Randall. One of those victories was a sixth-round kayo of former WBA junior lightweight titleholder Roger Mayweather in Las Vegas. The Mayweather fight was the main event in an ESPN-sponsored show and got the attention of the boxing world, as *The Las Vegas Sun* reported:

> It wasn't just another knockout. Pendleton unloaded a pair of right hands that could very well knock Mayweather into a career change.

Lolly and I had been working on Freddie's punching power, and the Mayweather fight showed that improvement.

Until then, few people had taken Freddie seriously, but now promoter Bob Arum of Top Rank said to a reporter, "I'm telling you, this kid can fight – he had bad management before, but now he's 3-1." A year later, Arum would begin to promote Freddie's fights.

❧

IN 1987 I HAD CONSIDERABLE SUCCESS with the All-Stars. One memorable moment came when three of my six fighters, including Pendleton, all won on the same card at Bally's casino in

Atlantic City. Holli was there that night, and it was thrilling for all of us. The *New York Times* even wrote a feature about me that year, telling about my early career and how I came to be a manager. I was 67 by then, and looking back on my life I had to marvel at its diversity, with so many interests.

It made me chuckle to recall how I'd probably seemed like a fraud to several tourists I'd socialized with around the pool in Acapulco. Writing in a column, "Neighbors of Note," *The Long Islander* newspaper's Joshua Botkin told the story:

[Gersh] made a habit of lying by the pool of the hotel at which he was staying, and each day he would chat with whoever was occupying the lounge chair next to his. "One day," Gersh remembers, "I would tell the guy that I'm a former history teacher and that I was the dean of a junior high school. The next day I would tell someone else that I run a day camp on Long Island. The following day I told a guy that I managed prize fighters . . . then I turned around and told somebody else that I own real estate in Puerto Rico."

"On my final day there," Gersh says with a smile, "I see all four men standing at the other side of the pool, staring at me. They must have been comparing notes and saying, 'God, what in incredible liar!'"

That year, Dave Metzger wrote an article about me that appeared in boxing publications. He quoted Lolly about my penchant for "falling in love with boxers," adding Lolly's statement that, "It's nothing for [Ed] to walk into a gym and go into his pocket for a fighter. But he's too soft. He's a patsy."

I understood Lolly's point of view, but I was enjoying life completely. I really wasn't as naive as Lolly said. Dave quoted me:

When I started in this business, I resented anyone who suggested that boxers weren't honorable people. But boxers can be whores. I've come into contact with so many who are only looking for what they can get. Many are prostitutes who will sell themselves to the highest bidder. But the same, of course, can be said of managers.

There is no sport and no profession as difficult as boxing. Look at it from the participants' viewpoint. They come from the lowest socioeconomic and cultural level of society. Anyone, almost anyone, with ability will do something else. Boxers starting from this level obtain their social and moral values at this level. Thus, [too often] they have no real morals. It's the same with managers and trainers who are ex-boxers. And instead of elevating them, sometimes [managers] sink to their level.

Despite all this, fighters need to eat, sleep, buy equipment, pay gym dues. I give them weekly salaries as loans. If they eventually make money, they can pay me back. If they don't I never get it back. At one point, boxing was costing me $1,400 a week. . . . I'm a businessman, and I don't like losing money at any time. But I haven't given up. It's definitely a labor of love.

Metzger continued with his own opinion:

Ed wants fighters to be like he was when he was fighting. He used to say, "I wish I had someone who could help me." Now, he's that guy helping them. [Yet] some fighters by nature are not the nicest guys. They think you owe them a living. So many become ungrateful.

In that same article, I said:

I'm the best manager any kid could find. No one is more equipped to make them money and invest it for them. I'm not too macho to fail to realize my own limitations, and

I've put together a top organization. I've been disappointed in my boxers. But I just want to be remembered as somebody who made a contribution. Someone who hasn't taken, but has given.

Boxing World published Dave's article, but the editors put their own title on it: "Ed Gersh: A Manager Who Brings Honor to the Boxing Profession." That title meant a lot to me.

It also meant a lot when, in the spring of 1988, the Suffolk County Society for the Prevention of Cruelty to Children honored me for my five years of work and contributions. The keynote speaker was South Huntington superintendent of schools and SPCC board member, Dr. Daniel Domenech, who said:

Ed Gersh has . . . continually devoted his time, money and expertise to help fight child abuse in Suffolk County. I know of no other individual who has worked so hard for this cause. This recognition of a fine humanitarian is truly deserving.

Coming from such a dedicated organization in so worthy a cause, this was an honor that I'll always cherish.

෴

From 1986 to early 1988, "Fearless Freddie" Pendleton, as he was nicknamed, compiled a 9-3-2 record, with eight knockouts. In April 1987, Freddie proved to be a top contender when he drew with former WBA lightweight champion Livingston Bramble – a controversial decision because Freddie deserved the win. His most remarkable victory was a 15-second knockout of well-regarded Sammy Fuentes in Atlantic City in February 1988.

This was one of the fastest kayos in pro boxing history. The *Atlantic City Press* said that when the opening bell rang,

Pendleton stormed from his stool, ducked under a Fuentes left and delivered a loaded right seconds into the fight. Fuentes' knees buckled, and he backed straight up into the path of two more rights. As Fuentes sagged to the canvas, referee Joe Cortez waved off the fight.

While preparing for this bout, Lolly had noticed something about Fuentes. Lolly told the *Sun-Sentinel*'s LaBelle that the knockout "surprised everybody but me."

There are certain things you pick up from watching certain fighters. There was one thing that Fuentes did that was a glaring mistake, and it left him open for the right hand. Freddie stuck him once, then kept on sticking him until the fight was over.

Unfortunately, I missed that amazing moment, because I was in bed sick with viral pneumonia. The next day, however, I worked out at the Fifth Street Gym – a friendly place to be after Freddie's knockout victory, which earned us lots of compliments. One of the gym's most prominent personalities was Beau Jack, the former world-famous lightweight champion whom I'd known from my Gleason's days. Beau was in his seventies then, and employed by the gym. Knowledgeable boxing people like Beau Jack appreciated what Freddie had achieved and what promise his future held if he were willing to work hard with the right attitude.

Soon after the fight, prominent boxing figure Chris Dundee told Florida sportswriter Jim Baker what he thought about me:

I've known Ed Gersh many years, and I've always found him to be a very decent and honorable man in a brutally tough business. I think any young fighter would have to consider himself very lucky to be associated with Ed Gersh.

I appreciated those sentiments, coming as they did from Chris, whose family had such success in training, managing, and promoting fighters. In turn, I can only compliment the Dundees for their outstanding careers.

In that same article – titled, "From the Classroom to the Ring, He Knows the Ropes" – Baker quoted me on why I was managing fighters:

Actually it's an avocation with me in the financial sense, but I take boxing very seriously. The vicarious thrill it gives me just can't be compared.

Holli was also interviewed, and she expressed her feelings about this passionate hobby of mine:

Ed is really too nice a man for this business, and it's heartbreaking to me when I think of some of the things that have happened. He deserves better, because he genuinely cares for his fighters and he provides for their needs.

Freddie was also quoted:

Mr. Gersh is the best thing that ever happened to me. He gave me a place to train, boosted my confidence and took care of my financial problems so I could concentrate on my boxing.

That sounded quite familiar to me at the time – harking back to Howard Davis, Jr., expressing gratitude for all my efforts on his behalf. I didn't want to compare Howard with Freddie, however, not even when Freddie publicly said he "owed me" a lightweight title and was going to get it. Instead of recapitulating the Davis affair, I was delighted to hear such resolve from Freddie, especially because he'd been improving with every bout, as I told Baker:

I'm not really interested in taking on any more fighters, but I really can't run away from a Freddie Pendleton. Boxing has turned out to be a very expensive hobby for me, but when I see a guy like him start to come into his own, it makes it worth the effort for me.

Baker also quoted Dave Metzger, who said I knew what it meant to be hungry and what it takes to win:

All he asks of his fighters is to train hard and give him their very best in the ring. If they do, he'll give them his very best in return.

I really did try to do my best for my fighters.

ও

FREDDIE'S WIN-LOSS RECORD OF 17-15 was still mediocre unless you considered what he'd achieved in the past two years. Top fighters were worried about facing him because if they lost to a guy with a mediocre record, that would hurt their stature and standings. They well knew Freddie was good and getting better, and none was eager to fight him. Freddie was ranked No. 4 by the IBF and No. 3 by the USBA in June 1988, when I publicly needled Bramble for ducking him. I said to the *New York Post*:

You would think every junior welterweight/lightweight would be anxious to fight him, but Livingstone Bramble turned down a rematch.

Bramble soon would accept that challenge. Meanwhile,

Freddie was feeling pretty good about himself, as he told the *Long Islander:*

> Every time I step in the ring now, I want to prove to Mr. Gersh that he's got a new fighter with a positive purpose. He and Larry Kent have proven to me they're doing their jobs. Now it's up to me to do mine.

Freddie did just that in July, when he fought Bramble in a 12-rounder in Atlantic City for the USBA lightweight championship.

The fight was close until the 10th round. We didn't know that Freddie was ahead on two of the three judges' scorecards, but we figured he needed to win all three of the final rounds. Early in the fight he'd inflicted a cut over Bramble's right eye, but also had taken some real good punches. I saw tremendous heart in that fight, as Freddie came back strong in the ninth and 10th rounds. Then in the 10th he caught Bramble with a left hook, opening the cut, and the chief physician entered the ring to examine it.

The physician stopped the fight, declaring a technical knock-out, and to our delight Freddie was the USBA's new lightweight champion.

We were immensely proud of Freddie, and it felt very good, personally, to have finally managed a fighter to a championship. It was, indeed, one of the happiest moments of my life – but it wasn't enough for me yet.

Edward and Holli Gersh, pictured soon after their marriage in 1987. Below, the West Hills founders are shown in front of the day camp's administration building in 1988: l-r, Gersh, Polanski, and Schnittman.

Darrin Van Horn leaps for joy in February 1989 as he is declared IBF light middleweight champion, outpointing Robert "Bam-Bam" Hines of Philadelphia at Atlantic City's Trump Castle. Manager Gersh also enjoys the triumph of his second champion.

Chapter 19

ANOTHER CHAMPION

JUST DAYS AFTER FREDDIE PENDLETON won the USBA title in July 1988, I signed up Darrin Van Horn, a young junior middleweight from Louisiana. At the time, Darrin was a 19-year-old sophomore at the University of Kentucky. He was good-looking enough to be a model, and good enough in the ring to be undefeated in a 36-0 pro career that had begun at just 16 years of age. Darrin's ring nickname was "Schoolboy," and some considered him a "Great White Hope," as promising white boxers often were termed.

From the start, Darrin had been managed, trained, and promoted by his father, G.L. Van Horn, a fast-talking ex-convict who'd been in San Quentin penitentiary for robbery. G.L. had brought his son along quite well, and now realized Darrin needed a well-funded management organization to guide his career. G.L. said he wanted to get out of boxing and offered sell me his contract with his son. G.L. said if I bought him out, he'd leave boxing completely. It cost me $50,000 to buy out Darrin's contract from G.L. – "Good Living," some said his initials meant.

Darrin signed a six-year contract with me, and promoter Cedric Kushner had the right to promote his fights – which was fine with me because Kushner could bring network and cable television broadcasts to a boxing show. Kushner was a native South African, an entrepreneur who'd made good money in the early 1980s promoting rock concerts. In a press release in 1989, Kushner stated that his "underwhelming resume included Boston laborer, Miami pool cleaner and New York messenger." He'd begun promoting boxers in the mid-1980s.

Darrin Van Horn was smart, courageous, and determined, exactly the sort of fighter I wanted, but behind the scenes the father retained the same dominating influence he'd wielded for many years. I brought Darrin along slowly, although he was a hot property – a white boy, well-spoken and educated, but street-smart and able to mix it up with black and Latino fighters. He was still very young, and I estimated he'd begin to peak at 22 or so. I engaged the veteran trainer Hedgemon Lewis to take charge of his development. Darrin knew how to punch, and we had to teach him how to box and move.

Darrin won twice more in 1988, then in February 1989 he had a title fight against IBF light middleweight champion Robert "Bam-Bam" Hines of Philadelphia. This was the first-ever boxing show at the new Trump Castle in Atlantic City, with NBC broadcasting the fight card. Promoters named the Van Horn-Hines bout the "Hassle at the Castle." We brought in well-known trainer Lou Duva to bolster our preparation, especially to help with attitude and motivation.

In a cover feature, *Ring Magazine* called Darrin the "Million Dollar Baby" because of his success in the ring and the intense interest in him on the part of Kushner and NBC television. That sort of interest meant good paydays for a prize fighter. Some people, however, had labeled Darrin a "catcher," a derogatory term meaning he caught too many punches. Skeptics were saying he wasn't tough enough to take really hard hits, especially not the blows that Hines, a very good inside puncher, was known to dish out. The voluble G.L. Van Horn, however, boasted to *Philadelphia Daily News* writer Stan Hochman before the fight that Hines was no match for his son:

> Show me a way that Hines can beat us. Hines can do one thing, punch. And we can do lots of things. We have more tools, more ammunition. Hines knows what it means to lose. He won't feel too bad to lose again.

Considering Hines had a 24-1-1 record, G.L.'s insults didn't make much sense. G.L. wasn't my fighter, though, so there was nothing I could do about his bragging. Television and promoters, of course, enjoyed such pre-fight hype, which supposedly stimulated a larger audience. Before the fight, the media from New York to Las Vegas gave G.L. lots of publicity, even more than Darrin. Fortunately, Darrin was more respectful of Hines than was G.L., and he was cautious.

In the first round Hines turned out to be "a lot stronger and quicker than I thought," Darrin later said. At the start of the fight, Darrin had moved inside and tried to land the big punch, but he soon realized: "Inside, I couldn't fight with him. His punches were too strong and sharp. No matter where I moved my head, I ran right into a punch."

Yet, Darrin's aggressiveness won him that first round unanimously. Then he changed his tactics. He began to lead with his right, catching Hines off guard and scoring points. And he kept just the right distance to make Hines come up short with his powerful jabs. Darrin proved the better fighter that night, as Hines, himself, admitted after Darrin was declared the winner by unanimous decision.

To my delight, the E. Gersh All-Stars had another champion.

❧

WITH OUR NEWFOUND SUCCESS, we entered another level of competition and a more competitive level of the boxing business. We had to position Pendleton and Van Horn to get big fights through promoters who had influence with television networks – and who also controlled the fighters we needed to be matched against.

Author Charles Jay, writing online for *Total Action SportsNet*, explained the relationships of boxers and managers to promoters, boxing venues (usually gambling casinos), and television:

> There are really two entities that "fuel" boxing promotions and the promoters who stage them. One [is] the casinos, who provide the "found money" for promoters at the venue itself. But that is "small potatoes" compared with the more important entity – television. It is becoming increasingly difficult to make any kind of profit promoting boxing . . . without the support of television revenues. . . .
>
> [T]he promoters who are able to secure television for their boxing shows are the ones able to develop the power base necessary to operate. Let's use an example to illustrate this. If a television executive were to grab any promoter, and I mean that – ANY PROMOTER – and tell him he was going to have 20 TV dates, guaranteed, for the upcoming year, along [with] the rights fees that go along with it . . . [this would] provide the promoter with the inside track on a couple of things: 1) the chance to sign fighters to promotional contracts, since he knows he will . . . have the money and the activity necessary to fulfill an obligation to the fighter, and 2) the opportunity to pitch a casino with the guarantee of getting nationwide TV exposure for a predetermined number of fights. . . . .

Jay continued, saying, "the people who run television boxing are in a position to make or break promoters" – and, may I add, managers.

Freddie Pendleton was being touted as one of the world's best in his weight class, and that should have brought him opportunities to contend for the championships of other sanctioning bodies. Also, we had more up-and-coming fighters in our stable who needed bouts that would be stepping stones to higher rankings. We had to be able to make deals with leading promoters, and we had high hopes when Bob Arum's Top Rank took Freddie on. Arum promoted one of Freddie's four fights in 1987 and three fights in 1988. Freddie won all seven. He fought twice more in 1988, both in California for another promoter. (My agreement with Arum did not give Top Rank exclusivity.) Freddie won the first of the California bouts and then lost the next – fighting up a weight class at junior welterweight – by a 10th-round kayo. Top Rank was very unhappy that we'd fought Freddie in a heavier class.

In 1989, it was a different story for Freddie. Top Rank offered a fight that spring, but Freddie became violently ill and had to drop out. Top Rank arranged two more fights, but both times Freddie was injured in training and again had to cancel. As it turned out, one prospective opponent was a southpaw, and I had always objected to Freddie meeting a left-hander, because it puts a right-handed fighter at a distinct disadvantage. I'd informed Top Rank several times that I wouldn't accept matches against southpaws. Freddie's injury would have made no difference because I wouldn't have taken that fight anyway, as was my right according to our agreement with Top Rank.

Matters now became complicated. Lolly Kent suggested three other possible opponents for Freddie, but Top Rank turned them all down as not being good enough. Meanwhile, Freddie was waiting on the sidelines, fighting only once in all of 1989. Such inaction was detrimental to his career, but we were hamstrung by Top Rank not arranging fights that were acceptable to us.

The boxing world is inherently difficult for fighters and managers to negotiate. For a start, pro fights are arranged by the promoters' "matchmakers," who are supposed to be honest experts capable of bringing the right fighters together. Good matchmakers offer exciting fights for fans and fair competition in the ring. But too many matchmakers have only the best interests of the promoter and the promoter's favored fighter in mind, as Charles Jay explained:

> The matchmaker works for a promoter, or is sometimes one in the same with the promoter. And the objective of the matchmaker is not necessarily to put on the best show possible for the paying public, but mostly to put on a respectable show while at the same time making sure the "house" fighters win. There is an art in that; make no mistake about it.

In an article for *The Nation*, longtime sports writer Jack Newfield said too many fights are "fixed in the matchmaking to make [the promoter's favorite] look good." Furthermore, the outcome of most bouts is determined by the scoring of a panel of judges, but there's no guarantee that the judges are objective and honest. Newfield explained the judges' frequent conflict of interest:

> In many cases the judges are paid by the promoter, including travel expenses. They know which fighter is under an exclusive contract to that promoter. They don't have to be told that if they favor that promoter's employee, they will get future assignments from that promoter. Can you imagine a baseball owner picking and paying the home-plate umpire in a World Series game?

Charles Jay further elaborated on these incestuous boxing relationships and how they undercut managers:

> [T]he promoter pays the fighter. And this makes the promoter more of an employer, with the fighter filling the employee role. . . . [T]he manager cannot necessarily prevent

the fighter from engaging in a particular contest, [but] the promoter CAN. The promoter has the absolute last word on where and when a fighter fights. . . .

To advance our fighters' careers, we needed to weave our way through the logjam formed by the promoters, venues, television executives, and the sanctioning organizations. There was no single national administrator – no objective "watchdog" – governing boxing, but instead dozens of state agencies were in charge of the sport's oversight. Elsewhere, Newfield referred to the "buccaneer, lawless jungle of boxing," and called for "Congress to create a national commissioner for boxing," which would be akin to the "central authority" that administers baseball.

I wholeheartedly agreed.

છે.

So, by late 1989 Arum and Top Rank were not providing Freddie Pendleton with acceptable fights.

My agreement with Arum expired in January 1990, and I turned to Main Events, the Paterson, New Jersey, promotion company run by the Duva family. The Duvas had control of 19-1 Pernell Whitaker, holder of the IBF and WBC lightweight titles, and I wanted Freddie to fight Whitaker for those titles. Arum and Top Rank couldn't promote that fight, so I went directly to Duva, who accepted on the condition that if Freddie won the title we'd go with Main Events for two return matches. My agreeing to that further infuriated Arum, who broke off our friendship.

Looking back on it, I realized it was a mistake to have accepted that exclusive arrangement with Main Events because Whitaker would have been required by the IBF to fight Freddie before too long. My uppermost concern at the time was to protect my fighter, however, to see he got the fights he was entitled to get. I personally was taking no part of my fighters' purses, but they needed to fight to make a decent living. I wanted to schedule enough fights both to give Freddie a chance at other titles and also to produce a financial return for him – instead of my having to pay for everything myself.

Past disappointment with Howard Davis, Jr., and several others was on my mind when I was interviewed by Florida sports columnist Cedric Harmon just before the Pendleton and Whitaker fight in February 1990. I told Harmon:

> Fighters are a very strange breed. Most of them are great when they need you. . . . You support a boxer for years; you're everything to him. You'll clothe him. You'll house him. You'll help him with all of his financial problems. And then when they start making money, they're out the door. No loyalty.

Unfortunately, some managers also had ethical shortcomings, I told Harmon, saying that too often a boxing manager "financially is a thief, a sneak, and no good, and [yet] seems to get ahead."

Harmon also wrote, "Insiders feel that Gersh has been the exception of today's standards of boxing managers."

Well, Freddie lost that championship fight to Whitaker in a 12-round unanimous decision. Although a real setback, it was one of the few times Freddie openly admitted an opponent deserved to win. Now, he was bitter, and he complained about Lolly Kent, demanding that I remove the sometimes acerbic Lolly as his trainer. This I refused to do. It's ironic to think that Lolly had been the one who'd convinced me to keep Freddie at the start.

In March, Freddie and I signed a promotion contract with Cedric Kushner, but Kushner and Freddie soon proceeded to arrange a fight without my consent, in fact against my wishes – a situation not unusual in the shady world of professional boxing. Fighter-manager contacts are often vulnerable. Contracts signed in one state between a manager and fighter can be void in another state if that boxing commission so chooses. Furthermore, few managers have the financial wherewithal to go to court to defend their rights against the lawyers of a bigtime promoter. Boxing is rife with stories of managers losing control of fighters to well-financed promoters.

Freddie Pendleton – via his lawyer – claimed he had the right to break our contract because I'd "abandoned" him, and he said I hadn't properly accounted for money due him from his purses. At the same time, he went with Kushner. I was very upset and filed a counter complaint with the New York State Athletic Commission, asserting that my rights as manager had been violated and my contract with Freddie had been breached. I retained Commack, L.I., attorney Robert J. Dinerstein to represent me to the commission. We provided a full accounting of my financial relationship with Freddie and contended that I'd never abandoned him. The adjudication dragged on for years.

I could have walked away, but I was determined not to give up without a fight after all I'd done for Freddie Pendleton. Darrin Van Horn, unfortunately, was also well on his way to breaching our manager-fighter contract and going off with Kushner.

પ્ર

AT TRUMP CASTLE IN JULY 1989, Darrin had a bout in defense of his IBF title against Italian fighter Gianfranco Rosi, whose record was 45-3-0. Rosi won a unanimous 12-round decision. We all were devastated, especially Darrin, who'd lost for the first time in his career. To help him recuperate, and to renew his spirits, I gave Darrin an all-expenses-paid vacation with his girlfriend to the Caribbean.

To my dismay, Kushner convinced Darrin that he didn't need a manager any more than Freddie Pendleton did, and with G.L. Van Horn also back on the scene, they proceeded to arrange fights without my permission. As with Freddie, Darrin claimed I'd abandoned him, which was absolutely untrue – I'd even given him that expensive vacation trip right after his loss. Again, I appealed to the New York State Athletic Commission.

At this time the commission was chaired by an old friend, former boxing writer Randy Gordon, who'd replaced the well-respected Jose Torres, a former light-heavyweight champion. I thought I'd be assured of a fair hearing since Randy knew me well and what I'd done in boxing. But to my disappointment he recused himself from participating in the decision on the Pendleton and Van Horn cases. I wasn't asking Randy for any favors, and he certainly could have been objective. I felt that his recusing himself from my cases was uncalled for.

Kushner testified to the commission that the breach in my relationship with Van Horn was my fault, adding that I knew little about boxing, and that I'd repeatedly rejected his advice and guidance. This, coming from a promoter of rock concerts.

The commission did not permit me the opportunity to rebut Kushner's testimony. Despite the signed contracts and the obviously false claim that I'd abandoned these fighters, the Athletic Commission found in favor of Pendleton and Van Horn. They went on their way with no compensation for me. The Athletic Commission had supported my grievance with Howard Davis, Jr., but not with Pendleton or Van Horn.

Indeed, times had changed.

It's no wonder that, nowadays, the major promoters routinely deal directly with the fighters and refuse to negotiate with the managers. When things go wrong, however, they claim the manager's at fault, but that's usually not true. Few feel any sympathy for the manager, even though he has supported a young man and developed him as a fighter and then is pushed out and left with nothing.

Of course, I did have those championships as manager. That no one could take away.

Darrin Van Horn lost again to Rosi in 1990 for the IBF light middleweight title, but the following year he won the IBF super middleweight championship, a heavier weight class. Darrin held that title until 1992. His record when he retired in 1994 was a remarkable 53-3-0.

Freddie Pendleton went on to a long career, retiring in 2001 with a record of 47-26-5. He successfully defended his USBA title several times and won the IBF lightweight title in 1993. Freddie had a number of title defenses and challenged for other titles, including an unsuccessful bid in 1999 for the WBA welterweight championship (a technical knockout in the 11th round of a 12-round bout). I was glad to see Freddie do as well as he did.

It was satisfying for me that my peers in boxing knew I'd been instrumental in helping Davis, Pendleton, and Van Horn be so successful as prize fighters.

As for Cedric Kushner, in 2000 he was banned from boxing for admitting to making payoffs to the IBF to manipulate the rankings of fighters. The New York State Division of Gaming Enforcement at first wanted to revoke his license, but Kushner helped investigators gathering evidence in the IBF case. After 18 months, the ban was lifted, according to an Associated Press article, "partly on the strength of statements by Division of Gaming Enforcement investigators, who said . . . Kushner fully cooperated in the probe."

Riding was a favorite Gersh pastime at their K.O. Ranch in Aspen.

Gersh and son Kevin spend time on the golf course together.

Chapter 20

CLOSING YEARS IN BOXING

IN 1990, FRIENDS OF OURS CONVINCED HOLLI and me that a visit to Aspen, Colorado, would be a great vacation for us. In fact, these friends had arranged for an Aspen real estate agent to send us sales literature about properties on the market there. We had no plans to buy, however, and just went out there for a visit. It was Halloween, and the whole town was celebrating, everyone dressed up, having one big party. We fell in love with Aspen, and of course the beautiful Rocky Mountains. One thing led to another, and before we left, we'd bought a condominium in downtown Aspen.

We kept our houses in Huntington and Boca Raton, but we were very much at home in Colorado, making new friends and enjoying the social scene. After we purchased the ranch, which was very run-down, Holli took the lead and worked with an architect, remodeling the main house into a gorgeous adobe. For the next few years we spent much of our summers at the "K.O. Ranch," and our children and their families enjoyed visiting. I often went horseback riding, as I had as a young man in the Catskills. Now, I was pretty much retired from the day-to-day operation of West Hills, which was being managed by our director, Mike Moore. Wilfred was still part of our extended family (he would eventually be happily married to a woman from the Caribbean to whom we introduced him).

I kept active with the All-Stars, but I wanted to avoid having to deal directly with the promoters. So, I decided to promote fights myself. It wasn't allowed to both promote and manage the same fighters, so Holli became president of H. Gersh Promotions, and we went into partnership with Phil Alessi, a longtime promoter from the Tampa Bay area, where his family had a bakery. Phil had a structure, an organization with boxing venues and connections. When we began to work together he'd already promoted more than 300 fights, including more than 150 national telecasts on network television. I put up most of the capital to fund the boxing shows Alessi promoted. I anticipated that network television broadcasts with their commercial sponsors would be financially beneficial to my fighters, who'd be featured in many of the shows. At the same time, I'd make sure our matchmaker arranged bouts that were right for my fighters' development.

The All-Stars included a number of fine prospects – Fort Lauderdale welterweight John Coward was shaping up as one of my best, but he prematurely faded because of problems with illegal substances. My fighters gave a good performance in any boxing show, and they improved from the experience, just as their rankings rose whenever they won.

Alessi shows were mainly in the Tampa-St. Petersburg area, competing with the Miami and South Florida fight scene, which was controlled by the Dundee family. Angelo and Chris Dundee had stimulated great interest in prize-fighting in Florida in the 1950s and 1960s. Having been Ali's trainer, Angelo was himself quite a famous boxing personality. By the 1990s, the Dundees had the Miami area locked up when it came to promoting boxing, but Angelo was supportive enough to us – or perhaps just curious – to attend our press conference announcing the Gersh partnership with Alessi Promotions, which soon became the busiest boxing promoter in Florida, with a dozen or so shows in Tampa in 1991.

One of the All-Stars' most successful prize fighters was middleweight Ronald "Winky" Wright, of Washington, D.C., for whom Alessi promoted 19 fights – all victories. Winky had a long and successful career well into 2005, when at the age of 33 he was still fighting and had a 48-3 record. He held the light middleweight titles of the WBA, WBC, IBF, USBA, and NABF, and previously he'd won and lost the WBO title. I split with Winky after those first 19 bouts when his trainer asked if I alone would manage his career instead of collaborating with Phil Alessi. Out of loyalty to Phil, I declined, so Winky left the All-Stars to go with other management.

Among Alessi Promotions' most important boxing shows was a 1991 Larry Holmes bout when Holmes was on the comeback trail after losing the heavyweight championship, which he'd held from 1978–1985. Holmes won that fight, defeating Eddie Gonzales, and continuing his comeback for another year until losing to Evander Holyfield.

As usual, Holli was in the thick of it all. We still often had boxers staying in our house in Boca in preparation for a fight. Our association with Phil and Alessi Promotions was enjoyable in many ways, but it was costly – I lost a lot of money because not enough people came to see the fights in the arenas we rented – very large arenas, such as the Orlando World Center and the Sundome. Also, we had only a regional cable television network to broadcast our boxing shows. National broadcast revenue is essential to the success of professional boxing, and we didn't get it.

To stimulate more interest in prize-fighting, Phil Alessi and I tried to start "The Ringside Club," where boxing enthusiasts could get together in a private setting to share their mutual interest in the sport. For a $100 membership, they could reserve discounted ringside seats, attend press conferences, meet fighters, managers and trainers, and be able to invite friends or business relations to ringside. We even offered a "Ringside Club" jacket – but we never did enlist enough charter members, and the idea didn't leave the ground.

વ્ક

IN THIS TIME I HAD VERY HIGH HOPES FOR DARRIN MORRIS, a junior middleweight from Detroit nicknamed "Mongoose." He'd previously been managed by the Dundees and had won the World Boxing Federation (WBF) title in 1992. He was being trained by 1964 Finnish Olympic bronze medallist Osmo Kanerva. By August 1994, Darrin was 21–2–1, having won his last nine fights – these under my management. Now Darrin was a genuine contender for the IBF crown. Coincidentally, a neighbor of mine in Aspen happened to be managing a top middleweight himself: Leonard "Boogie" Weinglass had junior middleweight champion Vincent Pettway, who fought from Boogie's business home base in Maryland. Pettway was ranked first by the IBF, while Darrin was seventh.

I publicly teased Boogie in *The Aspen Times:* "I'm challenging him and his fighter for the championship . . . anywhere, anytime."

My dare was all in good fun, but I meant it when I said, "We could even fight out here." I praised Darrin's ability and said, "But Boogie's afraid of me; he's afraid of my fighter."

The newspaper quoted me about Darrin being "very dedicated . . . hungry [and] he's got talent." It also explained that Darrin had hurt his hand in training and missed a recent fight that would have been televised. "[A]fter the hand heals, Gersh . . . expects Morris to make a legitimate run at the world championship."

Indeed I did.

Unfortunately, the next time I arranged a big fight for Darrin, he again said he'd been hurt in training and couldn't fight. Several fights in a row were canceled that way, with him claiming to be hurt. Disgusted, I stopped managing him. Darrin didn't tell me then that he had HIV. He died a few years later, at the age of 34. Darrin was my last fighter.

I withdrew from participation in Alessi Promotions and closed up E. Gersh All-Stars. I estimated that in my years as a manager and promoter I'd lost around $250,000, but I had no regrets about my boxing career at all.

Except, perhaps, for one.

In 1994, I expected to be named the next chairman of the New York State Athletic Commission – the chairman at the time still was Randy Gordon, appointed by the Democrats. I was a staunch supporter of, and a generous contributor to, the New York State Republican Party. During George E. Pataki's campaign for governor, Republican Senator Alfonse D'Amato – a fellow Long Islander and a power behind Pataki – well knew that a post on the commission would appeal to me. I had hopes of one day being able to change the weak governance of boxing in the state.

Pataki was elected for his first term in 1994, and while I was at a celebratory dinner with close advisors to Senator D'Amato, I was toasted as "the next chairman of the Athletic Commission." Later that evening, as I was taking a shower, I offhandedly called out to Holli and said, "I think I'm going to try to be chairman of the state Athletic Commission."

Holli gasped, and in the next instant stuck her head through the shower curtain, saying, "It'll cost you a three-bedroom apartment in Manhattan."

I laughed and replied, "How about a two-bedroom apartment?"

Holli agreed, and we purchased the former Howard Cosell apartment on East 69th Street. We would sell the K.O. Ranch in 1998 – it had been left vacant too often by then – and buy the home on Chestnut Hill Road in Woodstock, where we could be within two hours of Huntington, since I was becoming increasingly involved in West Hills once again. As the Pataki administration took over New York State, Holli and I were preparing for what we assumed would be a new phase of our life together.

ò▲

OF COURSE, AS A DONOR TO THE REPUBLICANS, I was vulnerable to accusations of being part of the spoils system, rewarded by the victorious politicians for my support. Yet, I was interested only in boxing, not in a patronage job. I didn't want or need a state salary or a prestigious office in the state bureaucracy. I intended to donate my salary to charity. Nor did I need to be invited as some political bigshot to boxing matches or receptions to rub elbows with famous fighters. I could do that any time I chose. And I certainly didn't need the headaches and hard work that surely would come with the chairman's job if I did it right.

As Athletic Commission chairman – knowing boxing inside and out – I could do a lot of good for the sport and for the prizefighters. Among other things, I wanted to set up a financial safety net for fighters after their careers were over. The prospect of being the most influential boxing official in New York excited me. It gave me hope that the sport I loved so much would have a better future, a new foundation.

In June of 1995, with no chairman appointed as yet, I wrote a proposal to the state Urban Development Commission, which had requested that I present a plan for improving the status of boxing in New York. I laid out my ideas for revitalizing the business of boxing and for protecting the rights of fighters and managers. I especially wanted to place controls and oversight on matchmaking, which too often was calculated to manipulate fighters for the sake of major promoters and gamblers. The many, many intentional mismatches and noncompetitive bouts were particularly detrimental to boxers, often resulting in serious injury that ended careers – and even caused death.

Further, I wanted to improve training for officials and judges and also to revise the scoring system to make it simpler. I also wanted to encourage small promoters and the development of local venues – the original cornerstones of boxing that had all but disappeared. I even intended to convince Madison Square Garden's proprietors to reactivate its boxing programs, especially the great Golden Gloves tournaments.

I closed my plan as follows:

It is my opinion, and the opinion of many knowledgeable boxing people, that the Chairman of the New York State Athletic Commission should be a successful businessman with a strong background in boxing. I fit both categories and I feel that I will rejuvenate boxing in New York State if given the opportunity.

I had my heart set on it, and was raring to go.

Later that month, however, former heavyweight champion Floyd Patterson was appointed chairman. As much as I admired Floyd, a great heavyweight champion from 1956–1962, and a fine man, I knew he didn't have the administrative experience to improve boxing and set it on a new track. Big financial contributors to Pataki's campaign received key places in the Athletic Commission staff – mostly politicos with little or no knowledge of boxing.

It was a bitter disappointment to me not to have the opportunity to reshape boxing as a competitive, much-admired sport.

With my managing of fighters also at an end, my boxing career was over. Nothing was the same in the sport that I'd loved so well. Even the old Fifth Street Gym in Miami closed up in this time, shutting its doors on my friend Beau Jack, the last former fighter to be found in the place in the final days before the building was demolished.

ã↑

ALTHOUGH I WAS OUT OF BOXING, I still followed developments – especially how the New York State Athletic Commission remained a do-nothing rubber stamp that allowed corruption and mismanagement to remain at the heart of the sport.

New York City and Madison Square Garden had lost their stature as the Mecca of boxing, and the commission fell under a cloud of disgrace as young fighters continued to die in the ring, at times as a result of administrative incompetence and lax control by referees and ringside physicians. As chairman, Floyd was no match for the politicians and hustlers who influenced and manipulated boxing as much as ever. Matters became worse when he apparently began to suffer from Alzheimer's, which brought on loss of memory. He continued nominally as commission chairman, with his staff running the show, and nothing said about his illness.

It was an embarrassment to Floyd and an indictment of both the state administration and the Athletic Commission when, in 1998, he was forced to answer questions, under oath, testifying in a lawsuit filed against the commission "by promoters of Ultimate Fighting, a controversial submission sport," as Middletown *Times-Herald-Record* sports writer Steve Pinto reported.

> Patterson had trouble answering a series of questions ranging from his secretary's name to who he defeated to win the heavyweight championship in 1956. Pataki officials said they may name Patterson an "honorary chairman" of the commission.

Floyd resigned immediately after this testimony.

Randy Gordon, Floyd's longtime friend, expressed the feelings of many of us who cared about the sport of boxing. Randy had encouraged Floyd from the start, even though Floyd had taken his job. Randy wrote an article titled "Always a Champ" for the *Cyber Boxing Zone* website:

> Now, not quite 34 months after being sworn in as the 15th Chairman of the New York State Athletic Commission since

its inception in 1920, Floyd Patterson has resigned because of an inability to properly do his job.

I feel bad for Floyd, much worse than I felt when he lost either fight to Liston. I feel bad for what was done to him for the past three years. Politicians used him. They used his great name. They used his goodness. They used his integrity. They used it all to make themselves look good.

Then, they stood by – like a bunch of ruthless cornermen waiting to count their share of the purse as their pug is hammered from corner to corner – as a skilled, sharp attorney picked Floyd apart on the witness stand . . . as he represented the New York State Athletic Commission. His corner should have thrown in the towel. They should have stepped in and stopped the carnage early. Floyd should have been spared the agony of what his political "friends" allowed this incredibly decent and sensitive man to go through.

Gov. Pataki has now said he's considering making Floyd an "Honorary Chairman" of the commission, with no decision-making responsibilities and no pressure. Wonderful! He should have thought about that three years ago!

New York's boxing insiders continued down a scandalous slope, as racketeering thrived and boxers died. In 2000, the *New York Post* ran a scathing and damning series of articles written by Jack Newfield and Wallace Matthews. An accompanying *Post* editorial stated that the series "revealed the commission in recent years has failed miserably – on all counts" with regard to supervising boxing. Worse than that, said the editorial, commission officials have been accused of corruption that sometimes led to serious injury for mismatched and even sick fighters.

Largely as a result of the *Post*'s allegations, the FBI later launched an investigation of the commission and of boxing, but the scandals continued to play out for years. In his 2001 piece for *The Nation*, Newfield wrote that the commission was

guilty of "incompetence, conflicts of interest and, most prominent, [of] repeated failure to protect the health and safety of
fighters." He went on about the shortcomings of the commission's patronage system:

> The counsel to the commission . . . was also the counsel to
> the state Republican Party[,] an elections lawyer who knows
> little about boxing. He ran the commission during the years
> that poor Floyd Patterson was used as a front – made chair-
> man in a cynical act that revealed contempt for a former
> heavyweight champion.

Newfield continued eloquently:

> Boxing has to be changed, even though there is no lobby for
> fighters and no constituency for reform. It is the moral thing
> to do. . . .
>
> The fact that almost all boxers are black and Latino makes
> it easier for respectable people to shrug and look away. It
> would not cost the taxpayers anything to regulate boxing at
> the same level every other professional sport is policed.
> Only the will is lacking. Nobody important cares enough.
>
> But the rest of us should, whether we are boxing fans or
> not. It's easy to avert your eyes and say, "Abolish the sport."
> But that won't happen. Instead, we should help these voice-
> less workers obtain the justice they deserve.

I agree completely.

Someday, I hope, boxing will again deserve the admiration
worthy of the efforts and talents of the many remarkable people
who have been associated with it. The saying attributed to the
Roman poet Virgil – posted on the wall of Gleason's Gym when
first I got there in 1941 – might one day again stimulate aspiring
young fighters, optimistic trainers, and dedicated managers:

Whoever has courage and a strong, collected spirit in his breast, let him come forward, lace on the gloves, and put up his hands.

ॐ

EDWARD IRWIN GERSH DIDN'T BECOME CHAIRMAN of the New York State Athletic Commission, but Holli and he were happy to have bought that home in New York City. If Ed Gersh were not to be found in Manhattan, Woodstock, or in Boca Raton – or off on a vacation trip somewhere – he'd likely be in the office at West Hills or playing golf, or visiting with his children and grandchildren.

In 2005, just after his 85th birthday, Gersh told a visitor to his Woodstock home that back when he was a struggling, penniless young man, he'd never dreamed he'd achieve the style of living he now enjoyed.

"I'm the proof that if you find something you're good at and work hard at it, there's no reason why you can't succeed. That may sound like a cliché, but my own life bears witness to the assertion that there's absolutely nothing in the world you can't achieve if you try hard enough."

Then he remarked that Howard Davis, Jr., had recently called, and they'd spoken for the first time since the 1980s.

"Howard said he was managing fighters, and asked if I'd be interested in considering a partnership with him."

The surprised visitor asked whether he really would want to get back into boxing again.

Ed Gersh smiled wistfully, then said, "I might."

THE END

The three remaining blood brothers celebrate Gersh's 80th birthday in 2000: Frankie Ganger is at left, and Bernie Jovans is at right.

ACKNOWLEDGMENTS

Thanks to Karen Bronzert, my secretary at West Hills, for her untiring assistance; to Burrill Crohn for his contributions, including a documentary video on my life; to Cynthia Allen, former manager of New York University's *Jews In Sports* website (www.jewsinsports.org); to Bill Brandon of Decalogue Books for his advice; to Carla Dellaporta, faculty administrative assistant at New York University; and to Wanda Hunter of the Cumberland Library, Fayetteville, N.C.

E.G.

❧

STUART MURRAY, a journalist and editor, has written more than 30 books, including fiction, biography, and reference works. He lives in Berlin, New York.

Edward I. Gersh

EDWARD GERSH and his wife Holli reside in Woodstock,
N.Y., and Manhattan, and spend winters at their home
in Boca Raton, Florida.